THE SOUND OF SEAS

GILLIAN ANDERSON
& JEFF ROVIN

THE SOUND OF SEAS

**SIMON &
SCHUSTER**

London · New York · Sydney · Toronto · New Delhi

A CBS COMPANY

First published in the USA by Simon 451, an imprint of Simon & Schuster Inc., 2016
First published in Great Britain by Simon & Schuster UK Ltd, 2016
A CBS COMPANY

1 3 5 7 9 10 8 6 4 2

Simon & Schuster UK Ltd
1st Floor
222 Gray's Inn Road
London WC1X 8HB

www.simonandschuster.co.uk

Simon & Schuster Australia, Sydney
Simon & Schuster India, New Delhi

A CIP catalogue record for this book is available from the British Library.

Hardback ISBN: 978-1-4711-3778-5
Trade Paperback ISBN: 978-1-4711-3779-2
eBook ISBN: 978-1-4711-3781-5

Printed and bound by CPI Group (UK) Ltd, Croydon, CR0 4YY

Simon & Schuster UK Ltd are committed to sourcing paper that is made from
wood grown in sustainable forests and support the Forest Stewardship
Council, the leading international forest certification organisation. Our books
displaying the FSC logo are printed on FSC certified paper.

THE SOUND OF SEAS

PROLOGUE

Vilu woke in dull sunlight.

With his eyes still half-closed, the young boy growled like a *thyodularasi* pup and stretched his bare, gangly limbs in unison. Then he deflated and lay for a moment on the narrow cot, feeling the warm new day from his fingertips to his toes. He squeezed his eyes shut then opened them wide, blinking away sleep. He snuggled down on the mattress filled with oiled sea sand and looked around the small, fragrant room. Like all the rooms in the complex, it was a tiny place, barely large enough for his bed and a standing closet for his few clothes and possessions.

The home in which he lived was shaped like a large wheel. It was constructed of heat-retaining basalt stones piled one atop the other and coated with thick plaster made from seawater and crushed jasmine petals. He inhaled the invigorating aroma deeply. Vilu once asked the house guardian, "Which wakes me first? The light of the sky or the warming of the new day?"

"Which do *you* think, boy?" the man asked.

"The warming," Vilu had replied without hesitation. "Because it not only warms, it makes the jasmine and the bed oils smell stronger."

"Then it is the warming," the man said, smiling.

"Anyway," one of the other boys, Sahu, had said later, when they played in the courtyard after lessons, "it is always daytime during this season. There is always light. That wouldn't wake you."

"It wakes the seabirds," Vilu had replied. "I hear them. Why not us too?"

"They wake because they are hungry!" Sahu replied dismissively.

"If that were true, *you* would never sleep," Vilu said, laughing.

Sahu had no answer for that other than to shrug and continue consuming the petal-flavored ice he had purchased.

But Sahu had a point. Vilu had learned in their school that at this time of the season the sun circled overhead like a block of ice caught in an eddy. Even the window shades, made of *opirati* skin, could not darken a room completely. Vilu would have to remember to ask their tutor if sleeping people could react to little variations in light. The Priests said that quiet minds were actually wiser than those that were fully awake. But the Technologists disputed that idea, as he understood it.

If adults cannot agree, then why bother learning anything? the boy wondered. Then he smiled. *I wondered that in my head! Does that mean the Priests are right?*

There were no lessons today and, lying lazily on the mattress, Vilu studied the dark, charcoal-gray light that rose on the walls. It barely illuminated the designs that reached from floor to ceiling. The designs had been cut in the plaster by the local Priest, hoping for Candescence to shine on this abode. A Technologist had added flecks of olivine to the eyes of figures in the design. Vilu didn't understand the markings. It told a story about designs in the night sky, about lights strung across Galderkhaan like phosphorous fish. The Priests recited it in words he heard nowhere else. A few of the older children found it interesting. He found it confusing and boring.

He stretched again and continued to lie in bed, listening to the soothing sound of the ocean as it sloshed against the coast. As dreamtime left, he began to hear the familiar sounds of voices along the wharf, of the airships' ropes creaking on the current, of the fishers returning from their predawn hunt—

Fishers returning? the boy thought with sudden excitement. *Then why am I lying here?*

Typically, the bell would have rung by now and he would be at the adjoining home taking lessons with one of the teachers, but this was not an ordinary day. It was a time of celebration, the Night of Miracles, and the scholars were all in the capital city of Aankhaan, representing the village of Falkhaan in the festivities. Several of his friends had gone, but Vilu did not want to make the long journey by cart and raft. Those conveyances were too slow, too dull.

A real Night of Miracles would be if things were exciting for once! he thought, only half regretting his irreverence. At least the morning had potential to be exciting *if he hurried.*

Vilu leapt from his mattress, its mushy surface retaining his shape. He pulled off his short white nightshirt, dressed quickly in loose-fitting drawstring trousers and a roomy pullover, and ran toward the flap that hung heavily in his doorway. Pushing it aside, he nearly tripped over his long blue pant legs as he sped through the corridor. He hitched them up and expertly rolled the bottoms as he ran.

Each of the eight spokelike sections of the circular home opened onto triangular communal courtyards between the residential arms. Here, young children could play with minimal supervision from the adults. The courtyards were protected from the street by heavy *opirati* skins that only the older children could raise.

Limbs churning, Vilu thrust himself through one of the skins like a force of nature. He had selected this exit because the communal caregivers were on the other end of the home, organizing recreations for when the children woke. Vilu did not want to be stopped and told to gather the little ones. For one thing, he did not want to participate in the games and plays designed to help children understand and celebrate what Vilu did not quite understand nor wish to celebrate. Only two things mattered dearly to him: the *thyodularasi* who he swam with in the sea and, more—much more—the airships, especially the well-known ones piloted by the really great Cirrus Cloud command-ers, the likes of *Femora* Loi and *Femora* Azha in the fleet of *Standor* Qala. Vilu had heard that Azha of the coastal city of Aankhaan was in very bad trouble, but he didn't care: she had once given him a ride in the clouds and he would always love her for that.

"I wondered when we would see you!" cried a fish seller wheeling his basket from the airship field to the market.

"You'd better hurry!" yelled another.

Vilu only had time and breath enough to wave with a circling mo-tion, showing respect to the older women. He was glad his mother's mother was not here, for then he would have to stop and bow to her. There were more rituals in Galderkhaan than a restless boy had time for.

Arms and legs pumping, Vilu squinted against the light but he did not turn from the sun. He wanted to try and spot the great airship of *Standor* Qala, see it soaring clear and proud before the massive vessel passed in front of *welaji*, the light in the sky—teaching that distant ball of magma just who had command of the air!

A large hollow sound echoed through the skies. Vilu felt it in his belly. *That was it!* He had to hurry.

Breathing hard, the young boy ran across the densely packed, sun-hardened sand, wishing he had paused to pull on his footings. But there had been no time, and hadn't the local Priest once said to the fishers that labor toughens the flesh the way strife toughens the spirit the way destruction had strengthened the Candescents? Isn't what they were celebrating today—the disaster that gave birth to all life?

Who am I to fret about the flesh of my soles? Vilu wondered. To the contrary: he embraced the pain, the hardening.

Other Galderkhaani adults who knew the boy laughed and dodged as he raced toward the sound of the sea. The vast waters were an un-likely beacon, his birth mother, Otal, had said, because the surface boats did not interest him.

"You were birthed in a tower in Mendokhaan—you should run to the sound of the wind!" she had said.

Perhaps she was right; he did not see the woman very much since she moved to Aankhaan, so he could not discuss it with her. But the wind was a tease. Now it was here, now it was there. What was the point in running after it? He always knew where the sea was, and where there was sea there were fish and where there were fish there were airships. Even his teachers approved of that reasoning—despite the fact that Vilu desperately longed to be in that selfsame fickle air!

It's like playing with a thyodularasi, he thought. Part of the fun was that you never knew what it would do!

Unlike most of the citizens of the coastal village, Vilu did not care about the water for any other reason. His one passion was for the great airship that launched from the tower on the warm dawn currents, then spotted the legions of fish and sea giants and signaled the smaller airships and boats. He loved *Standor* Qala's ship so much that he even began to learn the flashing mirror-talk they used to communicate.

The young boy swung past the other housing complexes and decided to avoid the market that was sure to be crowded. Leading with his head of dark curly hair, he angled into a net street where the large fine-mesh sheets were suspended on high horizontal bars for repair. Workers were deftly handling bone needles and large coils of sinew that came from the herds of lumbering *shavula* that were bred for food, clothing, and rope. The net workers who knew Vilu, including two of his mother's lifelong men friends, Moge and Ura, stepped aside to allow him passage as he approached.

"You're not going to make it!" Moge said, laughing as he jabbed a calloused finger at the boy. "The approach horn has sounded!"

"I *will* make it!" he gasped. "I am not old like you!"

Another horn blared across the rooftops and through the streets.

"The airship is at the mooring tower," Ura added tauntingly, using hand gestures as he spoke. "You'll have to run harder."

"I'm trying!" Vilu said, throwing his arms up in a universal gesture of emphasis.

Vilu heard the dull flap of the great airship's wings as it soared across the tops of the homes, following the coast toward an imminent docking at the tower. The great oval shadow of *Femora* Loi's vessel was followed by the shadows of the much smaller airships and the nets they used for cloud farming. The multitude of long tapering shadows covered the net street with a design that looked like spots on a sacred *ymit* as it slithered through the coastal sands. Vilu loved to see the coastal flagship of the great fleet move from the fishing vessels like a teacher leaving its young to play, but he did not look up, he could not.

Though it was frowned on, since many elders were still asleep, Vilu cut through the radial arm of a small home belonging to the *jutan*, the old man who represented their town in the capital city. He dashed through one flap and out the other before the servants even knew he was there. That deposited him in a dark alley where *thyodularasi* gathered to rest in the shade and wait for scraps from passersby. The head of one of the sleek creatures rose and it honked as Vilu passed. The boy waved, missing in his attempt to pat its head as he raced by. The animal barked after him.

Vilu smiled back at the animal, looked ahead, then stopped running so abruptly that he scraped the soles of his feet with the suddenness of it.

The boy was at the mouth of a large courtyard that was built around a great oval pool, a hip-high basalt construct where ice water was melted for the many homes. Within the encircling wall the pit was cut deep in the packed sands, with long spokelike lumps marking the location of underground pipes that carried water from this pool, and others like it, throughout the village. Typically, before and after school, children sat astride the mounds and rode them as if they were the heralds of the Candescents riding their winged, heat-breathing *opirati*. When the mounds leaked, those games included splashing until the repair teams arrived.

Today, there were no children or their parents, talking, often loudly, about matters involving lovers or some political issue concerning Priests or Technologists—issues that Vilu did not really understand or care about. The scene in the courtyard was like nothing he had ever experienced. Nearby, in the alleys and streets that were used by people—not like the one he'd just gone through, which was frequented by *thyodularasi*—he saw small groups of adults huddled, watching in uncommon silence. They too were staring into the courtyard, which was not quite silent.

Beside the pool, on the side nearest Vilu, was a stone hut where the water guardian lived. He was an elderly citizen whose job it was to make sure people did not swim or drown in the pool. Normally, when children were riding the mounds, the tall old man, Lasha, was outside, where he pretended to be Tawazh, the primary sky god, chief herald of the Candescents. He would wave his arms in large gestures, ordering his minions to survey the northern regions beyond the sea, the eastern lands beyond the mountains, look for signs of the high gods' return. Sometimes Lasha's companion, Fen, emerged wearing a white cloth over her head and declared herself to be a Candescent, the only one greater than Tawazh, and yelled at Lasha to stop playing and pay attention to the white, furry little *mensats* that had interrupted their morning walks to leap into the water at the far end.

Today, Fen was already gone to her job as a record-keeper at the House of Judgment and Lasha was not being godly. He was fighting with a woman—fighting and losing. His back was against the rear wall of his narrow hut, his arms raised to protect his face, his belly turned away, protected by his hip. The woman was scratching at him with stiff, sweeping hands, kicking with agile legs. When he wasn't trying to protect his eyes the old man was trying to grab and restrain the woman's wildly moving arms.

Vilu stared through the bright morning sunlight, just as the others were doing. The *thyodularasi* he had passed moments before waddled from the shadows of a doorway, thumping over on flippers. These ended with stubby, webbed fingers from which the animal could extend four sharp claws per flipper. Absently, Vilu brushed the animal away by its whiskered snout. It grumbled low in its throat and nuzzled the boy anyway. Vilu ignored it. He had never seen physical conflict and was riveted. Violence was forbidden, unworthy, punished with banishment—and the boy was suddenly more frightened than anything else.

Fighting, he thought. *Violence in Falkhaan of Galderkhaan.*

His mind could not process that fact—even as he began to move toward it, one leg before the other, the same way he waded through the waves at the shore despite the unknown creatures and dangers and long, serpentine *ymits* that lay within. There was something that drew him to the struggle . . . and to the woman whom he did not recognize.

As he approached, the blazing sun was no longer in his eyes and he finally saw the many faces in the windows of the adjacent homes, peering from behind the shades, from around the barely opened door flaps. Youthful faces, adult faces, everyone watching. Like him, most had never seen a physical struggle . . . except as play.

Minutes passed and Lasha continued to struggle, at one point falling into the pool. As he pulled himself out the woman looked around and extended her fingers as if she were pointing at something that wasn't there. When Lasha emerged from the pool, he stepped around the woman and then ran at her again. Vilu realized, then, that she had not been attacking him but was trying to prevent him from restraining her.

Just then someone came striding from one of the buildings toward the two combatants. It was a tall young woman with the posture of a great, proud statue. With a sudden intake of air, Vilu recognized her from glimpses at the airship mooring tower where he sometimes sat and watched the great airship being loaded before taking to the skies: it was *Standor* Qala, undoubtedly here because this was where she had apprenticed. No doubt she was to meet her prized vessel and fly it to Aankhaan for the night's festivities. Qala was one of Galderkhaan's four *Standors*, and the sole commander of the fleet that plied the skies above the seas—and was likely to remain so, now that *Femora* Azha was said to be in trouble for violence. Qala looked godlike in her airship regalia, a tight leather tunic and ankle-length skirt with silver bands and markings that caught the sunlight. A red cloth pouch hung from her belt and fishbone clips clattered in her dark, shoulder-length hair as she moved. The woman put her arms around the other woman's shoulders and pulled her back.

"Stop this!" Qala said at the same time. "Get back, Lasha!"

"She began the struggle!" the old man cried. Aided by the *Standor*, he sought to enforce his control of the courtyard.

Their communication was brief and superficial because their hands were engaged, unable to add nuance. All the while, the woman fought to get away from them. With powerful hands, Qala grabbed the woman's black tunic and pulled so hard that poor Lasha, whom the stranger was still clutching, went with her, stumbling to one side but tearing free of his assailant's hands. The woman's fingers remained in motion, however, moving fast and wide, a gesture that Vilu had never seen used in speech.

Because it is fighting, he thought. *The language makes no sense because violence makes no sense.*

Overcoming his surprise, the young boy continued to creep forward, staying in the shadows—not like a creature of the tunnels, afraid of the light, but because the compacted earth was hot from the relentless sun. He continued to look ahead, like a seabird fixed on prey, as Qala bundled the struggling woman into her arms and held her there. The woman, whose features Vilu could not yet see, continued to kick and shout and then scream so loudly that the alleyways began to fill with more and more people drawn by her voice. People were beginning to wonder aloud who she was, for they did not know her; no one was a stranger in Falkhaan. He heard someone suggest that she was here for one of the local Night of Miracles celebrations.

Vilu crouched lower and continued forward until he was close

enough to hear what the woman was saying. It was difficult to understand the precise meaning of the woman's words, since her arms were
flailing, unable to qualify what her mouth was speaking. But Vilu understood the gist of her anger:

". . . must go!" the woman cried. "Must get back!"

"Where?" Qala asked. She hugged her close, the *Standor*'s legs
wide to brace herself.

"My son . . . *let me go!*"

"First, you must calm yourself!" Qala ordered.

As the last of the shadows of the fishing fleet passed overhead,
releasing the sun and causing the pool to sparkle wildly, the woman
seemed to relax. She did not go limp but she ceased her struggles.
Nonetheless, wily Lasha stood ready with a hemp noose he had just
grabbed from the hut. He held it up, ready to slip it around the woman's throat, but Qala shook her head.

"She will be all right now, I think," the *Standor* said. It was as much
an order as an observation. She tilted her head, looked down into the
woman's wide eyes. "You will be, yes?" she asked, motioning gently.

The woman didn't answer but she stopped struggling. Vilu felt a
release of tension from the crowd. It was like the Priests said: people
could feel people's moods if they were open to them. Now Vilu relaxed as well. Too late, he recalled why he had come running out in
the first place. Shielding his gold eyes, he looked up at the great airship as it nosed up to the high mooring tower on the coast—his
heart seemed to grow huge as he saw the pride of Falkhaan roped
and planked to the *simu-varkas*, the highest column in western
Galderkhaan. The great ship's flipperlike wings rippled atop the envelope, catching the air, turning at the behest of the *femora-sitas*
working the hemp. The tiny, distant deputy commanders were pulling hard. It was majestic, and yet—

Vilu's eyes returned to the dying conflict there on the ground.
That struggle had power too. Something about it touched him inside;
not just fear as he had never known in his young life, but the unfamil-

iar wildness of the woman and whatever had been compelling her to strike Lasha, to cry out. He had seen people who inhaled dried, burning seaweed act strangely, dance, roll on the ground—but never violently.

The woman was tired and all but hanging limp in the *Standor's* arms. The larger woman's face was near her captive's ear.

"Can I release?" Vilu heard the *Standor* ask in basic Galderkhaani, since her arms were still occupied.

Her captive hesitated then nodded.

"First, tell who are you and why this anger."

The smaller woman was breathing heavily. She was looking ahead, scowling, as though she were trying to solve a problem posed by a numbers scholar. She seemed distracted and was moving her fingers as if they were weaving needles. Side to side, pointing down, tucking and untucking.

"Did you hear?" *Standor* Qala asked.

"Yes, yes," the woman said. "I—I want to get home. To my son."

"Where is home?"

"North," she said after some hesitation.

"You must be mistaken," Qala told her. "You cannot dwell 'north.' There is no town 'north.'"

"There *is*," the woman said, finding renewed life in her arms and gesturing emphatically. "I tried to tell that to this *other* one—"

"Noose her!" Lasha said, shaking the hemp with fearful enthusiasm.

"Quiet," Qala said to the pool guardian. She turned her face back to her captive. "You wear the dress of a digger," the *Standor* noted. "I will take you to the Technologists, perhaps they should be—"

"No!" the woman said, then laughed. She moved her pinned arms as much as she could. "My god, the Technologists. This is madness. I cannot *be* here. I don't *belong* here. I must go back!"

Lasha had made his way around the woman then bent cautiously close to her hand. She was wearing a bracelet carved from stone.

"She cut my cheek with this," he said as he studied it.

"Your cheek should not have been so close," the captive said.

Qala continued to examine the woman. "No arguing. You seem better now," she said.

"I can stand, if that's what you mean."

"And have a conversation," the *Standor* said. She bent and looked at the carvings in the stone. "'To Bayarma from Bayarmii,'" she read.

The smaller woman shook her head as the laughter turned to tears. "It isn't possible," she said. "I—I know that name."

"Which name?" the *Standor* asked.

"Bayarmii," she said. "That was the name of the young girl who tried to bond with the soul of Maanik, a young woman in another—place."

"Another place," Lasha said, snorting. "North, you mean."

"That's right. The girl who perished with her grandmother. Or . . . she will perish." Caitlin looked at her hands. "I cannot be her . . . the grandmother. These are not old enough. I must be the girl's mother."

"You are confusing me," Qala said. "Who are *you*?"

The captive looked from Lasha to the glistening pool to the little boy near it. Her expression softened when she saw him and a sob erupted from her throat. Her legs fell from under her.

The *Standor* held her upright with strong but comforting arms. "What's wrong?" Qala asked.

"I left a sweet young boy behind," the woman said. "I have to find him."

"And perhaps I can help with that," the *Standor* said. "First, you haven't told us who you are? Only who you are not."

"I am Caitlin O'Hara," she said, the name sounding strange in a tongue that was not her own, "and I must get home."

"To the north?" Qala said.

Caitlin nodded forlornly. "To the north . . . and a world farther than that."

PART ONE

CHAPTER 1

It was nearly dawn when an exhausted Ben Moss left Lenox Hill Hospital on Manhattan's Upper East Side.

Nothing seemed real to the British-born UN translator. But that was becoming the new normal ever since he and Caitlin had been delving into the long-dead world of Galderkhaan and its living emissaries—ghosts, spirits, energies, or whatever they were; during those few weeks he had lost his old perspective on what constituted "real."

No, that is not entirely true, he thought. *What is very real is that Caitlin is presently unconscious and nonresponsive.*

Yet even as he thought that, his arms moved. He had been spending all his spare time trying to piece together and translate the language of Galderkhaan—so *much* time that it seemed almost unnatural not to make superlative hand gestures as he spoke.

That too was a new normal. Along with watching people who unconsciously moved their hands as they spoke, wondering, *Are you descended from Galderkhaani?*

Ben walked onto Third Avenue, into the lamplit darkness of the New York predawn. It was late fall and, in addition to the darkness, a cold wind swept in from the East River, adding to his sense of desolation. He was unsure what to do next. That unfamiliar confusion frightened him. Typically, Ben followed the lead of the UN ambassadors. He didn't have to plan very much, to think further than the next few words. The one time he had tried doing that, as a student at NYU—loving Caitlin—it ended with an estrangement that lasted for years.

Galderkhaan had brought back all the old fears of wanting something, of planning *for* something, of being disappointed. Now Caitlin's life might hang on him reengaging.

Not being a family member, Ben was only able to get answers from attending physician Peter Yang because the linguist was the only one who could explain—more or less—what had brought Caitlin to this condition.

"You told the EMT that she was—self-hypnotizing in the park?" Dr. Yang had asked as they stood in the hospital waiting room.

"Yes," Ben had said. That was the only way he could think to describe what he suspected was going on.

"Do you know why?" the doctor had enquired.

"She was . . . she *thought* she might be able to contact spirits," he said. "It's become a professional hot topic for her."

"Why?"

"Several of her patients needed help in that area—she didn't tell me more."

"Several?" the doctor had asked.

"Similar reactions to psychological trauma," Ben replied.

"Coincidence, then?"

"That is what she was—exploring," he said carefully.

"I see. No mental illness in her past?"

"None."

"Do you know if she has experienced visions, hallucinations?"

That had been a question full of dynamite. Ben had thought carefully how to answer. "Yes, but I don't think there's a neurological—"

"You're a doctor, Mr. Moss?"

"No. But she chose to do these things," he said with some annoyance. He didn't like being challenged on translations, and he didn't like being challenged on this. "As I said a moment ago, Doctor, she was *self*-hypnotizing. A choice."

"All right, then," the physician went on. "What about drugs, alcohol—"

"No drugs, no alcohol in excess."

"Depression, schizophrenia, hysterical reactions, near-death experiences?"

He answered yes to the last two, explaining—once again, revealing as little as possible—that Dr. O'Hara had been treating patients who suffered from both of those and she had experienced a kind of empathetic blowback.

"Not uncommon with good hypnotists," Dr. Yang mentioned. "Is this similar to the trauma work she did in Phuket, Cuba, and elsewhere?"

Ben brightened. "You know about that?"

"I've read what she has published."

"Yes, that work and this are very much related. Back then she was seeking a way to—short-circuit PTSD, if you will. She was continuing where she left off."

The doctor seemed less alarmed when he learned there was a context for the experiments. The diagnosis, for now, was psychogenic unresponsiveness. Dr. Yang said they would keep her in the hospital for more tests, but that was all he would say. Ben would have to find out more from Caitlin's parents. He had phoned them, waking them, trying and failing not to alarm them. It was one of the few times his smooth British accent and composure had been a total fail. They were on their way in from Long Island.

So Ben left the complex, largely uninformed, not quite aware of what had happened, and utterly unsure what to do next.

There were no phone messages. He hadn't expected any; neither Anita Carter nor Flora Davies had his cell number. Anita was a colleague and friend of Caitlin's, a psychiatrist who had stayed with Caitlin's son,

Jacob, at the apartment; Davies was the head of the Group, an organization based in a Fifth Avenue mansion and which collected information and relics from Galderkhaan. Ben did not know anything about the latter. Neither had Caitlin before she went down to its headquarters, a visit that led directly to her collapse in the adjacent Washington Square Park.

Bundled against the cold, Ben decided to do what he always did: take small steps and see where they went. He paused in the doorway of an office building to call Caitlin's landline, to make sure Jacob was all right. That was what Caitlin would have wanted him to do.

Anita picked up in the middle of the second ring. She said that the ten-year-old was in his room, up early after a restless night, but that there was something more pressing.

"What's wrong?" Ben asked.

"There's someone here," Anita said with concern in her voice. "First tell me—how's Caitlin? *Where* is she?"

"In the hospital."

"Is she all right?"

"She's unconscious—doctors wouldn't tell me much."

"Shit."

"Anita, who's there?"

The woman hesitated.

"Just say it," Ben told her. "Nothing would surprise me."

"All right." She lowered her voice, said closely into the phone, "It's a Vodou priestess. And her son."

"Madame Langlois and Enok?"

"Jesus, yes!" Anita seemed caught off guard. "How did you . . . was Caitlin expecting them? I assume she met them in Haiti—"

"Not expecting that I'm aware of," Ben said. Caitlin had met the Vodou priestess and her *houngan* son while trying to help a young girl in Port-au-Prince. Gaelle Anglade was one of the youths whose trauma seemed linked to Galderkhaan. If the duo had been planning to visit, Caitlin would not have failed to mention it. "They just showed up?"

"About an hour ago," Anita said. "They flew in from Haiti, came right here, and the priestess flat-out announced that Caitlin is in the coils of a serpent."

"The great serpent!" Ben heard a woman's voice say in the background.

"Forgive me," Anita said, lowering her voice. "The great serpent?"

"We did not come right here," the Haitian woman added. "Should have. I do not like Miami. Too chaotic."

"Right, right," Anita said into the phone. "Ben, what the hell is going on?"

"I'm not entirely sure," he answered truthfully. He did not know how much Caitlin may have told her about Galderkhaan and did not want to get into that now. Leaving the protection of the doorway, he saw a cab, hurried to the curb, and flagged it. "I'm coming over there. Has Jacob been in his room the entire time?"

"Yes," Anita said. "He's been in there drawing a comic book about Captain Nemo . . . he's fine. Ben, I'm a pretty good psychiatrist and very good listener and there's something you're not telling me. What exactly happened to Caitlin?"

"Firefighters found her lying unconscious in Washington Square Park."

"Oh, Ben . . ."

"I know. There were fires—maybe a gas leak. Perhaps she was overcome."

"I got the alert on my phone, didn't put the two together. Should I call her folks?"

"Done. They're on the way to Lenox Hill."

"Jesus. What does the doctor say? Or wouldn't they tell you?"

"He was like the bloody sphinx, with occasional claws."

"Jesus," she said again. "Maybe if I call him, doctor to doctor?"

"From his questions, I don't think he knows much. I'm more concerned about Jacob and your guests."

"I understand. Look, I'll arrange with my office to stay here as long as I'm needed. Meanwhile, what *do* I do about . . . them?"

"Nothing, other than keep them away from Jacob," he said. "Have they asked about him?"

"No—but they're obviously involved in this whole 'thing' somehow," she whispered. "How else could they know that *something* was going to happen to Caitlin?"

"I just don't know," Ben said. "Look, Caitlin's got a can of mace in her night table if you need it. I'll be there in about ten minutes. And don't ask how I know that."

"Wasn't," Anita replied. "What's the doorman's name? In case I need him?"

"I think Elvis is on at this hour."

"*Elvis?*"

"Yeah. He's okay."

"What about you?" Anita asked. "How are *you?*"

"I have absolutely no idea," he told her. "Just moving ahead. See you soon."

Ben sat back in the cab, watched the video display in the seat, saw the news alert from Washington Square. There weren't just fires; there were floods, water-main breaks, crowds of students who were being hustled from dorms into the streets. The driver was talking to someone in Nepali on his Bluetooth. Ben couldn't even tune it out; he understood everything about the family's dispute with the city over a dangerous school crossing in Queens.

Noise and unrest, Ben thought. It didn't end with the tamping down of the tensions between India and Pakistan. It just went back underground, unsettling everyone at a low boil. Thanks to Caitlin and her commitment to helping, he was now acutely aware of it.

Caitlin, he thought, choking up for the first time. *What happened down there, Cai?* But it was more than wondering; it was pain and guilt. While Caitlin sought a way to rescue the kids who had been assaulted by Galderkhaani spirits—Maanik Pawar in New York, Gaelle Anglade in Haiti, Atash Gulshan in Iran—Ben Moss, linguist, had been pushing the Galderkhaani language on her, calling and texting and meeting with her to describe with great enthusiasm each new discovery or supposition. He had made her part of a quest that should have ended, for her, with the curing of Maanik and Gaelle. He tried—and failed— not to feel resentment at the way she had kept him out of her research and discoveries. It brought up old feelings about the way she had conceived Jacob with a man she had only just met on a relief mission, someone who later became the very definition of "absentee father."

Tears pressed against the backs of his eyes as he thought of the girl he had shared so much with, who he had strongly reconnected with over Maanik, who he was now helplessly in love with. He wanted her back not just from this crisis but in all ways, and he didn't know how to go about any of it.

Baby steps? Ben thought with sharp self-reproach. His limited research into Galderkhaan barely translated the fragments of ancient language they possessed, let alone provided insights into the existence of souls in the Ascendant, Transcendent, and Candescent realms. How was he supposed to help Caitlin with this?

Maybe the madame has insights, he thought then hoped. The priestess had been helpful in Haiti. *She certainly has some kind of second sight.*

As the cab sped west across Central Park, Ben tried to be useful— and consoled—by applying himself to the purely scholarly side of the problem. He was amazed at how much cultural overlap had been revealed among Galderkhaani, Vodou, Hindu, and Viking lore—peoples who had no contact in the dawn of our known civilization. Yet, the same cultural archetypes appeared. Inevitability? Or was it something deeper. Was there a connection that went back to this civilization that predated all others?

How can that not *be the case?* he asked himself.

Nor was this the time to figure it out. He did not see how that kind of research would help Caitlin.

By the time the taxi reached Caitlin's Upper West Side apartment building, the morning had already blossomed into early dog walkers, rattling breakfast carts, and loud delivery trucks. The bustle seemed to be happening outside a bubble, a combination of exhaustion and distraction. Even the driver's ongoing school-crossing issue seemed to belong to some other time and place.

And then, suddenly, there was a wave of fear—not unwarranted. No sooner had Ben emerged from the cab than a man stepped up to him. The newcomer was about five-ten, a little shorter than Ben, and in his forties. He was wearing jeans, work boots, and a black beret. His eyes were covered with reflective sunglasses with fashionable white frames. He held his smartphone in his left hand. His right hand was thrust deep into the pocket of his heavy leather jacket.

"Mr. Moss," the man said. It wasn't a question.

"Sorry, I'm in a hurry."

"I understand," the man replied politely, but firmly, stepping to block his way. "This will not take long."

The man's voice possessed a faint but distinctive accent, which Ben placed as Icelandic. It was uncommon here, and in spite of everything—or because of it—Ben gave the man his attention, but not until after he had looked around.

"There is no one else with us," the man said. "You will not be accosted."

"All right," Ben said. "You have my attention. Who are you and how do you know who I am?"

"My name is Eilifir," the man said softly, "and I followed you from the Group mansion, saw you speaking briefly with Dr. O'Hara."

"Followed?"

"I have a car. Actually, the driver followed you. I was busy watching."

"But you just said—"

"That there is no one with us, and there isn't," the man said. "We are alone. From the mansion I came here, replaced one of my people. I've been waiting to speak with Caitlin—or you."

"I see. You mentioned the Group. How do you know those people?" Ben asked.

"We—their sponsors and my people—once lived together."

"On Fifth Avenue?"

"No, Mr. Moss," the man replied with a little chuckle. His unshaved cheeks parted as he smiled for the first time. "Our ancestors lived together. In Galderkhaan."

Ben was a little rocked by that—not just the fact that someone else knew about the place, but obviously knew more than he did. Then his mind returned to what he had just been thinking about, what he knew of the postapocalyptic trek of the Galderkhaani up through Asia to points north, including Scandinavia.

"You say you 'once' lived together," Ben remarked. "That, plus the fact that you didn't go up to the mansion and knock on the door tells me that you are no longer very sociable."

"Their ideas are different from mine."

"Are you some kind of rogue scholar?" he asked.

"Not exactly," the man replied.

" 'Not exactly?' That's all I get?"

"For now."

"Uh huh," Ben said, and moved to go around the man. "Sorry, Eilifir. I have a lot to—"

"Not yet," the man said with a hint of menace now. He moved closer.

Ben hesitated. He had been around enough diplomats to know when polite insistence was about to shade into a threat.

"Do the doctors know what is wrong with Dr. O'Hara?" Eilifir asked.

"How do you know anything's wrong with her?"

"I have a man outside the hospital," the man replied. "You departed. She did not. Must we do this dance, Mr. Moss?"

"Caitlin is unconscious but it isn't a coma," Ben answered. "They don't know what it is. You probably know that, if you've been watching her."

"No, I only suspected," the man said. "We make it a policy not to crowd people. The others—they do that. Empathetic souls like Dr. O'Hara pick up on it." He turned his face toward the brownstone. "The man and woman who are upstairs, why are they here?"

"I don't know that either," Ben said. "How do you know about *them?*"

"Someone was here, watching, until I could relieve her."

"That's at least three people," Ben said. "You have a curious definition of 'alone.'"

"As you know, words have nuance."

"Right, but I don't have time for subtleties. So that there are no more surprises—how many helpers do you have here?"

"Too few," Eilifir replied. "Do you know Casey Skett?"

Hell, couldn't the man answer a question directly? "No," Ben said to move this along. "Who is *he?* Or is it a waste of breath to ask?"

"I guess you would call him our general," the man said. "He and I are the leaders of a handful of other field personnel who want to help you save Dr. O'Hara."

"From?"

"Becoming lost in the past," the man said.

"How do you know . . . *what* do you know?" Ben asked.

"That any form of *cazh* or the lesser mergings is tricky, dangerous, as I'm sure you well know."

"Is that what happened here?" Ben asked with alarm.

"I'm honestly not sure," Eilifir replied. "That's what we're trying to determine. If it has, then she is in great danger."

Ben did not tell the man that it was the second time that morning he'd heard that sentiment.

Eilifir drew his hand from his pocket, handed Ben a card. "Call me when you learn anything, when you need something."

"You seem certain that I will."

"No one can face these forces alone," he said, "the more so when he or she doesn't know what they are."

"Do you?"

The man was quiet for a moment—contemplative. "Not entirely, no. But we have tools you lack, tools you may need. And before you ask what they are, I can only say this: Caitlin O'Hara has forged an energetic relationship with just two Galderkhaani tiles. That was enough to send her soul through time and wreak havoc across several acres of New York." He moved closer to Ben until they were inches apart. There was a new, more ominous quality in his voice. "There are thousands of tiles buried beneath the South Polar ice. If Dr. O'Hara taps into them, wakens them in an effort to get home, the forces she will release would be exponentially more destructive than what we saw last night. And not in the past, Mr. Moss. She would pull that fury with her, into the present. It would travel *through* her. You can imagine, I think, what would be left of her after that."

It was as fantastic and sobering a monologue as any Ben had ever heard—and, in the United Nations, he had translated many of those.

"Where will you be?" Ben asked.

"Right here," Eilifir said, backing away.

Though the air was warming slightly, Ben felt cold inside. Without another word, he turned and went into the apartment.

CHAPTER 2

Mikel Jasso was very tired and extremely frustrated.

The Basque native lay in the cot that had been assigned to him until such time as he could be evacuated from the Halley VI research station. That would take weeks, but he had been ordered to stay out of the way of the thirty-nine scientists, medics, maintenance workers, and other personnel at the base. He was to remain inside the eight modules—which were connected caterpillar-style, like a train—not venturing outside, not observing experiments or research, simply doing nothing.

Doing nothing had kept him awake since his adventure under the Antarctic ice. He desperately needed sleep. But there was something he needed more desperately. He had been among the long-frozen ruins. He had interacted with tiles of staggering power.

He had communicated with the dead.

Mikel Jasso needed answers, not imprisonment.

And I need someone above ground to talk to about it all, someone to listen to me, he thought. There was a vast amount of knowledge out there. The technology alone could occupy him for years. Not just the olivine tiles but treated skins that were still fresh, the breathing apparatus that seemed to employ the mechanism of sea creatures to filter air from a maelstrom; all of that was extremely sophisticated. And he couldn't get to it, having made himself a pariah by causing the crash of a truck, the denting of a module it was pulling, and endangering the life of an expedition member who had elected to rescue him from an underground cavern.

Mikel also had a broken wrist, which made it difficult to do anything.

And so he lay there, his tablet at the ready, staring at the white ceiling, replaying the last two days for anything he may have missed.

The archaeologist had to laugh, at least inside. He was in a human habitation brought south, and to this spot, with enormous effort. Administered by the British Antarctic Survey, the Halley VI modules had just been successfully towed from a fragile section of terrain on the Brunt Ice Shelf to a more stable region twelve kilometers inland from the Weddell Sea. The accommodation building and garage had come with greater difficulty: not having been erected on skis, they had to be dragged across the ice by trucks and bulldozers struggling against unfavorable winds and cold. Yet nearby, an entire civilization had flourished in this miserable, hostile environment. Even allowing for climatic change, Antarctica was still quite harsh at the dawn of the Ice Age, at the height of Galderkhaani civilization. From what he had gleaned in the caverns, lava had been used to melt and control ice via a network of tunnels. Towers of basalt and other materials had been built. The air had been conquered by ships that spanned the vast continent, and perhaps beyond. Science and religion had struggled with an ambitious, deeply conflicted cultural project, the conquest of the afterlife . . . incredibly, with some success.

The anthropologist in him was puzzled by something even deeper: How did the Galderkhaani come to be here? When? By what chain of evolution? The answers would change human understanding of the world. Those answers, those profound truths were also out there, and Mikel couldn't get to them. He couldn't convince a group of scientists to help him investigate further. In fairness, Mikel was not being as cooperative, and thus as persuasive, as he might have been. His unauthorized descent into the ancient underground ice tunnels, and his insistence that he could not reveal much of what he had found there— not without the authorization of his employer, Flora Davies and the Group back in New York—had alienated the science team and most of the other occupants. The sole exception was Siem der Graaf. The young maintenance worker appreciated the fact that the archaeologist treated him like a colleague and not a high-priced repairman. Siem also appreciated Mikel's willingness to charge into the unknown in pursuit of knowledge. If not for the extreme climatic conditions, Mikel wouldn't be sitting here because of the Halley VI staff. But he wouldn't get more than a quarter mile without gear and assistance.

Making matters worse at the moment, he had been unable to reach Flora Davies, his superior at Group headquarters, her assistant Adrienne, or anyone else in the NYU-area mansion. The Internet was down, and phone service was poor though he still got into voice mail; for some reason, Flora wasn't calling back. He had seen on the news that the West Village in Manhattan was still reeling from unexplained fires in the area; no doubt that, and the water pumped at the inferno, had compromised the wires in old conduits beneath the mansion.

His forced isolation wasn't entirely contrary, however. Mikel used the time to create a written record of everything he could remember about his trip through the ruins of ancient Galderkhaan and his encounter with the spirits of the Priests Pao and Rensat. With one hand, he had arduously pecked out the log on his tablet.

The dead, he had written, are not dead—merely without bodies. The lowest of these appear to be "unascended souls." Like poltergeists in modern lore, they appear to be trapped in the place where they lived or died. I encountered two of these: Galderkhaani Enzo, who had a modern soul; and scientist Jina Park, who was held here, in her thrall. I do not understand by what mechanism either of them remained in the caverns below the ice. Perhaps by *choice? Perhaps by the means through which they died—intense fire? Or perhaps this is the Galderkhaani version of hell, a place where souls are punished for suicide or murder or other mortal crimes.*

In the happier order of things, the Galderkhaani believed that at death they ascended—single souls reaching a level of celestial epiphany I still don't understand. From my studies I learned that Pao and his contemporary Vol created a ritual they called cazh, *words and a ceremony that bonded souls, allowed them to shuck the body en masse and, together, rise to an even higher state of spiritual enlightenment—Transcendence, which I would equate with traditional angels or djinn in more familiar ancient lore. Their ultimate goal was to bring together enough souls to—well, transcend Transcendence and achieve Candescence, a state of bliss they believed would make them somehow "one" with the cosmos.*

Strangely, it did not sound lunatic as he wrote it. Mikel's livelihood was to conduct research for the Group, research that sought every fragment of knowledge they could glean about Galderkhaan. During that quest he had encountered many ancient and current faiths that, despite their subtle differences, all had an archetypical similarity: without fail, each of them believed that humans die and a spiritual part of them goes to an afterlife.

Who am I to dispute any of it, he thought as he added material to his tablet. *Either I spent hours speaking with a pair of transcended ghosts or I was delirious.*

That was possible too.

Mikel ached in every part of his body, having climbed through lava tubes and flown vast distances through a wind tunnel, which was where he broke his wrist, not to mention being thrown from a truck that was hauling a module. He had struck his head numerous times, so many times, in fact, that anything was possible.

But there is no disputing this, he thought as he typed. *Since touching those luminous olivine stones that lined sections of the tunnel and its towers, I have felt different. Not alert, because I'm still tired as hell . . . but more intuitive, I guess you'd call it.* He went back and erased that; it wasn't true.

He didn't know when someone was coming or what was being served for a meal. He wrote: . . . *but more aware of the lives that were lived here.*

Whether they were ghosts or angels in any real sense did not matter. Mikel felt as though, through the tiles, he had touched the past . . . that the past was still out there, somewhere, not dead but alive, not gone but eternal.

He didn't write any of that. The data wasn't there to support a living past, and the answers were elusive. He hoped, while he was still down here, he could learn more. However, he did add this:

I'm still at a loss to explain exactly what precipitated the pillar of fire that erupted perhaps fifty kilometers from where I found the Galderkhaan power center, the Source—whose early activation apparently precipitated the destruction of that civilization.

That wasn't entirely true. It *could* be explained.

Pao and Rensat had sought an American woman, Caitlin O'Hara, someone with experience in spiritual matters and Galderkhaani artifacts. They wanted her to help them save Galderkhaan from destruction by shutting down the Source in the past. Perhaps they had found Caitlin and she had done just the opposite—activated it here and now, or at least part of it, to obliterate the possibility of rewriting history. Or perhaps she made it burn hotter in the past somehow, and there was blowback in the present. Those details are the ones he lacked.

But he had no explanation to fit the geology and the narrative that had been unfolding. The deep, deep magma would have required a reason to suddenly "burp" at that location.

In any case, Pao and Rensat clearly had not succeeded. Otherwise, he would not be here. If Galderkhaan had survived, it would still be here. The concept of multiple timelines, of alternative histories, of parallel worlds was not something he was willing to consider . . . yet.

But then, a few days ago, the spirit world was not something in which you put much credence either, he thought.

He flexed his index finger, which he had been typing with. Below him, the module was not quiet. There was the ever-present hum of generators, the occasional hammering shriek of wind, and the creak of the structure as it endured those winds. Yet that was all background noise and Mikel started when his phone chimed.

"Finally!" he said as he saw Flora's personal number. He pressed the device to his ear and plugged a finger in the other to drown out the noise. "Hello—Flora?"

"No," the male voice said from the other end. "It's Casey Skett."

Mikel was instantly alert. For the last ten years Skett had worked with the Group disposing of biological "accidents" that occasionally resulted from their research. He worked for the New York City Department of Sanitation's "DAR" division—dead animal removal. That was the only reason he ever came to the mansion. Skett should not be using Flora's phone.

"Casey, what's going on over there?" Mikel asked with an unprecedented sense of foreboding.

"I want you to talk to Flora," he said, his voice crackling through the bad connection. "And then I want you to do me a favor."

"Put Flora on," Mikel said. There was something about Casey's tone that did not sound like Casey, the skinny and slack-eyed figure who rarely strung more than three or four words together.

A moment later Flora was on the line.

"Hello, Mikel. I'm afraid you're going to have to do whatever Casey asks," she said in a thick, slow voice.

" 'Afraid'?"

"He—he has shared information that I cannot, at present, divulge," she said.

"Why not?"

"Because he—he does not wish me to," she replied. "But you will cooperate with him, yes?"

This too was not the Flora he knew. But Mikel knew better than to question her. Not because she was always right, but because there was no changing her mind once it was set.

"Of course," Mikel told her. "I'll do whatever you need, Flora."

"Thank you, Mikel."

He was immediately aware of—and concerned by—a couple of slight catches he had noticed in her voice, brief hesitations. She was one of the most certain people he had ever known. Were those catches natural, or was she trying to signal him that all was not well?

"Before you go," Mikel asked casually, "how is my find behaving?"

But Flora was not available to answer. Casey Skett was back on the call.

"Your find is fine," Casey informed him. "It's under control."

"You've evidently been promoted," Mikel said.

"I could not resist the compensation package," Skett said. "And you, Dr. Jasso—you are a valued reallocated asset."

"Meaning?"

"That my promotion means you are no longer working for Flora but for me. And the favor I need is for you to go to the site where fire erupted from the ice."

Mikel didn't ask how he knew. The Group has access to satellites monitoring every area of the Galderkhaani continent. "Do you know what caused it?"

"Something in the past, I believe," he answered. "Or rather, something that began in the past and rippled through to the present. That process is one of the things I wish to understand."

At least he wasn't cagey about answering. "I have a broken wrist," Mikel said.

"You still have one hand that works? That's all you should need."

"True, if I could get out there," Mikel said. "But I've created problems down here—lots of them. No one is going to do me any favors."

"Find a way to compel them," Skett replied bluntly. "They're already trying to understand it—but from a distance, like the safe and incurious academics they are."

"How do you—"

"I saw it in a report filed by Dr. Bundy," Skett said. "I have resources too, Dr. Jasso. Aren't *you* curious about it as well?"

"Of course I am," Mikel said. "But I'm grounded, and frankly, I don't like being under the whip hand of someone who was until today a custodian, in effect."

"Who pretended to be a custodian, in effect," Skett said. "And spare me the hauteur. You took orders from Flora easily enough."

"She earned my respect. You haven't even begun."

"Dr. Jasso, pride has no place in my work. You will do as I ask and that is that. However, I assure you, my reasons are not hostile even if my methods seem to have been. Inform these scientists of yours that you can show them what happened out there. Assure them they will never figure it out just using instruments, but that *you* can explain it."

"Just by going out there?"

"Correct," Skett said. "By going out there and witnessing an experiment that I will be performing from here. Dr. Jasso, you know there's more to this phenomenon than geology. You were down there, among ruins. Don't bother to deny it—Flora told me everything."

"She couldn't have, Casey. She didn't *know* everything. That's what reports are for."

"Educate me," Skett said.

"Why? If you want my help, put Flora back in charge and tell me what *you* know."

"I know that Flora and her entire staff will die if you don't go," Skett said. "I'll tell you what: you can keep your secrets for now. Just get out there. You'll want to share with me in due course."

Mikel hesitated. Skett was right about one thing: the issue was Galderkhaan, not Group politics. He didn't seem to have many options.

"What are the risks?" Mikel asked.

"They are abundant, but you've taken risks before."

"I have, but I need a good reason to go out in temperatures that are negative thirteen degrees Fahrenheit and falling," Mikel said, glancing at the Halley VI weather app on his phone. He wasn't being entirely truthful: he would risk a great deal to be able to go back out there.

"I already gave you the reason," Skett said with growing impatience.

"And I've agreed," Mikel said. "But I need to come up with a really persuasive argument to get permission to use Halley equipment."

"Two words should do it," Skett said. "Actionable information."

"I just said, they have their procedures here—"

"And they have funding to consider as well," Skett said. "They have to produce results or the spigot runs dry. Now go and get this done, Dr. Jasso."

It was a simple but possibly effective argument. Among the twenty-three scientists, there had to be one who would back him.

"Put Flora back on," Mikel demanded. Then he added, "Please."

A moment later Flora was back on the phone. "I'm here, Mikel." The echo told him she was on speaker.

"Are you all right with this?"

"In theory, yes. I would have preferred more time for preparation, but Skett is running this operation at the moment."

"Flora, who *is* Casey Skett? Why is he doing any of this? Why *now*?"

"It is not just *now*," Skett said angrily, grabbing the phone and taking the call private. "My god, Dr. Jasso—it has been this way for centuries. The Group—do you think they are this benevolent research organization funded by the scions of the old East India Company?"

"So I've been told," Mikel said cautiously.

"It's a lie, Dr. Jasso."

"Let me hear that from Flora," Mikel replied.

"I'm afraid she doesn't know everything either," Skett said. "Now enough talk. Just get to the site. You will understand better when you see what kind of power we are exploring."

"We? Who else is involved in this?"

"There is nothing more to discuss," Skett said. "Call me when you are there."

"I need to rest," Mikel said. "I've been going nonstop for days."

There was a brief silence. "Take three hours, then go. I will expect your call."

Mikel heard a scream.

"Flora?" he yelled into the phone.

"Mikel, be care—"

But Casey had already terminated the call.

CHAPTER 3

This was not a dream. It was not a vision. All of this was real, and the physical stimuli were an assault on the mind of Caitlin O'Hara: the unfamiliar sights and smells, the loose touch of the clothing, the sudden and unfamiliar sense of agoraphobia—she wanted to be *home*—and her inability to will these things away . . . the onslaught drove her into a swift, ungovernable panic attack.

She struggled, she rose, she moved, and she remembered little of it until now.

Now? What is "now"? she wondered with considered clarity that was almost worse than the raw panic. *What is "is"?* She was obviously in ancient Galderkhaan in a body that was not her own. From the bracelet, she assumed it was Bayarma's body, the mother of Bayarmii.

Standing with her back to the tall, powerful woman who had restrained her, Caitlin breathed slowly and pointed the first two fingers of each hand at the ground. Her vision was sharper, the smell of fish and jasmine filled her nostrils, the air was cool to the point of chilly and free of pollen, and there were no mechanical sounds anywhere in the world around her, her arms and fingers felt different. The sky was a rich blue, the clouds the same as her own time, and there was a thin tendril of black smoke that came from somewhere in the distance.

But she did not feel the one thing she wanted desperately to feel. She could not find the active stones in her own time, and the tiles here appeared to be quiescent. Without them, she did not know how to return to her own time. The one other occasion she was here—protecting souls in her time from aggressive souls in Galderkhaan—she was disembodied, a spirit, a conduit for energy. Caitlin felt none of that now.

Because the tiles are all in harmony and balance, she thought. *Vol has not yet activated the Source. Who knows how many years—or weeks or days—until he does.*

Panic was replaced by helplessness. Plugging into the earth calmed her and she somehow managed to remain calm. Perhaps it was the balmy air, cool and refreshing, with the salty smell of a nearby sea. Maybe it was this *body*, which wasn't her own; it didn't seem to want to panic. It didn't seem to understand, even, what that was.

Caitlin was glad for all of that because she couldn't afford to lose control again. She did not know if there were psychologists here—there didn't seem to be a word for one, she realized, as she *thought* in Galderkhaani. The closest she came was *galdani*—a physician who heals with a kind of empathic energy. But she imagined that there were prisons and hospitals and she did not want to end up in either.

Being physically present in Galderkhaan felt different from being here in spirit. In her previous experiences with the Galderkhaani, Caitlin had felt like a hitchhiker. With Maanik, with the other children, she was not alive in a foreign body but merely observing through their eyes. Eavesdropping. This was not like that. She was inhabiting, controlling, this woman's body. The chronic numbness in Caitlin's hip, from childbirth, was gone. She looked at her fingers, saw the whorls of her fingerprints. The encroaching farsightedness, though slight, was also gone. She did experience a little difficulty breathing, however.

No, she realized suddenly. It wasn't difficulty. It was simply different. Either her lung capacity was less or the oxygen content was diminished.

As she continued to take stock—quickly, intellectually, like when she was an aid worker checking her gear before boarding a truck or helicopter—she realized that her arms were shorter, fingers more slender, but both were stronger. Her upper arms were toned, bronzed, fit, either from whatever work Bayarma did or from speaking in Galderkhaani with the constant superlative gestures that gave depth and nuance to every spoken word and phrase.

Caitlin noticed all this as the woman continued to hold her supportively, gently, despite the obvious strength in her big hands.

The woman asked if she could let Caitlin go. Caitlin indicated that she was all right now. Her captor finally released her and took a step back. Caitlin made sure she could stand on her own, then turned slowly and looked behind her. As she gazed at that strange, alien face, the flesh ruddy bronze with oddly elongated gold eyes, Caitlin fought very hard not to freak out again.

This is real. I am here.

But becoming agitated would not help her get home—if that were even possible—and she did not know how much time she had. If she perished with Galderkhaan, what would happen to her soul?

They spoke, Caitlin gathering her thoughts, not remembering what she said after she said it—she was still trying to find the tiles, to feel comfortable in this body. She continued to breathe slowly. There was a pool of water to her left. She extended two fingers toward the ground near it. She closed her eyes and, through the pool, tried to connect to any of the waters around New York. She did not feel her soul reaching outward as she had when she was on the rooftop and used the harbor to find Yokane, the descended Priest living in the city. She pushed her fingers hard, curled them, tried to pull something, *anything*, from the water. She heard the sound of the sea nearby, but could not feel it. She pictured her body lying in Washington Square Park—just that—and attempted to return to it, to the moment she fell. There had been firefighters, flame, water from hoses.

Caitlin felt nothing. She sought the bodies that had been buried centuries before in the potter's field under the park. Again, nothing.

Of course, she thought with rising horror. *I can't reach them because those bodies have not yet lived and died.* Manhattan and its waters—perhaps they're somewhere else on the globe in this era, nearer to the equator as they once were. There was no way of knowing.

My body has not yet been created, she thought with true horror. But then how did her *soul* exist? And not just her soul, but her memories. She thought about her son and tried to use that to get home. She imagined Jacob in their apartment. He was not born yet in this time, but his spirit lived strong inside Caitlin. That should help . . . it *had* to help.

It didn't. Once again, there was no vibration, no sense of anything beyond her fingertips other than the unfamiliar Antarctic air, the distant cries of seabirds, the receding sound of leathery flaps from the airship not far, the crashing of waves.

"You seem better now," the other woman said.

Caitlin nodded tightly. They spoke some more, she gestured as they spoke, she confirmed whose body she had . . . "borrowed." Caitlin definitely was not better but she had to find a way to appear so. She did that for her patients sometimes, when she had problems of her own and was not quite ready to hear those of others: she compartmentalized, and she had to do so now. She allowed herself to submit to the present . . . this present, not her own present, millennia hence. She relaxed her fingers.

Caitlin knew she would have to learn more about her surroundings . . . and, most importantly, what was holding her here. Had she flashed here from the tower where she had faced Pao and Rensat? Or was that in the future? Or the past? Were the tiles of that structure binding her to this place?

If so, why can't I feel them?

It was a struggle to remain focused, to try and prioritize.

They were talking about Caitlin's home, about her having come from the north. The psychiatrist found herself doing what she always did, what challenged Ben, concerned Barbara, occasionally shocked Anita: she was telling the truth, regardless of the consequences. Maybe that wasn't such a good idea.

Meanwhile, the woman in leather and silver regarded her quizzically. She returned to Caitlin's name, which she had provided just moments before.

"Cai-tah-lin Oh-ha-rayaah," the woman said thoughtfully. "The name and inflection are unfamiliar to me."

I am not surprised, Caitlin thought. *The language will not be created for tens of thousands of years.*

"As I said, I am not from around here," Caitlin replied.

"The bracelet," Lasha said accusingly. "Perhaps it is stolen?"

"No," Caitlin replied. "I—I would never do that. Maybe I *am* Bayarma."

"Ah, so now you are *two* people!" Lasha said, holding up a pair of fingers, one on each hand. "Maybe you are a *flendro* as well!"

"There is no need to be insulting," Qala cautioned.

Lasha grumped back a step.

"Tell me about your home in the north," Qala said.

"I—I can't remember much," Caitlin lied. She didn't want to alienate the tall woman who seemed intent on actually helping her. It was better to buy time, try and find out *when* she was, relative to the end of Galderkhaan. She looked at the cloth wrappings on her feet. They were bound with leather strips attached to a wooden sole. The edges were scuffed, old. She looked at her fingernails. They were worn, chipped. She could be a laborer of some kind.

"Do you wish to see a physician?" Qala asked. "There is one on my airship."

"No, thank you," Caitlin replied, gesturing sweetly. She didn't want to end up a guinea pig. She touched the bracelet. "This girl, Bayarmii. I should try to find her."

"As you wish," the *Standor* said. "Then I will leave you to Lasha— *provided* he promises not to noose you."

"I am a gentle man, my companion will tell you so." He wagged a threatening finger at Caitlin. "But she must swear on the scrolls not to misbehave. Can she guarantee that?"

"I am fine now," Caitlin assured them. "It was the shock of waking in this strange place."

"Or . . . it could be overheated fish," Lasha said accusatorily. "*That* could be the cause."

The *Standor* made a face at him. "Every time I see you, Lasha, you blame all the ills of Galderkhaan on fish or fishers."

"Not *all*," Lasha scowled back. "If you want to know whom I really blame it on—" Lasha began, then bit off the rest of the sentence. He looked around at the crowds still hovering in the shadows. "Well . . . the fish are the innocent heirs of poor decisions made . . . elsewhere."

"Another Khaana beater? Will you also blame the government for the way the air blows?"

"You don't think cloud farming and airships alter the currents?"

"Please, no politics or science," Qala said, raising her hand. "I have enough of that aloft, where I cannot escape the mutterings of the crew. I do not wish to speak of our ruling body."

"Or *Femora* Azha?" Lasha said, challenging Qala.

At that, Caitlin became alert. "I know that name," she said. Caitlin had to control herself from overreacting at the mention of the name. She knew Azha *too* well. It was that Galderkhaani's ascended soul that had directed her to Pao and Rensat, to the confrontation that had brought her here.

"I'm not surprised you've heard it," Lasha said. "The name is whispered everywhere in Galderkhaan."

"It will not be here and now," Qala said. She fixed a critical gaze at Lasha. "Criticize the fish if you will, speculate on shifting air currents if you must, but as a Khaana appointee I will not hear the rest." Her eyes shifted to Caitlin. "I wish you well. I am due in Aankhaan."

While Qala spoke, Lasha had opened and closed his mouth several times—like a fish, Caitlin thought. He seemed to want to say something, but before he could muster his thoughts, or his courage, Qala had turned and left.

"Thank you," Caitlin said after the woman.

Qala half turned and waved with a circular motion of leave-taking.

Caitlin took another moment to settle into her body and to accept the fact that she had understood and responded to everything that was being said. Some part of the mind of Bayarma was still obviously very present. The reference to Azha also helped her focus. If the woman had already acted against Vol, had failed to stop his premature activation of the Source, then the destruction of Galderkhaan was nigh. Caitlin couldn't afford to delay for that reason, or in case the captive soul of Bayarma was able to assert itself. That dynamic too was an unknown. If Bayarma returned, would Caitlin automatically be shifted home? Or would she just be kicked out, disembodied in limbo as she found herself after the conflagration in the park?

Lasha sat on a shaded section of the wall surrounding the pool. "Fen is right. My tongue will dig my place in the road. Just as it did for *Femora* Azha." He looked up at Caitlin. "You said that name sounds familiar to you?"

"Yes, as well as her sister and lover."

"I know nothing of them," Lasha said. "Not before Fen, but before her colleagues in the capital, Azha spoke against the rivalries that are chewing our populace to pieces."

"I thought she committed violence?"

"Yes, which is the only reason she was permitted to speak against the Priests and the Technologists and their mad hostility. She was exiled." He threw an arm toward the sea. "Now there are rumors from the fisher fleet that she is dead. I am not yet ready to ascend, so I watch what I speak before the likes of her." Lasha gestured cautiously after Qala.

Caitlin nodded. Now she had a better idea of *when* she was. It was after Azha's airship had crashed, after the Priest Vol had resolved to undermine the Technologists by causing the Source to explode, though with far greater destruction than he had imagined: it was this act that destroyed Galderkhaan. Caitlin did not know how long a period it was between those two events. It could be as little as a day; it could be weeks. Though the Antarctic solar cycle caused the Galderkhaani to frame their time differently from what she was accustomed to, Caitlin understood the terms that were in Bayarma's mind. They were close enough to contemporary times, based on the flow of the tides.

Caitlin took a moment to try and find Azha with her mind. The *Femora* had contacted her in the twenty-first century—her ascended soul had to be here as well. If it was, she could not find it. Perhaps she was busy trying to find some spiritual means to stop Vol.

"Your name is Lasha," Caitlin said, moving her arms now as she spoke. "And you . . . guard this pool?"

The man nodded gruffly, his leathery skin tight, his dark eyes narrowed. He looked like a purer version of Yokane, the Galderkhaani descendant Caitlin had met in New York. His features—like those of the *Standor*—were angular, narrow, the bone structure visible beneath the taut bronzed flesh.

"Can you tell me where I am?" Caitlin asked as a large gray-skinned creature scuttled toward the pool. She recognized the animal with its long, floppy ears and a tail; otherwise resembling a modern-day seal in size and general configuration, a kind of pet Bayarmii had. It was chased by Lasha with an adamant "Shoo!" The creature barked at him as it flopped off.

"Bold *thyodularasi*," he said. "And they're getting bolder! Too many fish being harvested, not enough for them to eat. This one is very smart. He endears himself to the children and they feed him." He stopped himself from another tirade and his eyes returned to Caitlin. "You asked a question. This is the port city of Falkhaan. We feed Galderkhaan, all of it. The fish below and the jasmine leaves grown in the clouds above. You—you look like a capitalist."

Hand gestures told her that the word had a very different meaning here than it did in her time.

"What makes you think I come from the capital?"

"Your clothes, hands, suggest you are a digger, but your slender arms do not appear to do much digging. So I think you are a supervisor in the tunnels."

"A good—" she sought but did not find a word for "forensics." She settled for, "A good analysis, Lasha. Let me think about it."

"I am sure of it," he said. He moved his hands as though they were rising on heat but said no words. She understood that to mean it was the way she carried herself, proudly.

"I thought you might be here as a representative of the capital for the Night of Miracles," Lasha added.

"What is that?" Caitlin asked.

The old man shook his head sadly, wriggled his fingers. "Your memory is truly vapor. It celebrates the dawn of the Galderkhaani, our rise from the fires."

"The magma," she said.

"Yes, the magma," he replied. "The storm from above, the rocks exploding within the fire, life released from the heat and carried forth on the smoke. At least, that is the legend. Told by whom, though, I ask you?" he wondered aloud. "If no one was here, how could we know?"

"Perhaps by studying the rocks?" she suggested.

"The Priests would have you believe that they've consulted with the ascended, but—a study of the rocks?" He seemed to have just processed what she said. "What would you do, hit them against your head?"

"I don't know," she said, smiling in spite of herself. Science was clearly not so advanced here in some areas. The celebration concerned her, though. Symbolically, that would have been the ideal time for Vol to make his move. And if this were the time when he was to act, there was something else on Caitlin's mind. Something so elusive she found it difficult to grasp: that conflagration was the time when she herself, at the United Nations, opened a door between her time, her world, and Galderkhaan. Could she, even in spirit, exist in two places at once?

"The capital—is that where the Source is?" she asked, hoping that knowledge of the project was common.

"The Source is there . . . and here," he said, stamping his sandaled foot on the packed earth. "That's what is heating the water—the run-off from the ice that is melting to the west. Do you have something to do with that dig? If so, I have much to say to you. Hot water is good for bathing, bad for fish."

"I don't know if I'm involved," Caitlin replied, suddenly thinking it would be a good idea to go where she knew there might be tiles, where she had faced Pao and Rensat in spirit. "How far are we from there?"

"A *timhut* by air," he said, throwing a hand vaguely behind him, to the south. "*La-timhut* on foot."

She knew, from the memories of Bayarma, that the first measure described a journey to be taken without need of sleep. The hand gestures indicated that it was half that. Five or six hours, perhaps? The second was about ten times as long. She would have to fly.

Caitlin rose suddenly. "The woman who just left—"

"Qala? The *Standor*?"

"Yes. Do you think she would take me? Or perhaps someone she knows."

"I don't keep her schedule!" Lasha said with annoyance. He ran to the other end of the pool to chase away a trio of *mensats* that were trying to claw up the wall to get a drink. He swatted the noose at them then flung it under his arm as if it were a martial arts nunchaku. "You'll have to ask someone at the tower. Her ship is one of our proudest and is almost certainly headed there for the celebration."

Caitlin was still a little too unsteady to run after her; then she remembered the boy she had seen before. He was still staring at her from the shadows. Caitlin suddenly felt very protective of him. She smiled sweetly, sincerely, and motioned him over.

Lasha laughed. "Good idea!" he said. "Vilu needs no excuse to talk to the *Standor*!"

Vilu welcomed the acknowledgment. He approached tentatively, his eyes on the woman. The *thyodularasi* waddled over behind him, huffing eagerly through its whiskers as it sniffed the boy's moving ankles.

"Your name is Vilu?" Caitlin said.

The boy nodded.

"Vilu, would you do me a favor?" Caitlin asked.

Lasha cut through the negotiation. "Boy, run and ask *Standor* Qala if she could delay a moment. This lady wishes to speak with her."

The boy grinned and took off as she had seen Jacob run in the park so many times—bent low, head down, arms churning, legs pumping. Vilu seemed so free. Caitlin's heart ached for her son, but also for this boy.

Soon he would most likely be dead, she thought, *along with every living creature in Galderkhaan*. And while she wouldn't be the reason—Vol would—the interference of her future self with the *cazh* would prevent their souls from transcending, from living together as spirits. He would be an ascended soul wandering alone for eternity. She wondered if wisdom and maturity came with that state or if he would be locked in boyhood and fear for eternity.

Caitlin turned away, tears behind her eyes.

"What is it?" Lasha asked.

"I'm still uncertain of my body," she replied, neglecting to gesture to express the kind of uncertainty she was feeling. It was sickness, deep in her belly, in her soul.

"You may sit in the hut, out of the sun," Lasha said. "That might help."

"Thank you." Caitlin was about to turn in that direction when she heard a small voice behind her.

"Mom?"

Caitlin spun and stared at Vilu. The boy had stopped running after the *Standor*. He was standing unsteadily in the bright sun, his arms repeating a gesture that meant "birth mother" in Galderkhaani.

"Did you say something?" Caitlin asked.

"Yes, Mom," he said, signing, not in Galderkhaani but in English. Just like the words he spoke. "I would much rather we go to the capital by Nemo's submarine."

And then he fell to the ground.

CHAPTER 4

Ben Moss stood in Caitlin's living room. Anita Carter was behind him, just closing the door. She introduced Ben to the others.

Ben was looking down at Madame Langlois, who was sitting in a rattan chair that Caitlin kept by the south-facing bay window. The Haitian's son was standing behind her, protectively. The woman was dressed in a colorful orange skirt with embroidered patterns of interlocking half-circles—like "S" shapes, but overlapping. She was wearing a wool sweater. The tall young man, Enok, wore blue jeans and a leather jacket that was still zipped to the chin. Madame Langlois held a tall glass of ice water in her hand. Ben noticed a serpent tattoo that wound from the tip of her right thumb down the back of her hand then around and around the little he could see of her forearm.

"I am very pleased to meet you both," Ben said, though he did not immediately move forward. "Caitlin has spoken to me of you both." His eyes were on the woman. "Madame Langlois, you said that Caitlin is—"

"The doctor—her serpent came to me in my sleep," Madame Langlois said in a casual voice.

" 'Her' serpent," Ben said. "How do you know it was Caitlin's?"

"It was the same as she saw in a vision. It was very active. It coiled around me then they bid me come here. *Very* active."

Anita Carter was standing well away from the group, near the dining room table, hovering in front of the hall that accessed Jacob's room. She had been very upset after Ben had phoned and told her what had happened. Now that she'd had a few minutes to collect herself, she was trying to understand where their guests fit into that.

"You said 'they' bid you come," Ben said. "Was there more than one?"

Madame shrugged in a noncommittal manner. "One who is many."

"I don't understand," Ben told her.

The woman said "eh" and shrugged again, as if Ben failing to understand was neither a surprise nor her concern. From the corner of his eye Ben saw that Anita was frowning. But he had worked at the United Nations too long to be insulted by the madame's dismissiveness; he was busy trying to find a place in Galderkhaani lore for the imagery she had described, and also for the designs on her clothing, which seemed to fit somewhat into the research he and Caitlin had been doing on Galderkhaan. There was a strong resemblance of her tattoo to the dragonlike prow of a Viking ship that Caitlin had drawn after experiencing a profound and terrifying trance . . . in Haiti.

Madame Langlois turned to stare out at West Eighty-Fourth Street, her dark eyes settling briefly on the rooftops of the brownstones across the way.

"The leaves are dead here," she said. "The branches are sad."

"I'm not too happy either," Ben said.

"Why? You do not die every year," she said.

Ben didn't know how to respond to that, so he didn't. He also wasn't in the mood for verbal or philosophical game playing. Then she leaned her head into the bay window and looked toward the part of Central Park she could see. The sun was just rising above the nearest line of trees, casting the tips of the bare limbs in a light, almost glowing, shade of bronze.

"But they are God's fingers, and the promise of resurrection," she said.

"You're still talking about the trees?" Ben asked.

Madame Langlois appeared reflective. "He fashion *all* living things, push them from the earth to the sun," she said.

"From darkness to light," Enok added in a quiet monotone, almost as though it were the response to a prayer.

"All right," Ben said with fast-growing impatience, "what does this have to do—"

"But too much light is death," the woman went on as though he hadn't spoken. She turned back toward Ben. "Dr. O'Hara saw the fires."

"Yes. I was with her when she did," Ben said.

"Not here," Madame Langlois said. "Somewhere else. Some time else."

Ben started. Caitlin had been to Haiti *before* she had witnessed the destruction of Galderkhaan. This woman could not possibly have known about the incident at the United Nations. Even if they had been in contact—which Ben doubted—Caitlin probably wouldn't have mentioned it. Her experience in Haiti was not a pleasant one.

The woman's bracelets rattled as she held out a bony hand to her son. Enok Langlois dutifully reached into a large satchel he carried and removed a cigar, handed it to her.

"Dr. O'Hara does not permit smoking in here," Anita said firmly.

"The airplane did not allow my matches," Madame said. "They fear fire too. I will just hold it for now and smell these leaves, remember the smoke." She put the cigar in her mouth, looked back at Ben, and said nothing. Apparently, it was his turn to speak.

He turned slowly away from them, looking to Anita for direction. The psychiatrist had nothing and shook her head. Ben glanced at Enok, who did not look happy to be there.

"What can you tell me about the snake, about what Caitlin saw and did in Haiti?" Ben asked.

Enok remained defiantly silent.

"We await the snake," Madame announced. "We wish it to show us things. Then we can say more."

In an environment where nothing should have surprised Ben, that did. "Are you saying . . . it's coming? A snake?"

The woman nodded once. "It ask me to come. To witness things. I did. Now it must tell more."

"What *kinds* of things are you supposed to witness?" Ben asked with growing exasperation. "You came all this way because you felt there was danger. You flew up without even knowing if anyone would see you—"

"Didn't matter," she said, looking back out the window. "Would have waited out there. There is movement all around. I still feel it."

"What kind of movement?" Ben asked.

In response, Madame waved her hand in a small, circular motion like the Queen of England waving. "I felt Dr. O'Hara open a door." She jabbed a finger upward. "There."

"The roof?" Ben said.

Madame lowered her hand. "And then, as we crossed the water in a taxi, she opened a larger one. This new door, Dr. O'Hara went through." She touched her chest with an open palm. "This part of her left us."

Anita gasped. "What are you saying?"

"She is not dead," Madame Langlois assured her. "She is very much alive."

Ben regarded the priestess with a blend of confusion and awe. She knew things—or, more likely, intuited them—that she had not personally experienced.

"Madame Langlois, Enok," Ben said, "at the risk of pressing you on matters you are unwilling to discuss—"

"Except leaves," Anita muttered.

"—have either of you heard the name Galderkhaan?"

Madame shook her head once. Enok remained still. Ben took that as a no. They did not ask what it was or why Ben was inquiring. It frustrated him that they weren't curious about anything outside their sphere.

"Ben," Anita said, "before Caitlin's parents get here, I think we should put these two in a cab and send them back to—"

Suddenly, as if from a great distance, Ben heard a clacking sound, like dice in a cup. Anita fell silent. It took a moment for Ben to realize that the sounds were coming from Madame Langlois, from around her neck. Mostly concealed by the sweater was a necklace of black beads and hematite tubes. Enok bent over her shoulder and gently pulled the necklace from beneath the white wool. At the bottom of the necklace was a thumbnail-sized human skull artfully carved from what appeared to be polished bone.

Ben watched with growing disenchantment. The beads were vibrating because the woman was shaking—very slightly at first, as if she were shivering, and then more pronounced. There was nothing mysterious or supernatural about it, or about her.

She shut her eyes. Ben wanted to ask what was happening but he didn't think she would answer, or she would respond with one of her riddles, and Enok would remain mute. Ben didn't understand how Caitlin had survived a full day of being stonewalled like this. He just watched through eyes that burned with exhaustion, with a mind that was struggling to make sense of anything.

Then Madame Langlois spoke.

"They seek . . ." she said around the cigar in a raspy whisper, raising her index and middle fingers together. "They . . . seek . . ."

Anita moved toward the hallway as the madame's extended fingers turned in that direction. Two long, bony fingers swung around slowly but firmly like the compass on a needle. They were not quaking like the rest of her.

"Ben, you have to stop this," Anita said as the fingers moved closer to the hallway. "Ben?"

"Caitlin pointed like that," he said. "Let it play out."

"There's a *boy* here, Ben!"

Ben heard her but he motioned for her to remain calm. Madame Langlois's hand seemed to be floating on the air, rotating slightly about the wrist, following the extended fingers. He was suddenly fascinated by her motion: now he recognized absolutely some of the moves Caitlin had executed at the United Nations, when she was making her spiritual journey to Galderkhaan.

"Have you ever seen anything like this?" Ben quietly asked as he sidled up to Anita. "The movement, I mean."

"What? Ben—this is a *show!*"

"I'm not convinced of that. I've seen Caitlin hold her hand like that. And mesmerists. Even Dracula, in movies."

"Jesus, vampires now?"

"Actors being intuitive, that's what an archetype is!" he said. "Please, just answer me."

Anita frowned, struggled to focus. "In the park, I guess—Columbus Park, in Chinatown," she said. "Weekend tai chi. It looks a *little* like that."

"In what way?"

"Floating hands. You move until they feel like they're separate from the body, carrying—" Anita stopped as she realized what she was saying.

"Carrying what?"

"All the energy of your body," she said. "As if your body and arms no longer exist."

Ben nodded. That, like what Madame Langlois was doing, could well be part of the common human experience. It was the same with language: the elements that show up over and over separate valid experience from affectation and trickery, like the need to shout an oath, not just cry out, after hitting your finger with a hammer. These are buried in the human condition though no one knows why or by what mechanism.

Perhaps they were rooted in Galderkhaan.

Ben pushed aside the woman's obduracy, watched her with fresh eyes. Madame Langlois's shaking subsided; she was slipping into some kind of relaxed trance yet the hand itself seemed to be floating, like a cork in water, the fingers moving in unison as if guided by an outside source. He saw the shadow they cast on the area rug but suddenly noticed the angle of the shadow relative to the fingers was increasing, somehow. It was as if the shadow were hooked like one of the curves on Madame Langlois's skirt, the base of the finger pointing straight ahead, the tip crooked toward one of the rooms.

Toward Jacob's room.

Anita noticed it too. "Ben!" she said in a loud, insistent whisper. "I don't care about the academic value of this. You've got to stop it." The shadow grew longer and Anita's breathing came faster.

"Enok, tell me what's happening or we must intervene," Ben said.

"Stop her and the snake will move freely among us," the man warned stoically.

"What?"

"We do not want that, I think," Enok said quietly.

"How do you know that will happen?" Ben demanded.

"I have seen it," he replied. There was respect for the process in his voice, if not in his expression.

Either Enok was correct or Anita and Ben were sharing a delusion. The shadow began to wriggle though Madame Langlois's fingers remained steady. It was not Ben's imagination, it was not a hallucination, and from Anita's frightened expression, she was realizing that as well. The darkness of the serpentine shadow seemed to deepen, obscuring what was beneath it, as they watched it crawl along the rug. And there was something else within it: what looked to Ben like glitter, only it was something transitory. There were tiny facets that appeared and reappeared in roughly the same places, the same relationship one to the other as the shadow moved.

With a back-and-forth motion, the head of the serpent pulled the rest of the body toward the hallway, to where Anita had solidly placed herself.

"Get it away," she warned, choking on the sentence as she spread her arms and legs.

"It will not hurt you," Enok said.

"It's not me I'm worried about," Anita said, her eyes fastened on the shape.

"It will hurt no one," he insisted.

"How do you know?" Ben asked.

"That is not its way," Enok replied.

"More double-talk," Anita said. "If you don't make her stop, I will!"

"Let it play out a little longer," Ben said. "We can always take Jacob and go."

"Can we?" she asked.

"It's not solid, Anita," Ben pointed out. "It doesn't appear to be noxious."

"It looks radioactive!" she said.

"That's not likely," Ben said. "Anita, please . . . this is happening for a reason."

The serpent expanded, thickened, seemed to take on size but not substance; it was like thick smoke with curling eddies of darkness becoming visible within. The tiny fireflies sparked and faded within as the inner clouds moved. Otherwise without features, the snake moved from the rug to the hardwood floor, writhed just feet from Anita where it suddenly stopped. It was almost as if the outer shape had suddenly frozen, while the turmoil and lights continued within. Ben began to walk toward Anita, slowly, around the shape, not sure what he was going to do. He stopped as the black snake rose like a cobra, turning toward him. Its head floated higher, bobbing from side to side until it reached the level of his eyes. A few moments after Ben stopped, the shape turned back toward Anita and moved forward, trailing neither glitter nor making a ripple on the floor. There was terror in the wide set of the woman's mouth but she did not scream. She placed her hands hard against the frame of the hallway entrance, set her legs, and had no intention of moving.

The shadow came right up to her, face-to-face, but it did not advance. It puffed even wider, as though pressed from within, its circumference increasing.

As the dead, flat head of the thing continued to hover before Anita, Ben heard Jacob moaning in his room. Anita heard him too.

"Goddamnit, get him *now!*" she said.

"You go," Ben said, edging around the serpent and taking her place. If it moved, he intended to walk through it, waving his arms in an attempt to disperse it. But the shape just remained there.

Anita turned and moved quickly down the hall, her footsteps on the hardwood floor the only sound in the apartment. Even the cat, Arfa, was missing, cowed by the serpent.

Staring at the thing just inches away, Ben could swear he saw coil-like shapes moving within it, but they were indistinct, like images only visible from the corner of the eye, vanishing when looked at directly. They were hypnotic, wormlike and writhing. But they were not like maggots feeding on a carcass; they were a dark, tightly coiled network from which the serpent seemed to be made. That must be what the madame had meant by "they." He saw now that where the coils touched, the sparks appeared.

Ben looked at the featureless head, studied the tiny whorls nearest to him. Each one seemed to grow as the snake inflated and then there were smaller snakes inside those other snakes, on and on, deeper into the black pall—

He heard a thumping sound from behind.

"Anita?"

"Shhh!" she said. "Come."

Ben backed slowly from the serpent. Jacob's door was the first on his right, Caitlin's room beyond it. The bathroom was across the hall. He edged backward but the serpent didn't advance. He didn't think it was because his eyes were locked on the thing; it had to be something else.

When he reached the bedroom door, Ben saw Jacob standing on the bed, amid the strewn pages of his Captain Nemo comic book. He was facing the wall between his room and Caitlin's. The boy was sobbing and drumming on the wall with the heel of his palm.

"Mom . . ." he wept softly. "Mom . . ."

Anita shook her head hard, as if to say *don't wake him*. She hovered nearby, her arms open to catch him in case he fell backward. Whether it was a nightmare or night terrors, Ben left that up to the therapist. He turned from Anita back to the serpent.

It filled the entrance to the hallway but did not approach. It undulated slightly, diffusing the sun but not dimming it: the serpent seemed to have a nimbus, an amber glow as ephemeral as the snaking shape itself. It reminded him then of Wadjet, the Egyptian snake goddess whose images he had come across while researching the Galderkhaani language in ancient hieroglyphics.

Ben stole a quick look back into the bedroom, saw Jacob standing very still now. Then he turned back to the hallway—

The snake was gone. Clean, healthy morning light once more filled the room, illuminating the familiar, creating normal, comforting shadows behind the sofa and under the table. It was as though the apparition had never been.

With a small exhalation, Jacob collapsed to the bed. Anita caught him, lowered him to the mattress, and knelt quickly at his side. She took his pulse, listened to his breathing.

"Call for an ambulance," she said as she felt his forehead.

"Does he have a high fever?"

"No, but you just *saw* what he did—"

"His mother said he does this, knocks on the wall in his sleep," Ben said.

"His mother's not here and I didn't bring my medical bag," Anita said. "Call or get my damn phone and I—"

"No!" a voice burst from the hallway.

Madame Langlois was standing at the entrance where the serpent had been. Enok was beside her, holding her elbow. They were silhouetted by the light, but it struck her necklace in a way that made the beads seem uncommonly bright.

"Screw you!" Anita said, still holding Jacob. "You did this!"

"I did not," the woman replied. "*They* did. And medicine will harm him."

"They who?" Ben asked.

"I do not know them," Madame Langlois admitted. "But they have vast power. Greater than yours."

Ben approached her. Anita moved to the door of the bedroom, a protective eye on Jacob, an angry turn to her mouth.

"We should get him to a hospital where he can be monitored *properly*," Anita told him.

"I don't disagree," Ben said. "But I want to make sure we don't do more harm. His mother's in a hospital and they have no idea what to do." He turned to Madame Langlois. "Why shouldn't we get help?"

"Because help cannot help."

"*Why?*" Ben pressed. "Madame Langlois, please help us here!"

The Haitian woman stayed where she was. She raised her hand again, extending her forearm into the hall, the two fingers once more extended. Anita and Ben both tensed as the single wall-mounted light near the front door threw a dim shadow on the long rug. But the shadow did not grow or move. It stayed, simply, the shadow of a finger.

"The serpent sleeps—they sleep within," she said. "Nothing happens now."

Ben was neither reassured nor enlightened. He took a step forward and Enok moved toward him protectively. "It's all right," Ben assured him. He looked at the man's mother and continued in a conciliatory tone, "Who are 'they'? At least tell me that. Tell me what you know, even if it's very little."

She lowered her hand. It flopped at her side. "They tell you when they wish," the woman said.

"Of course, you charlatan," Anita said. "You and your ridiculous conjuring, your tricks. What the hell did you *do* to Caitlin in Haiti?"

"Showed her things."

"You got in her head!" Anita charged.

"Anita, please—" Ben said.

"No, I've had enough," she said. She went to move around Ben, saw the landline in Caitlin's room, moved toward it. Ben took her wrist, stopped her. She wrested it away. "I'm calling 911. We need an ambulance and we need cops." She pointed toward the hallway. "They're leaving."

"They can't," Ben told her. "We need them."

"Why? To create more bullshit drama? Shaking, pointing, probably releasing some kind of hallucinogenic—"

"Anita, I'm angry too, but Caitlin helped to create this problem, this dynamic," Ben said.

Anita looked at him with disbelief. "Are you high, Ben?"

"Dammit, no. Caitlin sought it out, invited it in. She ran headlong into this, ignoring every goddamn stop sign. I know, I was there. I was the one pointing at the flashing exit signs. What we really have to do is learn more before we do anything."

"How, Ben? I'm listening."

"And I'm *thinking*. Jacob's breathing normally?"

"For a kid who's unconscious, yeah." She glared at Ben. "And that crap about Caitlin seeking this? She and I talked about that too. She was trying to provide care for a bunch of kids. She didn't ask for her boy to be endangered."

"You don't have all the facts," Ben said.

"Okay, I'll ask again: What am I missing?"

"This 'thing' Caitlin was dealing with," Ben said. "It targeted children of trauma. Jacob was caught in the backwash as soon as his mother got involved, that very day. Whatever it was got some kind of claws in him. She realized the first time she looked at this that there were forces neither of us even remotely grasped. But as you say, there were children at risk so she went ahead. I didn't want her to go to Haiti. I didn't want her to go to Tehran. Things came back with her, Anita. Things we thought—no, things we *hoped*—were gone. But they're not, and doctors—doctors as smart and experienced as you, Anita—can't help her or Jacob." He moved closer. "Anita, I'm sure that right now Caitlin is trying to fix *something*, again."

"She's. Unconscious."

"As far as the doctors know," Ben said.

Anita made a sound of disgust. "You're just guessing now, and it's a dangerous guess."

"Actually, I'm praying that's the case. If it is, then we have to let this play out, at least a *little* longer. If Jacob shows even a hint of change, then we do it your way."

"Define 'hint,' because he looks pretty pale *right now*."

"Paler," Ben said. "If his temperature rises or his breathing slows or he shows symptoms that are something other than the kind of re-action to a bad dream."

"He was awake, remember?" Anita said. "This—this show may have put him in a reduced metabolic state."

"And drugs are not the answer," Ben said. "There is something bad out there, something doctors won't be able to fix."

Anita exhaled angrily and looked back at Jacob, who was sleeping again. They moved away from the door, into Caitlin's room, and spoke softly.

"I just don't like it," she said. "And I don't trust those two. Caitlin's in a coma and I think this woman knows why. I want her to tell us."

"I believe she will, in her own time and in her own way. She helped Caitlin heal the girl in Haiti. And she cared enough to make arrange-ments to fly up here."

" 'Cared enough,' " Anita sneered. "About what?"

"What do you mean? She *sensed* there was a problem—"

"She may have already been here," Anita said.

"What are you, the INS now?" Ben asked. "You want me to check her papers?"

"No, I want you to consider the possibility that she may have *caused* this, all of it. Starting in Haiti and continuing here."

"Why?"

"I don't know!" Anita said. "A shakedown. She saw a gullible, well-off woman down there, got her bony little talons into her, saw a way to make some money. I mean, she's just over there, waiting. Offer her money, see if she talks."

"I don't believe that's why she's here," Ben said. "I think she's being careful. She could be afraid."

"Yeah, of being found out," Anita said.

Now Ben was getting frustrated. "I'll say it again, Anita: there are phenomena at work. Genuine get-thee-from-me-Satan stuff. You heard Caitlin last night. You heard her here, in this apartment, when she was physically downtown. Christ, she gave you a message for me!"

"It was a phone, a device, an open line, something," she said.

"Do you really believe that?"

"I do. I have to."

"You saw the snake—"

"I saw a smoky shape," Anita said. "Now that I think of it, maybe there was something in that cigar—"

"Which Madame Langlois didn't light."

"Not all psychoactive drugs are delivered by heating," Anita replied. "The bark of Virola trees are used to create powdered hallucinogenic snuff—she puffed it our way then led us with her fingers, the simplest kind of hypnosis. You said it yourself: Count Dracula stuff."

Ben shook his head. "You're not hearing me. I've been with Caitlin when things have happened. Weird things."

"The *only* weird thing is that I'm not tearing loose on these two and demanding answers," Anita said. "And I'm not the only one."

Ben gave her a quizzical look.

"Arfa doesn't like them either," Anita said.

"Right, where is the cat?"

"Exactly," Anita said. "He doesn't like other animals in the apartment. If there was a real snake out there, he would've been hissing and spitting."

"My point exactly," Ben said. "It was not a 'real' snake."

Ben turned away from her. He was typically rational, yet here he was trying to argue against a traditional explanation. He shook his head.

"I have to go to work," he said. He glanced at the clock on the night table. Caitlin had had it for decades, since they were students at NYU. It was not digital: the numbers flipped over on little plastic cards inside the white case. He missed his friend . . . he missed those days. There were times, like now, when he ached with that longing. "It's six forty-five," he said. "Caitlin's parents will be here in an hour or so and I have an idea. I think. I will bring Madame Langlois and Enok to my place."

"You'd trust them?"

"With what—my fridge and flat-screen? We can't leave them with the O'Haras, so it's either that or we turn them out."

"I still vote for the latter," Anita said hotly. "People who want to help . . . *help*. That's what Caitlin did."

She saw Ben's sad eyes, quickly realized her mistake, and corrected herself. "That's what Caitlin *does*. They don't play games like our Vodou lady, they don't talk without listening." She continued in a softer voice. "Caitlin is a humanitarian. She doesn't deserve what happened."

"That's a separate topic and there, at least, we agree," Ben said. "But that doesn't solve the immediate problem."

Anita's comments had sounded too much like a eulogy and Ben had to get away, not just emotionally and mentally but physically. He went back into the hallway to prepare to get the Langloises over to his East Side apartment near the United Nations. He looked in at Jacob again, resisted gathering up the boy's drawings. Jacob and his mother shared a strong bond and there might be subtle, subliminal clues as to what happened. But the boy might wake and look for the sketches: in a world made suddenly very unstable, Ben wanted him to have at least that anchor. He left and headed back down the hall. Arriving in the living room, he swore through his teeth.

"What is it?" Anita asked, hurrying in.

"You got your wish," he said, turning to the front door, pulling it open, and looking out into the empty hallway. "Madame Langlois and her son have left."

CHAPTER 5

Vilu lay sprawled on the hard-packed sand of the courtyard. He was lying on his back, his eyes shut, his mouth open.

Caitlin ran to him. Surrounded by slowly encroaching Galder-khaani, she forgot her own plight when she bent over him. For an instant, like the scrape of a knife along her breastbone, she felt that it was Jacob falling, needing her help, needing her comfort.

Lasha had followed with a bowlegged gait and a loud huffing. The other citizens were clustering tighter, trying to see what the woman was doing as she knelt over the prone boy.

"Is there a physician?" she asked Lasha.

The man looked back at the gathered faces. "Weta? Does anyone see Weta?"

"She is in the birth center!" someone shouted back.

"Run! Get her!" Lasha said then turned to Caitlin. "That building is at the far end of the village, away from the sea chill, and Weta is aged. It will take time."

Time. It kept coming up, seemed to be Caitlin's enemy in every possible way. She focused on the boy. She didn't bother to explain that she was a doctor herself: what she wanted immediately for the boy was a bed, shelter, and someone to watch him after she did triage. Most likely they had herbs or compounds, though she didn't know that any of them would work. Ancient medicines and cures were hit-and-miss. When they missed, they often made the patient worse.

She also prayed, audibly, under her breath, that her worst fears weren't realized—that this was not a transference of souls.

Her first thought was that Vilu had suffered heatstroke or dehy-dration, and she told Lasha to bring water. Unbending with a grunt, the old man turned and scurried back to his hut for a ladle.

Motioning for people to step back and give Vilu air, Caitlin saw that he was perspiring and, feeling for his heartbeat, found it normal. So was his temperature—assuming that the Galderkhaani "normal" was the same as that of modern humans. It wasn't heatstroke, but that forced open the door to those other, deeper concerns. Jacob had been reading *Twenty Thousand Leagues Under the Sea*. She prayed that that had nothing to do with what this boy had uttered, but in her heart she didn't believe it.

He followed me here, she thought ominously. *There can be no other explanation.*

Lasha arrived with an *alok*, a wooden, short-handled ladle that he'd filled from the pool. Apparently, they knew nothing of bacteria or parasites in Galderkhaan. Nonetheless, she took it and wet the boy's lips from a bony rim. He responded weakly and she put a hand behind his head to support him as he tried to take more. The feel of his hair seemed so familiar. Caitlin struggled to keep back deep, heaving sobs. But she could not help herself from looking down at the sweet face, the ruddy skin with just a hint of pale white freckles, the dark hair that fell in natural ringlets over a broad, innocent forehead. Caitlin used the sleeve of her loose-fitting tunic to dab away the sweat that was beading under his eyes and on his cheek.

His four-flippered friend waddled through the legs of the crowd.

"Shoo!" Lasha growled, kicking lightly at the *thyodularasi*.

Without taking her eyes from the boy, Caitlin passed the ladle to Lasha.

"What could have happened?" the old man asked, peering over her back.

"Excitement," said a teenaged girl who was looking on. "He so loves the airship."

"Then why did he say—*what* did he say?" Lasha asked. "Sybamurn?"

Caitlin realized with a jolt that the boy had spoken it in English; Lasha had uttered a Galderkhaani approximation.

"Submarine," Caitlin clarified without thinking—also in English.

"What is that?" Lasha asked.

"I don't know," she said, trying to forestall any further questions. "That's what *I* heard."

The woman fanned the boy with an open hand, blew gently on the sweat, touched his warm flesh. She used her body to block the harsh sun. Someone yelled that Weta would come as soon as possible. Caitlin was considering what to do next when the crowd that had gathered parted slightly and a familiar figure returned, tugged along by the *thyodularasi* Lasha had chased away. *Standor* Qala patted the thigh-high creature on its elongated snout and it released its grip. She strode through the group and crouched beside the boy, beside Caitlin.

"It was all too much for Vilu, I see," Qala remarked.

"This has happened before?" Caitlin asked.

"Not like this," Qala admitted with a half-smile. "Usually he just jumps around. Ever since *Femora* Azha took the children aloft in a fisher's airship, his life has been about flight."

"There is no blood, no injury," Qala said after reaching softly behind the boy's head. "Do we know if he'd eaten?"

No one answered. Reaching into the sashlike pouch at her side, Qala withdrew an oval pellet that looked like a ruby and held it just below the boy's nostrils. Qala adjusted it so the rays of the sun were striking it directly. The sunlight illuminated small, dark, opaline facets inside. Fragrance rose from the crystal, which began to decay as the scent grew stronger. Caitlin saw now that it was not mineral but vegetal, the surface made of petals crushed around slivers of what looked like dried berries. Oil dropped from the shrinking object, absorbed by the boy's flesh, just under his nostrils.

The boy stirred but his eyes remained closed.

"Odd," Qala remarked as the pellet finally fell to pieces. "I've seen the *dumatta* awaken those who were near death from drowning. This appears to be a different kind of sleep."

Qala allowed the lingering *thyodularasi* to lick her fingers. Lasha frowned.

"Don't *feed* it," the pool guardian said with exasperation.

"Quiet, Lasha. She deserves a reward for her loyalty."

"Loyalty! She's loyal to those who *feed* her!" Lasha shook bony fists at the animal, which snorted at him. "Perhaps it was spoiled fish that felled the boy! The fishers used to feed *those* to these beasts—now they sell them!"

"Complain about the fish again and I will see you assigned to a fisher ship in the western freeze zone," Qala said as she scooped up the boy, put him over her shoulder, and rose. "I'm taking him to the airship physician."

"I'm going with you," Caitlin said.

Qala regarded Caitlin. "I thought you had other business."

"Not now."

"Perhaps you know him?"

"I—I don't know," Caitlin said. "But everyone else on the airship will be busy. He may need a nurse."

The word she used was *xat*, which literally meant "health observer." All that mattered was she would be near him.

Qala turned to Lasha. "Inform his caretakers. I will send the boy back when he has recovered."

"But you're leaving, *Standor*," Lasha pointed out. "Aren't you? Imminently?"

"I am," Qala said, holding the boy a little tighter. "Let them know that as well."

The water guardian seemed perplexed but would rather pass the word to simple fishers than to ask for further clarification from a *Standor*. It wasn't as if the official carried any authority outside the operation of her airship. But the romance of her profession, the loftiness of her title, and Qala's personal popularity would make it difficult to muster popular support against her. Even mad Azha had been given every opportunity to atone for her murderous efforts and foreswear any similar actions in the future. A common Galderkhaani would never have been heard before the full council in the Aankhaan House of Judgment.

Turning from Lasha, *Standor* Qala looked at Caitlin. "Perhaps the physician should look at you as well."

"Let's take care of the boy first," Caitlin said.

They made their way through the crowd, which parted eagerly and respectfully. Qala was thoughtful as they walked.

"It is rare, in Galderkhaan, for children to receive the kind of priority you've suggested," the *Standor* finally remarked.

"Is it?" Caitlin replied.

"If riders in an airship are injured during a storm, who should be tended to first? Those who can manage the ship or suckling babes?"

"I did not realize we had such a crisis on our hands," Caitlin said. She wondered if her sarcasm came through in the exaggerated hand gestures.

Qala was quiet for another long moment then said, "Perhaps you have mothered before? In this place you know you're from, yet cannot seem to remember."

"Perhaps," Caitlin said.

They left the courtyard, Caitlin still a little wobbly under Qala's watchful eye. But she managed to keep up. She thought of Ben, imagined what he would give to be here, studying, listening, learning. Or Flora and her . . . her pirates. For all the intellectual sanctuary they took in their lofty, erudite trappings and ways, she did not believe it was scholarship they sought. It didn't take an enlightened soul to feel that way. Like too many people she had met over the years—especially autocrats—they reeked of dangerous self-interest.

Caitlin's gaze shifted from face to face among the locals who were working outdoors on small boats, on sails, nets, and mirrorlike devices she didn't recognize—perhaps a form of solar power, she thought. Some were walking with others, holding hands, holding children, accompanied by the seals. Ratlike creatures flitted in the shadows, long, froglike tongues whipping out at large insects that rested on the walls. She noticed mounds that ran alongside the streets. Did those humps conceal pipes that carried water? Sewage? Steam from magma? She couldn't be sure. A few citizens were eating at standalone buildings that were comparable to twenty-first-century taverns. A few of the people seemed to notice Caitlin—or Bayarma—and tilted their head to the right as she passed.

"You acknowledge no one," the *Standor* observed.

"I—I thought they were greeting you," Caitlin said. "Or the boy."

"The boy?" Qala laughed. "He's not conscious."

"They might have been wishing him well."

Qala frowned. "Then they would nod forward," she said. "They are greeting a newcomer, inviting you to return. The other way," Qala tilted her head to the left, "would be a sign of disapproval, such as the Technologists receive in Glogharasor."

"The Priest stronghold," she thought aloud.

"That's right."

"And Belhorji is for the Technologists," Caitlin said.

They were names she had discussed with Ben during a nighttime walk in Paley Park. For a moment—gone before she even knew it was there—Caitlin almost felt as though she were back there. It came as a very strong—"snapshot" was the only word that came to mind. A rich image accompanied by a frisson, a tickling at the base of her skull.

"So you *do* remember something," Qala said. "Perhaps your memory is returning?"

"Possibly," Caitlin replied. She sought to reconnect with the park, with Ben, with anything during that night. But it was all gone.

There was speed but no sense of urgency in Qala's long stride.

Though the boy was in need of care, Caitlin recognized the *Standor*'s manner as typical of command: she had seen it at disaster sites around the world, where men and women moved with purpose to instill confidence, alleviate fear, and to preserve calm. This woman was not just a leader, the lingering eyes of onlookers told Caitlin that she was widely respected.

As they walked, Caitlin to the left of the *Standor*, where Vilu's head lay on her shoulder, Caitlin was able to see the boy's face. He would be all right physically, she believed, but his condition *now* was not what concerned her. If she permitted the destiny of Galderkhaan to take its course, Vilu would most likely be dead very soon—unless she informed the *Standor* what was to come and got him away from here.

But even that, like my presence here, may alter the course of future history, she thought. *What if the Standor uses what I tell her and tries to prevent the catastrophe?*

As they continued toward the shore, Caitlin briefly felt another tingling at the base of her skull, this one slightly longer than the previous experience. It had a pulsing, electric quality and only lasted a few seconds, but it *had* been there. There was no image associated with it, but when it left, Caitlin felt as though she were more alert, more present, more *guarded*, as though she'd had a shot of espresso.

She didn't know what it was, but she knew what it wasn't. It was not an assault, like being in the subway when she first saw Yokane causing her energies to come alive; it was not a reaching out, as when she channeled the power of the stones in Washington Square Park. This was something that came from within her, on its own.

Is it me or is it Bayarma trying to assert herself?

Uncertainty filled her soul. She did not want to leave if some part of Jacob were here, in this boy. And the question of what would happen to her soul if Bayarma reasserted control was anyone's guess. She didn't think she would just skip into another body—Qala's or whoever else they might encounter. She had bonded with this family once before, and now she had connected with Bayarma for a reason.

Whether Caitlin wanted to or not, she was going to have to try and hold on long enough to determine whether it was Vilu or Jacob who was in the boy's body.

"How is your strength?" Qala asked as they walked.

"All right, so far," she replied.

"The tower is quite near," the *Standor* said. "But if you like, I can send a carrier for you."

"I'm able to make it," Caitlin assured her.

Caitlin had no idea what a "carrier" might be until they reached another courtyard. The open, sun-drenched area was at least three times the size of the pool yard and there were at least twenty cigar-shaped airships about the size of minivans. She focused on the objects, not the light; it was disorienting to imagine that this is the same sun, the same light, that would one day shine in her own welcoming apartment, light the breakfast table she shared with her son.

The airships were hovering an average of ten feet above the ground. Plants that resembled modern jasmine were being unloaded from nets that hung tightly between them. Indeed, the balloons themselves bore a slight resemblance to their cargo: there were leaflike fins high on the envelopes, fore and aft, presumably to control the vessel in the strong atmospheric currents as it hovered in the clouds.

Jasmine, she thought. It had been present in some form since she had first met Maanik in the Pawars' apartment. Was she drawn to it, it to her, or was it a coincidence? Or was she simply noticing it in her time because its presence here was informing the future . . . her future?

Caitlin couldn't quite grasp that idea, the *mechanics* of that idea, so she forced herself to stay mentally rooted in this place—observing, collecting information, seeking some way to rekindle her energies.

Beyond the courtyard, down a wide, open road to the shore, Caitlin saw dozens of surface vessels, their small nets full of fish. They were riding waves that had a different action from any she had ever seen: the sea was smooth and then, about ten yards from shore, waves rose up and smashed down as if they were pumped from some deep coastal trough. She had no way of knowing whether it was a local or continental phenomenon. Local, most likely, since ships were coming to shore off to the sides. She wondered if it were artificial since the breakers created a breeze that blew a refreshing coolness into the courtyard and chased away the smell of fish. Heat, odor, and spoilage—as heralded by the obsessed Lasha—*would* be a problem during interminable hours of daylight.

Caitlin also saw more airships high in the sky, among the clouds. The same kinds of nets were strung between them with foliage of all kinds crowded against all four sides of each. Apparently, the clouds were a more accessible source of freshwater than whatever ice surrounded Galderkhaan. From the barrels that lined the streets she assumed that the harvest here was primarily jasmine, which must grow readily in this climate, by these means, and was light enough to be supported by the airborne nets.

It was a small but impressive spectacle of agrarian and oceanic commerce, as well as simple but effective engineering. Yet the tableau was almost unnaturally quiet, at least to her New York–accustomed ears; even Haiti and Phuket had more ambient noise than this with cars, radios, jets, helicopters, cell phones, and the other trappings of modern civilization. As far as she could see there weren't fuel- or even steam-powered apparatuses; all the work was being managed by well-oiled pulleys, by weights and counterweights, and by hand. She also did not see smokestacks or chimneys, or even a hint of pollution corrupting the blue of the sky. Given what she knew of the Source, and what Lasha had said, the dwellings in Galderkhaan were apparently warmed during winter by subterranean pools of magma and water.

It was a clean, efficient way of living—more so, it seemed, than other ancient civilizations of more modern times.

And it is about to end, she could not help thinking.

Caitlin felt sick in her soul, even as she reminded herself that it was a Galderkhaani who would cause the catastrophe. Though she could not help but remember, with awful clarity, the vision of the dying as they tried to save their souls through the ritual of *cazh*, even as their bodies turned to ash, and how she had worked so hard to prevent that ascension—

"Now that we're away from the others, I would like you to tell me the truth about the bracelet," the *Standor* said. "About where you come from."

"I don't understand."

"You don't look like a thief. And I do not think you are a liar."

"It's true, I am neither," Caitlin assured her. "At least, I don't *think* I am a thief. I truly do not know. What prompted you to ask?"

"Your jewelry is not made of Falkhaan silver." She regarded Caitlin. "I have friends who are miners here. I know the local minerals and their impurities. The name on the bracelet is someone not from around here, or she would be known. You yourself say that you are from elsewhere. That you have a son elsewhere. Yet you also have some connection with this boy, who has never left this village. I saw it in the way you touched him."

"That is true."

"And being true, there must be an explanation."

"I wish I had one," Caitlin said, and meant it. "I felt as if I know him. *Standor*, maybe you can help me. You must have traveled the continent. Have you ever met anyone who has lost their memory?"

"Once, when I was still a novice," Qala said. "I met a Priest. He was experimenting with a ritual and emerged from it saying strange things about other lands . . . nothing anyone could understand. And he couldn't remember who *he* was, even when others told him."

"Is this Priest still alive?"

"I don't know," the *Standor* replied. "The last I heard of him, his body was alive but he neither spoke nor responded to any kind of stimulus." Qala regarded Caitlin across Vilu's back. "Do you think you participated in an experiment of some kind?"

"Again, I don't know," Caitlin replied.

"And . . . north," the *Standor* said. She looked out across the sea. "I have flown a considerable direction to the north. There is nothing. Nothing except floating mountains of ice, great sea beasts, and no birds. If there were land, there would be birds. Yet you say you come from there."

"I—I may have been confused," she said.

"I believe you have made yourself a crossed net line," Qala said.

"I'm sorry?"

"When an airship turns suddenly, without notifying its companion, the net between them gets tangled," the *Standor* told her. "I suspect you just told a lie to protect a truth."

Qala didn't press Caitlin, for which the psychiatrist was grateful. It was the mark of a wise and seasoned commander. Reading about the Vikings to try and understand Galderkhaan, Caitlin had learned that hands were axed for theft. But shipboard, one-handed sailors were of little use, so captains learned to accept small lies told from a crew that dipped, without permission, into the stores of grog or cheese. Qala had just done that for her.

They rounded the end of the street and turned to a road along the coast. The waves were indeed tame beyond the natural horseshoe-shaped harbor, but the sudden expanse of blue-white ocean was not what caught her eye. Caitlin and the *Standor* were making their way toward a column that was roughly three hundred feet high. It was a smaller, slimmer version of the tower of the *motu-varkas*, in which she had confronted Pao and Rensat. Her pace slowed as she took in the spectacle of the great airship moored to the top, like some tamed, dark storm cloud, its envelope being replenished by tubes that ran from the nose into the depths of the tower. The airship was, in effect, a highly elongated hot-air balloon, elegant in its simplicity.

"Majestic," she said.

"The sight of it always stirs me—and others," Qala agreed.

Caitlin didn't understand her meaning until she followed the woman's eyes to Vilu.

"Now we know that the boy is well asleep," Qala said.

Caitlin leaned toward the boy as they walked. His breathing was normal, the inhalation of sleep, not unconsciousness. She touched his hair.

"We are going to the airship, sweet one," she said softly. "If you open your eyes, you will see it."

The boy stirred slightly—

Because of what I said, or because it was my voice, my touch? she wondered. She took his fingers in hers. *Please, Jacob, if you are in there let me know.*

The straight line of the boy's mouth curved into a small, sweet smile. Caitlin kissed him as they continued to walk.

The path to the tower stretched about a quarter mile ahead, along a rocky, heavily eroded section of beach. At least two dozen wharves had been erected there, beyond the horseshoe harbor, each extending about a hundred feet from the shore. On this side of the tower was a sliver of beach: black sand where Galderkhaani presumably enjoyed recreation, though not this early in the morning. Perhaps it was reserved for the crews who had limited downtime.

There was no longer compacted sand underfoot but large square slabs of stone about a yard on each side. They appeared, like the tower, to be carved from basalt. There were designs cut in many of them—the names of Galderkhaani. Though Caitlin could read them, she had no idea who any of them were. As they crossed over one, she noticed Qala shift her grip on Vilu so that he was nestled in the crook of her elbow, leaving her hands somewhat free. She touched her forehead lightly with her left thumb while holding her other hand flat toward the ground.

To you who sleep.

Caitlin initially thought they were the equivalent of commemorative steles honoring the dead. Perhaps the one they had passed was someone Qala had known. But that idea changed as she peered ahead, into the morning mist that still clung to sections of the shore. The road of stones stretched into the distance as far as she could see along the coast. These weren't just road stones, she realized: they were most likely graves. Considering their size, either the people within had been cremated or they were interred vertically. Or perhaps the sea claimed the remains from below, through liquefaction.

"Where are you truly from?" Qala asked suddenly.

The question was asked with greater insistence than before. "As I said, I can't seem to—"

"You do not honor the ascended," Qala remarked. "You cannot have forgotten something so basic—not when you know how to speak, to read, to minister to a child. If you are not lying, then you are certainly withholding information."

Caitlin quickly replayed Qala's words and gestures in her mind, realized with a jolt that she had missed it: the "ascended" Qala had used in her gesture was plural, not directed at a specific individual but at all of them. It was a custom, no doubt, to pay homage when one set foot on the road. Caitlin should have been present enough, at least, to mimic the salute, even crudely.

She did not consider saying that her mental state had caused her to forget. Qala was not a fool. And it occurred to Caitlin, then, that she might need an ally for whatever was coming, especially one with an airship. She hoped it was possible to explain some things without revealing them all.

Caitlin stroked Vilu's hair once again, then turned toward the strong gaze of the *Standor* and fixed those gold eyes with her own.

"You probably will not believe what I am about to tell you, *Standor* Qala," she answered as they continued along the path, "but I *am* from the north. Only not from this place . . . or time."

The *Standor* made a face. "Is this more wordplay?" she asked. "Another 'time'?"

"Yes," Caitlin said, gesturing carefully, seeking superlatives that could help her state precisely what she meant. "I am from the distant future, not by design but by accident. I am here because a pair of transcended souls forced me to come."

CHAPTER 6

Mikel slept heavily, as though he'd been drugged.

After setting his phone to wake him, he collapsed, sprawled across a bench in the library of the module that served as a social and recreational area of the base. He did not dream, did not get to think of "things" before he drifted away. Casey Skett had relieved him of having to make any decisions. All that Mikel had now was an assignment and he had to be clear-headed to make it happen.

The ibuprofen Mikel had swallowed before sleep kept the pain of his broken wrist from being much of a distraction. The screeching winds were now the equivalent of white noise. Mikel stayed put until the alarm sounded.

Waking with the beep, Mikel found the room still and quiet with only distant sounds as the team of scientists and engineers went about securing their relocated base and undoubtedly researching the phenomenon they'd witnessed—the pillar of fire, biblical in dimension, that inexplicably erupted from the ice. Mikel knew they would not come close to understanding it without his help. Now he had to go down there and convince them of that.

Rest kept his eyes from drooping, but it provided neither clarity nor focus. He was still bombarded with random thoughts, things that sleep had allowed to bubble to the surface. He went back to his log to make a few final additions.

Several things occur to me now that I've had a bit of rest, he typed. *They are puzzles that must be solved. I do not know whether the ascended soul of Enzo remained trapped in the magma of the Source, burning for millennia, or whether her soul somehow leaped immediately from her death ages ago to exist in the present. I am sure the answer could be found somewhere in the olivine tiles, but if I encounter them again I have—and will continue to have—too much respect for them to do more than skim the surface. When triggered slightly, just the single artifact that was appropriated from the geological survey vessel in the Falklands liquefied a human brain. I am not prepared to play Galderkhaani roulette.*

What I know for certain is that the dead are somehow able to interact with the living, but, curiously, not with each other unless they cazhed. Otherwise, Pao and Rensat would have been able to communicate with Enzo. And I would not be alive to write this journal. I suspect the impediment was something the Priests suspected: that transcended souls are quite literally in a different time, realm, or dimension from ascended souls. Yet all can interact with the living—Pao and Rensat with me, Enzo with Jina Park. What is it about living matter that is a conduit, a conductor?

Clearly, Casey Skett wanted answers to those and similar questions. And while Mikel would welcome an ally, the risk was not just seeking to obtain knowledge; it was what Skett might do with it.

Now that his head was a little clearer and he had a chance to process his conversation with those in New York, there was the startling revelation about the Group. Mikel had been recruited straight from Harvard by Chairwoman Flora Davies. A Pamplona-born archaeologist, Mikel had indeed believed they were originally underwritten by a wealthy merchant who discovered Galderkhaani relics on a journey to Bengal in 1648. Mikel had seen those artifacts—shards of pottery with strange writing and pieces of an unknown skin that Mikel now knew were parts of the *hortatur* mask he had donned to help him breathe.

The idea that the story was a lie, or at the very least incomplete, was disturbing. Especially when Mikel thought of the power the Group, or Skett, was on the verge of possessing. They still had two tiles in New York: by themselves, they were devilishly powerful.

Which one of the groups do you help? he asked himself.

Walking away was not an option. This had been his professional life's work and there were profound questions he and only he could still answer. That was why there was no question about going out there, by bulldozer or Ski-Doo, or even on foot if it came to that.

So, he thought. *Time to try and convince either base commander Eric Trout or chief scientist Dr. Albert Bundy to let me have one or the other.*

Trout was the least likely. The burly, mustachioed former Royal Marine commando engineer was a hard-nosed manager, in charge of everything that wasn't science. Mikel had nearly wrecked a key module of the base: Trout would not give the man access to anything with wheels or treads. The Oxford man was the better target. Bundy had previously given Mikel what he wanted thanks to Flora's connection with the RAF—though that was before the base suffered its series of setbacks. Bundy would be less receptive now. Moreover, if the ice shelf had been compromised—and there was as yet no indication that the new location was secure—then it might be necessary to move again. Every means of transportation would be required.

The key may be assuring him that you can answer his questions as well by going back to where it all began, Mikel told himself.

Feeling cautiously optimistic, Mikel slipped from the bench. He walked past the rock-climbing wall that was used for exercise then headed down the spiral staircase to the cafeteria. Several of the staff had gathered there, hungry after the long hours of relocation and data crunching. Dr. Bundy was among them, sitting with several of his top scientists. The six-foot-seven-inch frame of Siem der Graaf was alone at a separate table, which was how and where Mikel had first met him. The maintenance worker was visibly stiff from having shared some of Mikel's adventures.

"How's everything going?" Mikel asked, pausing beside the table.

The young man looked up from a bowl of pea soup. His disinterested expression brightened slightly.

"I'm okay, my crazy friend. How's the wrist? And, how are you even standing after the fall from the truck? I feel like a sack of corn."

"I've learned to ignore superficial bumps and bangs," Mikel answered. "A hazard of the trade. Also, I'm sort of built like a cat. I bend."

"You under six-footers have an advantage there," the big man said. "I move like a log. A hungry log," Siem added as he returned to his soup. But his eyes remained on Mikel. "Speaking of which, you have a rather hungry look. Not for food, I think."

"What kind of a mood is Bundy in?" Mikel asked, his eyes on the scientists' table.

"Not bad. He seems to *like* having a crisis to manage," Siem replied. "I don't mean moving the base, that was mostly Trout. No, I've been hearing things like, 'What bloody caused this instability?' and 'There isn't a bloody computer model that predicted or can explain this!' " Siem said, mimicking Bundy's stentorian British accent. "Oh, and he doesn't believe it has anything to do with global warming."

"The greenhouse effect wouldn't quite explain a column of flame."

"Apparently, none of the satellite images or data suggests any cause, which is why they started spitballing," Siem said. "A new Russian superweapon. Shifting interaction between the Van Allen radiation belts and the plasmasphere. Dragons."

"Dragons?"

"Yes. That was Dr. Cummins's suggestion. She meant it in jest, I think. I hope. We don't have armor-piercing weapons at the base."

"Good God, Siem, why would you kill a mythical creature come to life?"

Siem snickered. "That's a very good question, you know? Too many movies, I guess. And I never was much of a conservationist. I'm a big fan of the Industrial Revolution."

Mikel smiled as he continued to watch the group. They either didn't know he was there or were ignoring him. "Is Bundy planning to go out there?"

"Not yet, as far as I know," Siem replied. "They want follow-up satellite imagery and more data from the remote automated systems before making any decisions."

"Whatever happened to eyes-on scientific reconnaissance?"

"Gone with the insurance documents we all signed to be here," Siem said. "They want to make sure it's not going to go off again."

"It isn't," Mikel replied quietly.

Siem looked up again. "How can you be sure? It's happened three times already. Nerves are a little unsteady."

He was referring to the initial appearance of the flame, the one that killed scientist Jina Park, and to the flare they had all seen while preparing to move the base.

"Because I know what caused that last flare-up, and I know it's burned-out," Mikel said. "The trick will be convincing them."

"Just on your say so?"

"In addition to being a lousy spelunker, I am a first-class PhD," Mikel pointed out.

Siem snickered again as he picked up the bowl and drank down the remainder. "Friend Mikel, I like you. And I might very well believe you. But even I wouldn't risk a research party on your say-so."

"We don't need a party," Mikel said.

"Just you?" Siem said knowingly.

"Just me."

"Good luck," Siem said in earnest, then wiped his mouth. "But if you wouldn't mind—what *did* cause the explosion?"

"It was an ancient power source, fueled by deep-flowing magma that's still under the ice," he said.

"What kind of power source?"

"A mineral," Mikel said. "One that is extremely powerful and apparently unique to the region."

Mikel didn't bother adding that the blast was actually the result of an ascended soul releasing its hold on a portion of that energy. Ascribing the incident to lava was cleaner.

"A new mineral?" Siem said dubiously.

"That's what brought me down here in the first place," Mikel said. "A sample I found, from the waters off the Falklands."

"You have it?"

Mikel shook his head.

"Too bad. But the other part of your theory is a problem too," Siem went on. "Lava would be difficult to overlook, and I don't believe anyone has found geologically active pockets out there. It would be talked about. I would have heard about it."

"The minerals may be screwing with their instruments," Mikel said.

"Ah."

Mikel also did not want to explain that the magma was not active *now* but in another epoch. He looked over at the scientists. "I should probably talk to Bundy about this."

"Probably," Siem said. "And I wish you luck. I do." His eyes held Mikel's. "You were pretty wild down there, Mikel. Are you convinced that you didn't strike your head when you broke your wrist? Or perhaps the air was toxic?"

"I don't blame you for being cautious, Siem—"

"It isn't caution," the maintenance engineer replied. "Frankly, it's doubt. I'm a mechanical engineer." He rapped the table. "Reality, not speculation. Also, I have some concern."

"For?"

"Whatever you do out here will follow you when you go home," Siem said. "I studied Antarctica, its history, before agreeing to accept this appointment. For centuries—going back to the seventh century, if you believe some accounts—people have come to the South Pole and left with crazy ideas. I've read about those ideas and their adherents. Holes to the center of the earth, spaceships of ancient aliens, living dinosaurs, dinosaurs from space living inside the earth. Trust me, Mikel. Careers have been ruined."

"But imagine the contribution to science of the first researcher to find a prehistoric beast down here—even a frozen one."

"And, with it, an ancient bacterium for which there is no known cure," Siem added.

"The price of science," Mikel replied. "How do you know there aren't *any* of those vessels or creatures out here? You yourself, the others—you all saw a burning face."

"We *think* we did, which is my point exactly," Siem said. "The air, the cold, the magnetic pole, the movement of vast oceans around us and under us—the *isolation*. I've listened to the scientists as I work on the gear. It all affects the mind. That's why we rely on impartial equipment, on data, to tell us what is real and what is not. And there is nothing that confirms a jot of this right now."

"As I said, there won't be," Mikel replied. He was still looking over at the scientists. Two had left, leaving Bundy and glaciologist Dr. Victoria Cummins alone with their laptops. Mikel clapped his good hand appreciatively on Siem's shoulder.

"Thank you for your advice, my friend," Mikel said.

"You are welcome," Siem replied. "Good luck getting out of this with your life," he added as the archaeologist walked away.

Mikel didn't know whether the engineer was referring to the impromptu meeting with a hostile scientist or the mission he proposed to undertake.

Probably both, Mikel thought. Siem was not wrong. But Casey Skett had left him no other opitions.

Dr. Bundy was facing Mikel as he approached. The geologist looked drawn but his brown eyes were as lively as ever. His natural frown deepened as Mikel neared.

"Speak of the bloody bête noire," the middle-aged scientist said.

Dr. Cummins turned. Her gray eyes were pale against skin that was still bronze from a long, very recent research trip down the Amazon

River. A glaciologist, she had spent four months studying the drop of sea levels in the region during the last ice age. Dr. Cummins was in her midforties, her dull red hair streaked with gray and pulled into a single tight braid. She said she had used it in Brazil to swat flies, like a horse.

"Doctors," Mikel said in the conciliatory tone he used when he needed something.

The woman nodded and flashed a thin smile. Bundy looked back at his colleague as though they hadn't been interrupted.

"Exhausting all preliminary, standard explanations for a jet of flame in the South Pole," Bundy said, recapping, "and categorizing, for now, as a form of mass hysteria the shape that *appeared* to be a face of fire we all saw before *that*, we also happened to be talking—Dr. Jasso—about the way you hijacked my truck just *before* the explosion, as if you knew the bloody thing were about to happen."

"I didn't," Mikel said. "Not exactly."

"Meaning?"

"While I was in the caverns, I saw a ball of fire," Mikel said. "It appeared to be—well, looking for a way out."

"Consciously seeking an exit?" Dr. Cummins asked.

"It didn't act like any flame I ever saw," Mikel said evasively.

Bundy pinned the archaeologist with a look. "To be specific—a quality you seem reluctant to embrace—you referred to that phenomenon as being, and I quote from vivid memory, 'What a soul looks like when it is sent back to hell.' Since you happen to be here, *despite* being uninvited to my table and a private meeting—"

"In a public space," Mikel pointed out.

"Public for members of this party," Bundy said. "Putting that aside for the moment, would you care to explain and elaborate, Dr. Jasso?"

Before he could speak, Dr. Cummins said, "Mind you, I am very much inclined, as I just told Dr. Bundy, to ascribe the face to some version of Saint Elmo's fire." She tapped her laptop. "There was a coronal discharge and a very strong electric field in the region at that time. The crackling could have been mistaken for a voice."

"Which supports my theory of collective hypnosis of a sort," Bundy said, resuming their previous debate as if he had not spoken to Mikel at all. "We heard a voice and, therefore, we saw a face."

"But Dr. Harvey's point about rising gas catching and refracting sunlight must also be given consideration," Dr. Cummins said, more to Mikel than to Bundy. "The motion of the gas and the sun itself would cause it to appear to move."

Mikel pulled out a chair and sat easily to avoid shocking his bruised posterior. "It was not any kind of gas or luminous plasma, Dr. Cummins. The fire was not an illusion from out there." He motioned vaguely toward the ceiling and the sky beyond. "The flame was real, it came from below."

"Bloody rubbish," Dr. Bundy said. "There is nothing active down there. Nothing that would have caused fire to spit up like that. We are still not reading any kinds of energy bursts, nor are any of the other outposts we've contacted. The RAF is looking into a possible missile strike, or space debris."

"They can look all they want," Mikel said with confidence that bordered on calculated smugness. "It was geologic."

"This is not goddamn Yosemite," Bundy said with rising anger. "We are not sitting on a bloody supervolcano."

"Not now, no," Mikel agreed.

Bundy exhaled, loudly. "You know, I keep hoping for bloody *science* from you," he said, "and am constantly denied." Then he spat a series of expletives. Despite his long string of degrees, the man had the mouth of a North Sea oil-rig worker, which is how he put himself through school. It was also the reason he made a point not to mingle with anyone who didn't have a PhD. That part of his life was done. It was the only reason Mikel was allowed at the table, despite the strikes against him. If not openly blacklisted, Siem and the other engineers were definitely graylisted.

Dr. Cummins turned fully to the new arrival. "I don't disagree that there is some kind of latent, potential danger out there," she said quietly. "That is precisely what Dr. Bundy and I have been discussing. But what do *you* mean? What do you know? As far as we and our very sophisticated, very expensive instruments can tell, there is nothing down there, no caldera, no ancient lava flows, nothing even extinct."

There was a hint of sarcasm in her voice. Mikel didn't mind; at least she was asking questions.

"The key phrase is 'As far as we can tell,' " Mikel said. "There are lava tubes down there. I've been in them. There are massive wind tunnels. That is how I got this." He raised his slinged arm.

"Dormant!" Bundy said. "Not presently *active!*"

"And, if I have been correctly advised, all of that seen in the dark, in the cold, by a battered and confused man in an environment where the senses might be easily confused!" Dr. Cummins said. She nodded toward Siem. "That, from a man who was with you part of the time."

"Exactly so," Bundy said. "Where is the bloody *proof*?"

"That, Doctors, is why I am here now," Mikel said calmly, cutting through the debate. "I want to go out and get it."

"You want to go back *out*?"

"I want to conduct firsthand research," Mikel said. "That's what archaeologists do. Research. In the field."

Bundy laughed. "Brilliant. And you want my blessing?"

"If not that, then at least a conveyance of some kind, even a very modest one."

Bundy was still laughing. "As much as I would love to be rid of you," he replied, "what you propose is absurdly unsafe. Even if the winds were calm—and they're fickle, having just today approached sixty miles an hour and climbing again—we don't know the status of the ice cover around that crater. It may not hold a vehicle of any kind. Or even a man."

"Better to risk that than the modules," Dr. Cummins noted.

Bundy shot her a critical look. "You agree with this?"

"Yes, but for very practical reasons," she said. "We may, quite literally, be on very thin ice, even here. If we don't know the root cause, we won't know how to prepare—or for what, exactly."

"You'll never know what's out there unless I go," Mikel added quickly. "And over days, over hours, important data may be lost."

"Or the entire base could be lost," Dr. Cummins added, addressing Bundy.

Bundy shook his head once. "Go out there and *you* may be lost," he said. "Again. And this time Siem won't go rushing out to save you."

"I'm not asking him to save me, or to save anyone for that matter," Mikel said, "except maybe the research station. Look, I'm not an official part of this team. I can walk out of here if I want."

"And bloody good riddance—"

"Fine, I accept full responsibility for myself and for any damage or loss you may incur," Mikel said. "Just a Ski-Doo, that's all I want."

"And those people who were going to pay for the last damage you caused?" Bundy asked. "The ones in New York? I suppose they will cover this too?"

"Working on it," Mikel said.

"You're all empty promises and hot air," Bundy said. "That's a boy talking, a boy caught in a half-truth, not a scientist."

Mikel looked over at Dr. Cummins. "Do you agree with him?"

"I don't know," she admitted. "You propose to do this with one functioning arm?"

"If I have to."

"You'll never survive," Bundy snapped.

"That's my concern," Mikel replied.

"Not when my equipment is involved it bloody isn't," Bundy said. "No, absolutely not."

"I'll go with him," Dr. Cummins said suddenly.

Bundy fired off yet another critical look. He seemed to have a bottomless supply. "Are you bloody serious?"

"Positively sanguine," she told him. "Look. We've been sitting here for hours, getting nowhere. *I* want to know what's down there too. But of more immediate concern, the ice around the pit *is* cracked. The melted ice inside may have solidified and secured it, but we don't know. The satellite images don't tell us that much. Furthermore, they don't tell us what kind of areal degradation may have occurred below the surface. That's where melting begins, along the ground line, and thanks to that flame geyser we saw—and maybe some we didn't see—we *could* be sitting on a section of shelf that is weaker than we know. There could be hairline fractures or crevasses due to oceanic erosion. We must know the cause and we must try to determine the extent."

"Which is the reason I'm imploring you to let me go out there," Mikel said. "If there is a 'next time,' we may not have time to evacuate."

"Or a place to evacuate to," Dr. Cummins added. "I'll admit, Dr. Bundy, that frightens me."

The face of the geologist relaxed slightly. Mikel could be denied; a fellow scientist was different. Especially one who voiced legitimate concerns. He looked at Mikel.

"This man frightens *me*," Bundy said. "He is impetuous. And I don't think he's telling us everything."

Dr. Cummins turned to study the archaeologist. "Dr. Jasso, I agree with Dr. Bundy. I believe you know things that we do not. Let me tell you, I have no patience for deceit. I worked with a botanist along the Amazon who sounded *just* like you. Same careful phrasing, same hesitation, same *urgency*. He said he had to take our raft, double back and study some rare flower he thought he had spotted growing near a tributary. I later discovered he had seen mud flecked with what he thought was gold. It turned out to be iron pyrite. I know because I had one of the natives watch him. He no longer had any credibility with me, and I sent him packing, Dr. Jasso." She examined the scientist. "What is it with you, Doctor? What are you not telling us?"

Mikel was silent. But his expression registered respect for the scientist and she saw that. She fell silent as well.

"That was unilluminating," Bundy remarked. "Dr. Cummins, I wish I shared your enthusiasm for this course of action. I do not. Dr. Jasso, since your arrival it isn't only the ice that has eroded. My authority has gone to bloody hell. Research is—*must be*—systematic or it is useless." He shook his head. "But I'm tired . . . too tired to argue about this. Until we know *something* about what is out there—which, right now, amounts to very, very little—I cannot and will not personally authorize an expedition." He placed his pale hands on the table and rose. "Now, I am going to sleep. We will revisit this matter later, after we have heard from the British Geological Survey, the U.S. Geological Survey, and other organizations whose job it is—not *ours*—to assess the situation."

"A situation on the ground that they will only study from outside the atmosphere," Mikel said disgustedly.

"At last, you understand," Bundy said.

The barrel-chested scientist departed. Siem had also left, leaving Jasso and Dr. Cummins alone.

The glaciologist rose suddenly. "Come on."

"Where?" Mikel asked, startled from his sudden dejection. He wasn't looking forward to trekking out there.

"To the garage," she said. "Your friend is preparing one of the trucks."

"My friend?"

"Siem. Good lord, I hope you read archaeological signs better than you read human ones," she said. "Dr. Bundy is a scientist. A good one. He wants answers as much as we do, and he wasn't saying no. He was simply abrogating responsibility for the decision I made to take you out there. Meaning, it's my ass if we screw up. Your friend Siem was watching, saw my eyes give the order, and left."

Mikel continued to stare at her. Dr. Cummins was correct. He had missed every piece of that.

"I understand that you work for a woman, the head of a small research organization," Dr. Cummins went on, rising with some effort; she too was tired. "Going forward, we are not, are we, going to have a problem as to who is in charge?"

"We are not," Mikel said, "with one caveat."

The woman froze, her mouth turning up in a not very surprised half-smile. "You've got spine, I'll give you that. What's the caveat, Dr. Jasso?"

"You defer to me regarding a single matter."

"Which is?"

"The ancient civilization that once held absolute sway over this continent," he replied.

She took a moment, just staring at him. Then she said, "A . . . civilization?"

"Yes, quite large and advanced well beyond where the Aztecs and Mayans were at their height," Mikel said. "A civilization that is not quite dead and is definitely not quiescent."

CHAPTER 7

Standing in the sunny but otherwise empty living room, Ben was not just tired and angry, he was perplexed. The Langloises were definitely gone; not only couldn't he hear her jewelry here or in the hall—he opened the door to check—but he noticed Arfa emerge from under the sofa and leap gracefully onto the windowsill. The cat skillfully nestled in the small space between the flowerpots.

Against his strongest instincts, Ben Moss phoned Eilifir. He couldn't think of anything else to do.

"Mr. Moss, what can—"

"Have you been watching the building since I went in?" Ben asked.

"Yes—"

"Did you see the Haitian couple leave?"

"No—"

Ben swore and ended the call. Eilifir called back but Ben ignored him. He tried to think of where the Langloises could have gone—and then it occurred to him: they would have followed the energy. Not that of the smoke snake, but the one Madame Langlois herself had referred to.

Leaving Anita in the apartment, Ben dashed up to the roof. Madame Langlois was now sitting on a lawn chair that was bolted to the roof and Enok was behind her. She was facing south. The smell of cigar smoke reached Ben as he approached.

"I thought you said you had no matches."

"Someone had a birthday recently, there were matches in the kitchen," she said.

Ben noticed them, now, in Enok's hand. "It was Dr. O'Hara's birthday," he said absently, longingly. He had to admire the woman's resourcefulness. "What made you come up here?"

"You never know where a habit may take you," she said.

Ben eyed the woman. "Is that all?" he asked. "This is just a place to smoke?"

"Smoking is never just to smoke," she replied. "It helps me think. And I think that Dr. O'Hara was up here."

"Many times," Ben replied.

"I say recently," she said, raising her arm and pointing to the southeast while she puffed on her cigar. "Very recently. The snake flows there. It tells me of a death."

"In the past or future?"

"It already happened," she said.

Ben peered out. "That's the direction of the park where Caitlin was found."

"It is not she who is dead," Madame Langlois said confidently.

"Do you know exactly when she was here?" Ben asked, approaching her under Enok's watchful eye. "Or rather, was she here in body?"

"In body and soul," Madame Langlois assured him.

Ben looked back at the woman, disapproval in his expression. "Madame, I'm sure you understand how frustrating this is for me."

"You are in love."

"Yes. Yes, I am. You say Dr. O'Hara is alive but in danger, yet that isn't much to go on. Can you please tell me anything more?"

It was Enok who answered. His eyes were hard, his voice even harder.

"You must learn to listen," he said as the smoke from his mother's cigar swirled past his face. "You do that for your livelihood, I am told, yet you are lost in words and not meaning."

"I don't agree," Ben said. "I struggle every minute with nuance and subtext—"

"You deconstruct, that is all you do," Enok said. "Dr. O'Hara *tried*. She was fully committed. She heard. You talk about going to your job. You only hear your own voice." He touched his own forehead, right between the eyebrows.

"The third eye?" Ben said. "That's a Hindu concept, the seat of wisdom—"

"It is present in many cultures," Enok told him. "I was with the doctor when she heard other voices. Heard, not just listened."

"I was with her on one of those occasions as well," Ben shot back, "and Dr. O'Hara—Caitlin—has now paid a price for 'hearing' without fully understanding."

"She saved the child from the serpent," Madame Langlois said pleasantly. "We here are not ready for it."

"Are you talking about a cult?" Ben asked. "Snake worshippers?"

It sounded trivial as he said it. Not silly, but small. Madame Langlois confirmed this impression.

"Not worshippers," she replied. "The most important *loa* himself."

"The god?" Ben said, making sure he understood.

"It is so."

"What is he doing?"

"You saw," she replied. "Damballa, the serpent *loa*, the Sky Father, the creator of all that live—he sent his herald. His endless coils that fill the heavens—*they* are coming."

"I saw lights inside the smoke," Ben said. "I thought those were what you meant by 'they.' "

"The *loa*'s skin will be shed again, not to create the seas but to create new living things," she continued as if she had not heard. She blew smoke at the sky. It formed a sinuous shape before dissipating to the southeast. She cackled low in her throat. "He is gone. He must go to his job too."

Ben was more confused than ever. He did need to go to work, not just to work but also to clear his head. He turned to Enok.

"I have to leave and you cannot stay up here," he said.

"Why not?" Enok asked.

"Because Dr. O'Hara's father is coming and he will not understand. Would you agree to go somewhere else?"

Enok deferred to his mother. She shrugged. "Okay. *Loa* knows me. He will find me wherever I am."

Ben didn't like that, and now he wasn't sure he wanted to take them to his apartment. He did not believe his renter's insurance would cover the kind of damage a giant Damballa made of smoke could inflict. He also wasn't sure his neighbors would understand. But he suddenly had another idea.

Motioning them to come along, Madame Langlois carefully extinguished her cigar on the roof then tucked it back in her pocket. Then the Langloises followed Ben down the stairs, Enok hovering attentively by his mother as she descended between the two men. Ben stopped by the apartment to let Anita know he had found the couple and was taking them somewhere else. Then he texted Eilifir and told him to meet them at the front door of the brownstone at once. When Eilifir asked why, Ben said he would let him know when they got there.

Ben walked ahead of the mother and son. A brisk wind had kicked up while they were still on the roof, and even the bright sunlight could not dampen the chill. Eilifir was waiting by a tree just west of the door to Caitlin's building. He remained there, his smartphone in his left hand, his right hand in his pocket. He kept it there even after Ben had emerged, followed by his guests. Ben approached the man, watching Eilifir as he would watch a diplomat at the United Nations: with innate mistrust.

"Have you ever seen these people?" Ben asked.

Eilifir peered over his sunglasses. "Only photographs taken by the individual I relieved," he said. "Who are they?"

"Vodou practitioners from Haiti," Ben said.

"You *have* made some interesting friends," Eilifir remarked as Enok and his mother walked up.

Ben introduced them. Eilifir acknowledged them with a slight dip of his head.

"Caitlin met them there while working on . . . this matter," Ben went on. "They came here because, according to Madame Langlois, they knew she'd be in danger."

"Great danger," the woman corrected him.

Eilifir smiled. Ben did not.

"The woman has some kind of connection with Caitlin O'Hara," Ben went on, "though I'm not sure how that works: snakes seem to be a key. This woman says a snake god is coming."

"*Is* coming," she said with emphasis.

"Caitlin saw a snake in a vision," Ben went on. "The madame invoked some kind of snake—a mirage, I guess you'd call it, upstairs."

"A harbinger," the woman gently corrected him again.

"That's the foundation of—what word did you use? A 'connection'?" Eilifir said mockingly.

Ben nodded. "I have to agree it's not very impressive, except for one thing. The arm motions in Galderkhaani, the curlicue designs in their writing—they're all very serpentine."

"So are the movements of a ballet dancer, and the art form did not originate in Galderkhaan," Eilifir remarked. "It is of fairly recent vintage. I have season tickets to the Kirov."

"There's more, but I can't go into it now," Ben said impatiently.

"I'm certain there is," Eilifir remarked. "What would you suggest I do with this information—and them?"

"I can't leave them here and I can't take them with me to work," Ben said. "I assume your people have a base somewhere, a headquarters."

Eilifir regarded Ben. "Are you pumping me for information, Mr. Moss?"

"Jesus, no," Ben said. "Friend, I don't give a good damn about you and your associates. In fact, I've had it with cloak-and-dagger, and I certainly have no patience for it now."

"You know, I believe you, Mr. Moss," Eilifir said. "But I am supposed to watch this building. I can't take charge of them. Anyway, I think you got what you wanted."

"I don't follow."

Eilifir cocked his head toward the two. "Them, out of the house. Do you care if they stay here on the street?"

"I do," Ben said. "I tell you, there's something between them and Caitlin."

Eilifir grinned. "I believe you. I just wanted to make sure."

"God, can I just have my life back without the games?" Ben asked. "Listen, nothing will be happening here, I assure you. Do you think I'd be leaving if I thought Caitlin would be coming back for breakfast? All you're going to see happening here is her parents arriving. That's it. They'll be coming to take Jacob O'Hara to school and they'll be here when he gets back. You will also see an exhausted, frustrated psychiatrist named Anita Carter leaving."

"Madame Langlois seems to believe something else will happen," Eilifir pointed out. "Snakes."

"Like Saint Patrick, the snakes will go where she goes," Ben said. "I'm sure of that too. They've only appeared in her presence."

"As far as you know," Eilifir said.

"Yes. As far as I know."

The shorter man gazed at the Haitian pair. Madame Langlois had gone back several paces to sit on the stoop of the building. Huddled in her sweater, she had resumed staring at the dying leaves of the trees. Enok stood at the foot of the steps and watched the two men with unflinching eyes. His face looked, just then, like a skull.

There was a ping. Ben's eyes dropped to Eilifir's phone. It had been dark. Now it was beaming with a text. Eilifir looked at it and then at Ben.

"All right," Eilifir said. "I will take them to our sanctuary."

"You had me on speakerphone?" Ben asked.

"I did."

"Nice of you to let me know," Ben said. "With whom?"

"My superior," Eilifir said. "We host, but the two of them must go willingly. And they remain with us."

"You have a deal," Ben said, pushing his indignation far to the side. "Where—and what—is this sanctuary? Is it a religious institution? A fortress of some kind?"

"Nothing as formidable as that," the man replied. "It's an estate in Connecticut. Very large, very comfortable, very isolated. There is an SUV on Central Park West. I will call it to come and collect them."

Ben exhaled. "So now I have to persuade them to take a ride outside the city."

"All you *have* to do is persuade them to get in," Eilifir said. "I won't force them to do that."

"No," Ben said, "and you will definitely want their cooperation. Hers to get Enok's. Where in Connecticut?"

"Right on the Long Island Sound, in Norwalk."

"Water," Ben said. "I think she'll like that. All right, give me a moment to talk to them. And Eilifir? The intrigue aside, thank you."

Eilifir grinned. "The intrigue is not even what makes this work intriguing," he quipped.

Ben acknowledged that with a nod and Eilifir watched as he walked over to the Langloises. Enok's eyes followed Ben like those of a predator watching prey. Conversely, Eilifir did not seem interested in Ben; Ben didn't know whether he should be flattered that he seemed trustworthy or insulted that he suddenly seemed beside the point.

Ben stopped in front of Enok and his mother, took a moment to collect his thoughts.

"Madame Langlois, Enok—the gentleman behind me is a colleague who knows more about this situation than I do," Ben said. "Would you consider staying with him outside of New York while I—"

Madame Langlois held up a hand and Ben stopped. She removed her necklace, aided by her son, and peered through it at Eilifir.

"I see him still," she announced. "I feared he might be *bokor*. He is not. We will go."

Enok placed a restraining hand on her shoulder. She lightly shrugged it off as she replaced the necklace.

"We came so far," she said. "We must go farther." She waved a hand above her. "And I am cold here." She leaned around Ben. "Have you tea?" she yelled to Eilifir.

"I will make sure you get some," he responded with a smile.

Ben stood there watching as Madame Langlois raised her elbow and, taking it, Enok carefully helped her to her feet. Together, they walked over to the man. As they did, Ben googled the word she had uttered on his phone.

He was not surprised. *Bokor* meant sorcerer. The woman might have her quirks and magick, but she was consistent. She really did seem to believe.

Eilifir texted the driver of the SUV, then told the pair a car would be there momentarily. Madame Langlois asked if she would be free to smoke. Eilifir said she would. He asked what she was smoking. She told him it was a Cuban cigar.

"We have not enough land to farm our own," she informed him.

Enok said nothing.

Walking over, Ben said, "They must like you. Until now, they kept to themselves."

"Not true," Madame Langlois said, retrieving her cigar and addressing no one in particular. "Everyone knows us in Port-au-Prince. Everyone."

Ben wanted to give up. He didn't know whether Madame Langlois was being difficult or whether she was just *that* literal. It didn't matter. In a moment, she would be Eilifir's problem, at least for a while.

While they waited, Ben leaned close, facing away from the Langloises.

"She was afraid you were a sorcerer," Ben said. "Why?"

"Shouldn't you ask her?"

"I don't have time for more riddles, from them *or* you," he said. "Is there something in your past, from Galderkhaan, that she might have picked up on?"

"Probably," Eilifir said.

That caught Ben off guard. "Care to explain?" he asked.

"I apologize, Mr. Moss," Eilifir said. "But one must be authorized to divulge information to outsiders."

"I freakin' read Galderkhaani," Ben said. "How am I an outsider?"

"Being a scholar does not make you of our blood," Eilifir said.

"By 'blood,' you mean Galderkhaani?"

"You already know my heritage," Eilifir said.

"Right. And I'm asking if that's what you just meant. Or by 'blood' do you mean something else, something clannish?"

"I will request permission to tell you more. If it is granted, I will contact you."

As they spoke, a white SUV pulled over and double-parked near the tree. Eilifir turned; Ben grabbed his arm gently.

"These two people are not bound by your rules of omertà," Ben said. "I want—I would *like* to know if they say anything that could help Caitlin."

"Of course," the man replied as he turned to open the door.

"One more thing," Ben said, still holding his arm. Eilifir turned back with less patience. "You said earlier that your ancestors once lived with the Group members, yet you don't communicate with them now. I assume you're rivals."

"Our argument is not with the personnel of the Group as such, but—what you said would be somewhat accurate. And now, that's all I can say."

"So your dispute is with . . . their sponsors," Ben continued to press.

The other man was silent.

Ben released his arm and took a step back. Without saying anything, the man had confirmed what Ben had already begun to suspect.

Excusing himself, Eilifir prepared to put Madame Langlois in the SUV while her son examined the inside. Only when he stepped back did she get in.

Eilifir shut the door, then went to the passenger's side and climbed in. He nodded a farewell. Ben briefly saw himself reflected in the dark window as the vehicle pulled away. He looked like crap. He felt like crap.

Plus now he was truly frightened. The world as he knew it had suddenly ceased to be. Despite his silence, Eilifir and his companions were not just descended from any Galderkhaani. He didn't know which was which, but they were descended from either the Priests or the Technologists.

And they were still at war.

CHAPTER 8

Hearing Caitlin's claim that she was from the distant future, brought here by transcended souls, *Standor* Qala stopped so suddenly that she had to throw an arm across Vilu to keep him from slipping off her shoulder. A half-smile quickly settled on Qala's face, as though she couldn't decide whether what Caitlin had just told her was a joke or whether she was mad. It certainly couldn't be the truth. Undecided, the air officer continued walking toward the tower.

"The idea is absurd," Qala said.

"No less absurd than Candescence."

"*That* is irreligious."

"As your comment is ill-informed," Caitlin replied.

Qala slowed, studied her as they continued toward the tower. Her eyes were suddenly like tiny machines, studying her . . . evaluating her.

"You are in earnest," Qala said. It wasn't a question. She wasn't insulted by Caitlin's remark. She wasn't afraid that someone might overhear them questioning the foundation of Galderkhaan's religious faith. The *Standor* was genuinely curious.

"I am quite serious," Caitlin replied.

"Are you going to tell me you are Candescent?"

Caitlin had not been expecting that. She frowned. "No. I don't think so. What I can tell you is that I am new to this culture, its language, its religion. Events here will occur that impact people I know, far from here in time and place."

"In this future time. From which you say you come."

"I *am* from the future."

"And you have somehow dropped into the body of another."

"That is correct, by means I don't entirely understand."

The *Standor* was quiet again, contemplative rather than doubtful. "The *Drudaya* were forbidden," she said. "Do they return?"

There was no English word that matched. The closest would have been a phrase: the children of the earth.

"That name is unknown to me," she said.

"If such is true, then it is best that we not speak of it."

"Why?"

"Did I not just say they are forbidden?"

"I'm sorry," Caitlin said, deciding not to press the matter. She wanted to try and find out everything she could in order to understand why she was here, in this city . . . and whether she should remain in Falkhaan or go to the capital. Because Bayarma was not present when Bayarmii and her grandmother died, Caitlin was reluctant to place this body anywhere near there. It might change events, cause them to transcend, alter the way Caitlin interacted while she was trying to protect Maanik. The young Indian girl might be lost as a result.

Nothing must change, Caitlin told herself.

Yet if Vilu were going to Aankhaan, there was no way Caitlin would not go with him. The burden was ferocious in its complexity, and Caitlin was still fighting hard to accept the reality of what was happening.

The road was wide enough for two, or for one of the many bicycle-like carts that passed them. They seemed to be constructed of tightly woven vines covered with some kind of smooth, brown pitch.

The wheels were made of some kind of rubber substance. Perhaps sap or animal fat or even skin. She had seen some citizens with masks around their necks that appeared to be made of a similar substance.

Nonetheless, once the conversation was ended—as Qala made clear by the forward set of her head—Caitlin fell in directly behind the *Standor*, now and then touching the forehead of the unconscious boy. As they walked, it was deeply distressing to Caitlin when she considered that the person she was desperate to return to had not yet been born. That thought made her want to scream—and yet it also had an unexpected, calming quality.

If Jacob does not exist, he cannot be missing me, she thought.

It was a strange, elusive comfort but it was the only one she had and she forced herself to hold on to it. She failed. Her memory was her reality. She also wondered about Ben, what he must be thinking, trying, fearing. And her parents. It occurred to her, with a flash of horror, that she still had a body in her time. She suspected—hoped, prayed—that it was still alive and that Ben would somehow see to its care.

If it is dead, then there will be no "me" to go back to, she thought with deep horror.

And if the spirit of Bayarma began to push, tried to reclaim her body, where *could* the spirit of Caitlin O'Hara go? Would she be like Azha, ascended, stuck in limbo?

No, she told herself. Azha was *cazhed* with Dovit. She had transcended. A single soul would merely ascend—alone, witnessing without experiencing, moving through eternity with mute awareness.

Would I have to wait millennia to see myself, and Jacob, alive? Could I go wherever I want? Or are the ascended locked in one time, one place?

There wasn't a thought that didn't chill her, didn't make her want to scream. And now she had the added burden of being with someone who, at best, wasn't sure she could believe Caitlin; at worst, might think she was crazed.

The familiar sea and sky around her made the strangeness of the situation even worse. There were differences, but nothing alien. She had looked up at the blue sky and clouds from Central Park, had looked out at the Atlantic Ocean, with Jacob, from Coney Island. They had appeared more or less like this. Caitlin felt that she should be able to close her eyes, open them, and *be* in one of those places. But as much as she pointed her fingers down while she walked, the energy was gone, or at least depleted. Her spirit was inert.

Her curiosity about Galderkhaan was even less than that. She did not know how these people came to be, who they really were, how long the civilization had thrived. She should be asking questions, making careful observations in case she did get back. Ben—she actually chuckled a little maniacally inside when she thought of this—would probably be watching every gesture, noting every word, looking at every marking, satisfied just *knowing* more than he did.

But he doesn't have a child. He doesn't have other children who depend on him. He has ambassadors, most of whom he doesn't even like.

What touched her, maybe even helped to anchor her a little, was the realization that Ben would swap places with her even knowing he might be booted out of this body and cast into limbo. He wasn't a loving soul, but she knew he loved her.

Caitlin forced her brain to stop thinking. She was here because she wanted to help others, and she had succeeded. That was her job. *Whatever has happened, you earned this, the gold star of collateral damage,* she thought.

The walk to the tower was brief . . . or at least it seemed so, as Caitlin contemplated other things. When she had been at the *motuvarkas* it was dark, she was being assaulted by Pao and Rensat, and she was unable to appreciate the construction of the tower. Though smaller by about one-third than that largest of the columns, it was nonetheless an imposing structure. Constructed of blocks that resembled granite but were possibly volcanic basalt—and lined, she knew, with olivine tiles—the tower tapered slightly as it rose, with two inverted V-shaped structures on either side of the mouth: these were the moorings for the larger airships, of which there was only one at the moment. The vessel was about three hundred feet in length, with a long, open gondola suspended beneath the dark gray balloon. A large platform similar to but wider and longer than a window washer's scaffold was suspended from ropes that hung from a long, pointed prow.

A prow with a dragonlike carving on the front. It was similar to the one Caitlin had drawn while doodling on the airplane while returning home from Haiti.

That was too much to add to the mix, so she didn't. How could she possibly have *anticipated* seeing this? Unless she was remembering from the past . . . ?

Good God, don't try and make sense of this now, she told herself. *Stay in the moment.*

A second scaffold was suspended from the rear of the airship. Hoists lowered bags that she assumed were filled with waste or casks that needed refilling. It was a clean, efficient operation powered by weights like elevators in some of the older buildings in New York.

The trio was quickly under the shadow of the airship. Caitlin felt a chill going from bright sun to gray shadow; it had nothing to do with a change in temperature but a sense that recess was over. Unprepared as she was, events were about to become far more challenging. And though her instincts told her she could trust this woman, Caitlin still had no idea what *Standor* Qala meant to do with her. Perhaps Qala would lock her up in the airship. Still, Caitlin allowed herself to go forward.

The scaffolding that was lowered from the front of the airship was for personnel. She was correct about crew having time on the beach to stretch their legs and wet their feet. From what she overheard, with its fish-spotting duties done, the airship would be making cargo runs to other locations in Galderkhaan on its way to Aankhaan. The plan seemed to be to arrive while the celebration was just beginning, adding even more majesty to the night.

They boarded the lift at the base of the tower. There were hip-high metal rails around the sides and Caitlin held one with both hands in anticipation of the platform being jerked aloft. To her surprise, the ascent was quite smooth. As they rose, the splendor of Falkhaan, of ancient Antarctica, revealed itself in epic pieces. Ahead and below was the village itself, a collection of some two dozen wheel homes and courtyards and a roused populace going about their day. To her right, which was north, was the sea—windswept with choppy breakers in the horseshoe, smooth without. Neither wave nor wind posed a peril to the small crafts on it. In the distance, large fish leaped from the seas in unison, smaller fish among them who were seeking safety from albatross-like seabirds. There was a great deal of hunting and pecking from the birds' large beaks as they tried to nab the smaller prey. Some succeeded, some failed, but even failure left some fish wounded. These fell back and were easily carried off from the surface.

The small airships above were silent, save for the flapping of the finlike projections that obviously controlled their rise and descent, others that managed forward and backward motion. Nets maneuvered into position to catch the leaping fish. To her left, beyond *Standor* Qala and Vilu, was a very distant vista: a plain of ice and distant peaks. She had no idea whether settlements like Falkhaan were created by channeling magma from the Source and melting the ice or they were simply oases in the ice sheet. As they neared the top of the column she saw another village some two miles distant with what appeared to be another cemetery road connecting it to Falkhaan. The village looked to be a cluster of farms growing something that resembled cotton, definitely a fiber of some kind. Carts laden with cloth were moving along the cemetery road that stretched beyond it into a hazy valley.

The wind was louder up here, not quite thundering in her ears but making it very difficult to hear anything else. The slight smell of something sulfurous also became more pronounced as they neared the top. She likewise felt an increase in the heat, the little that drifted down instead of rising.

That must be the magma of the Source located in the belly of this tower.
It caused the vista of the harbor city to ripple gently.

Soon to be leveled . . . all of it, Caitlin thought with a fresh sense of horror. She did not want to be a part of this. She did not want the responsibility. *I'm going to wake, I have to wake—*

"Mother?"

At first, Caitlin wasn't sure she'd heard the whispered voice speaking in English. She had been looking away from Vilu. Now she turned toward him and saw his eyes partly open. The boy was smiling thinly.

"Mother," he repeated, not as question this time but as a statement.

Caitlin started, did not know how to respond verbally. She touched his forehead comfortingly and returned his smile. Despite her expression, she prayed she had misheard, that this was not Jacob.

Standor Qala heard the boy as well. "Did he say something?" she asked.

"I'm not sure," Caitlin lied.

The *Standor* turned to the boy just as the elevator scaffold reached the top of the column. She stepped onto the far side of a ledge below the large inverted V. The platform was nestled firmly against the side of the tower. There was a ramp that led from the center of this platform into a gated opening in the side of the gondola. The gate was open. The gangplank wobbled slightly as they stepped on it, and a moderate wind blew across them. Caitlin was glad for the handrails along the sides, and held them as she followed Qala. Vilu's eyes were on her the entire time. The gangplank was about a dozen feet long. Halfway across, the boy stretched his arms over Qala's shoulder, toward Caitlin. Qala twisted her head around slightly. Her eyes followed the small hands, saw the fingers wriggling playfully.

"What's going on?" the commander demanded.

"It seems the boy is awake," Caitlin said as matter-of-factly as possible.

"It is not like Vilu to be more interested in a stranger than an airship," Qala remarked. "What is going on?"

Caitlin remained silent.

With a disapproving look, Qala turned her eyes ahead and strode forward, Vilu squirming to keep his eyes on Caitlin, his hands reaching for her. A guard at the open gate saluted by touching the fingers of his left hand flat against that side of his head. Qala bowed her head slightly in acknowledgment.

As soon as they were both on the open deck of the gondola, Qala turned to Caitlin. "I asked a question," the *Standor* said.

"Let's talk after we see the physician," she suggested.

Qala hesitated. It was a look of a woman who was not accustomed to having her orders replied to with an alternate suggestion.

"The boy first," Qala agreed. "Then you will share what you know."

"Even what you might not believe?" Caitlin asked.

"Everything," the *Standor* said, strongly emphasizing her words with a movement of her hands.

Caitlin nodded firmly.

Draped over Qala's shoulder, looking at Caitlin, Vilu responded by signing at her. Caitlin's heart began to rise in her chest: once again, the gestures were not Galderkhaani.

"This is not the *Nautilus*?" he said. "Am I dreaming?"

"You are awake, sweetheart," Caitlin replied.

"I can hear," the boy continued, in signed English. "I know it's you—but why don't you look like you?"

"It's . . . complicated, baby," Caitlin replied in English. She suddenly felt her grasp of the Galderkhaani language slipping, and not because she was communicating in English. The tingling had suddenly returned to the back of her neck.

"Kuvez ma tulo?" Qala asked, turning the boy's face from Caitlin.

She looked at Qala sharply. "I . . . understand . . . not," she said in broken Galderkhaani, her arms fumbling with gestures that had been so easy a moment before.

"Buz eija lot?"

"Christ God, no!" Caitlin responded in English, grabbing for Vilu.

But her fingers found no purchase, either falling short or else she had turned—she couldn't be sure, for at the same time Caitlin's vision grew misty, as if she were seeing through tears. And then she *was* seeing tears, weeping and screaming inside and out as the world swirled away and she fell to the floor of the airship gondola and found herself once more in blackness.

The last word she heard was "Mother!"

•   •   •

"Mother?"

Caitlin awoke looking into her mother's eyes. They were framed in a familiar, worried face that was barely visible against a bright overhead light.

"Doctor!" Nancy O'Hara called.

Caitlin heard her mother, heard her own voice through the folds of a stiff pillow that was bunched up against her ears. There was something in her nose, something in her arm, something on a finger—

"Ja-Jacob," Caitlin rasped. Her throat was raw, sore, not at all like it felt in Galderkhaan. The air was machine-blown, unnatural, unhealthy. Everything around her reeked of illness. Her shoulders ached as though her arms had been pulled at, hard. When she opened her eyes she had to blink several times to clear away a thin film of gunk that was on them. Her face smelled of rubbing alcohol, beneath which there was a hint of—ash? Smoke? In her hair?

Why was that there? she wondered. The last thing she had felt was clean air and tears. The last thing she had smelled was the strong smell of hemp. The last thing she had heard, and the last thing she had seen—

"Vilu . . ." she wept softly. "Jacob."

Nancy O'Hara had turned away and didn't hear her daughter. Caitlin heard her calling for someone. She tried to get up, felt—

That isn't the handrail of a gangplank, she thought with horror that made her recoil. They were the aluminum bars of the hospital bed. Her eyes coming into focus now, she became aware of the equipment blinking and humming to her left. She saw her mother, but did not recognize the figure moving toward her through the open door.

A man in a lab coat bent over her, looked into her eyes. They still felt gummy; the tears she had felt had belonged to Bayarma, in Galderkhaan, not to her. The white light of an ophthalmoscope seemed to pin the back of her skull to the bed. She fell back as though she'd been shot. She tried to blink but two fingers firmly held one eye open, then the other. The man said something she couldn't quite make out.

". . . haf pen anywar?"

"S-sorry?" Caitlin said. "I don't . . . don't understand."

"Do you have pain anywhere?"

"I—I don't know . . . arm . . . IV?"

"Yes."

"No . . . I'm numb. Shit, I'm back."

"Just rest," the man said as he killed the light. The hospital room came into clear focus. Caitlin saw an Asian man and her mother's face.

"Jacob," Caitlin said to Nancy O'Hara. "Where is he?"

"Honey, Jacob is home, with your father," Nancy assured her.

"No!" Caitlin cried. "I mean—his soul. His spirit. *Him*. Where is he?"

"Where? Caitlin, I promise you, he's home, he's all right," she insisted.

"No, please listen," Caitlin said. She tried to rise again from her pillow, from the bed. "Something has *happened* to him!" she said, her fingers fumbling with the bedrail. "He needs me!"

There was talk, there was movement, there were hands on Caitlin's shoulders and legs. Caitlin struggled against all of it.

"Let me go! Ben? Ben!"

"Calm down, Dr. O'Hara," a male voice said soothingly. "You've inhaled a lot of smoke and were nonresponsive—"

"Dammit, I'm fine! *Fine!*" Caitlin yelled. "I am *not* suffering from disorientation, confusion, delirium, or any goddamn thing else!"

"... five milliliters," she heard the doctor say over his shoulder.

"Mom, *call* Dad—ask him to check on my boy!"

There was a pinch, an injection of diazepam, and Caitlin stopped struggling almost at once.

"Goddammm," she slurred. "Please! No! Must ... get ... back ..."

And then she slept.

PART TWO

CHAPTER 9

Mikel Jasso couldn't believe his good fortune—or his bad luck.

Casey Skett, master of dead things, apparently knew people better than Mikel did. It was too early to say how any of this would turn out but, against the odds, the archaeologist had gotten more than he asked for. Indeed, now that Mikel thought of it, Skett was more artful and clever than any of them: he had fooled Flora Davies for years. *That* took skill.

As he and Dr. Cummins made their way through the station to where the truck was parked, the scientist was busy checking the latest images of drifts and ice cracking along the proposed route to the pit.

"The fractures don't seem to have made it this far," she said. "Readings from our remote automated systems say the heat has quite receded."

"It's fickle," he said.

"You talk as if it has consciousness," Dr. Cummins remarked. "Does it, Dr. Jasso?"

"Thoughtful fire? What would Dr. Bundy say to that," he answered without answering.

Dr. Cummins *hmmmed* as they walked on in silence.

Mikel was peering ahead, through the alternating light and dark of the interconnected modules, his mind back on Skett . . . and Flora. He was not sure how he even felt anymore about Flora and the Group. He did not believe it was incumbent on any employer to keep employees informed on the inner workings of the firm. Either you trusted your superior or you did not.

But this *withholding . . . that's a big one*, he thought.

Mikel had trusted Flora and now he did not, and he wasn't sure where that left him. If she didn't know everything about the Group's past, she had to have known—and withheld—at least some vital information about why they were seeking Galderkhaani artifacts. That was a dangerous secret to keep from agents in the field. Mikel and the handful of others should have been given the option of whether to risk their lives to obtain and turn over such powerful tools for something other than pure research.

What was more troubling was that he couldn't even be sure she was not playing Casey Skett or both of them playing him. Bad cop, worse cop.

Nonetheless, he had no choice but to let this play out as Skett had laid things out. At the very least, Mikel told himself, he *would* learn more about the power of the stones.

The truck assigned to Dr. Cummins was a Toyota Tacoma. It sat hefty and fat on the ice just outside the exit of the central red module.

"I was hoping for a dozer," Dr. Cummins said. "The treads are good for getting over small crevasses, the plow for filling them in."

"Maybe Dr. Bundy doesn't want us to get where we're going," Mikel suggested.

The woman shook her head as she pulled on a wool cap then tugged her parka over it. "He's a snob, and gruff, but he's devoted to science and learning and, believe it or not, to this evolving mission."

Mikel would have to take her word for that. He found it appropriate that while he had lost faith in one woman, he did not hesitate to trust the judgment of another. That was the bequest of his grandmother in Pamplona, a borderline mystic who knew her Bible inside out and also read everything she could find about obscure religions, talked to every priest she ever met, bounced new ideas, strange ideas, off her only grandson. Her interest in the arcane was what spurred his own fascination with ancient civilizations and set him on his career path. Even if his father hadn't been in prison for armed robbery, Mikel couldn't have had a more compelling and substantial role model.

The truck had been refitted for driving across the uneven Antarctic terrain. Resting atop forty-four-inch wheels with thick axles to absorb the rugged thumps and dips, the truck had an indomitable suspension system, side skids to prevent the truck from rolling over into a crevasse or sudden break in the ice, thirty-two gears for shifting out of almost any landscape, and a reinforced passenger cabin to protect the occupants against unlikely falls and landslides. There were also forward and rear winches, solar panels to supplement the 2,200-liter fuel tank, several additional tanks of gas, and a powerful V6 engine. On the roof rack were two insulated cases. One was filled with bottled water, oxygen, first-aid supplies, and battery-powered heaters. The other carried shovels, axes, ropes, pitons, blankets, flashlights, flares, spare clothing, and other gear.

No one had bothered to unload the truck from the last move; station personnel were still busy restoring communications and restarting the electrical systems that had been shut down during the unexpected transit. Dr. Cummins brought along a backpack filled with extra water and snacks; as soon as the vehicle was fueled, it was ready to go. Siem was busy taking care of that from a tank that was still attached to the skis that had been used to haul it here. He waved as the two scientists boarded.

The truck's solar panel had been left on and the inside was warm when the occupants settled in. The parkas, gloves, and scarves came off immediately. Though the gear had been needed for the fifteen-foot trek to the Tacoma, their skin would heat very quickly inside the truck. They didn't want to perspire, since sweat would heat and chill their flesh to dangerous extremes.

Dr. Cummins raised her sun goggles just long enough to poke on the GPS. The coordinates had been entered from inside the radio room; the truck could practically drive itself. Before they got underway, the scientist looked at Mikel through her dark-tinted goggles.

"You are preoccupied," she said. "With the mission?"

He nodded unpersuasively.

"But also by something else."

He nodded again. "Political stuff at the nonprofit where I work," he told her.

"Ah ha," Dr. Cummins replied. "You know, Dr. Jasso, it's dangerous out there—"

"I'm focused, Dr. Cummins. Believe that. I won't do anything to jeopardize this mission."

"I'm glad of that," she said. "However, there's one more thing. How to put this?" She stopped everything for a moment and looked at Mikel. "As I indicated back there, I've been on many, many expeditions with fellow scientists. All ages, all nationalities, all kinds of temperaments, all kinds of *agendas*. I know when *not* to press a colleague for information. Many of them—and you too, I believe—are often uncertain about what they are about to undertake. They might be concerned about a vague goal, worried about censure for a radical idea, afraid because they flat-out lied to get funding, said they knew more than they did. That's Fieldwork 101. So all I'm going to ask is this: Which of those has caused you to clam up?"

She put a little extra burr on the last two words so they came out "clahm oop" and added a touch of levity to a serious question. Mikel smiled a little, then exhaled and stared out the window at the jagged expanse that headed to a rolling horizon.

"All of the above?" she prompted.

"That's a very fair analysis," he admitted. He looked back at the weathered but compassionate face. "Dr. Cummins, I don't like clamming up. I don't learn anything when I can't share. So now that we're alone—we are, aren't we?"

"No hidden mics or open lines," she assured him.

He nodded once. "Here's what I can say with certainty. I have spent my professional life studying a human civilization that, as I began to tell you, thrived approximately thirty or forty thousand years ago," he said. "But it's possibly older than that. Much older, if they went through an evolution similar to our own." He shrugged. "Even that may not be the case. I know absolutely nothing of their origins."

He paused to let that sink in. Dr. Cummins needed the respite: she said "hmmm" three times before she nodded for Mikel to go on.

"My colleagues and I, and those who came before us—at least four centuries of researchers—thought the occupants of this land might have been protohumans of some kind," he continued. "Recent experiences I had out there—" he pointed almost accusingly toward the ice, "have proved that idea to be incorrect. These people, the Galderkhaani, were modern in every sense of the word, with sophisticated structures and language, with ships that sailed in the air and sea—"

"Galderkhaani," she said, making sure she got the name.

"Yes."

"How?" she interrupted, "How?"

"You mean, what was the scientific mechanism that created ancient technology, or how did we not know an advanced civilization was out there?"

"All of that!" she said. She switched on the ignition and the truck hummed loudly, a fine vibration tingling through the seat, as she put it into drive and set out. "For starters, just biologically speaking, there is no model of evolution that places modern humans in that time period."

"I am very aware of that," Mikel said.

"Have you seen a likeness? A carving."

"I have seen . . . yes. They had ruddy, exotic eyes, but . . . well, they were groomed, clothed in togalike garments. They had a complex language. They were not Neanderthal or Cro-Magnon. They were *Homo sapiens*."

"Dr. Jasso, are there remains out there?"

"There is *so much* out there," he answered. He needed to lay a little more groundwork before diving into the spiritual nature of his contact with the Galderkhaani. "As I sit here, looking out at the world, our world, I can hardly believe the things I've seen and heard. But it's all real. More to the point, that explosion we saw, it *is* linked to ancient conduits that ran beneath the cities, powered by various mechanisms using the heat and flow of deep pools of magma. Something caused the prime conduit, what they called the Source, to overload and destroy the entire civilization. Pompeii writ very, very large." He nodded ahead. "The pillar of fire we saw was a surviving part of that."

"And the face within?"

"A surviving spirit," Mikel told her.

That stopped her, again. After a long moment she asked, "You've seen it?"

"Yes," he said. Then went on: "And others."

"Living Galder . . . Galderkhaani?" she asked, pressing him.

"No," he said. "They were spirit."

Now she made a face. "That's just great."

"I didn't imagine it, hallucinate it, or make it up," he said.

"You broke your wrist, bruised your face. You appear to have taken quite a beating—"

"So I could have hit my head and imagined everything I just told you? Yes. That is possible," Mikel said. "Only that isn't what happened."

He held off telling her about the olivine tiles that were like sophisticated living neurons. He didn't want to hand her so much seeming fantasy that she turned back.

"Fine, Dr. Jasso, you didn't dream these things and they're not the result of a concussion. But what evidence do you have for any of it?" Her expression, like her voice, was suddenly very dubious.

"It's all out there," he gestured ahead. "If you go down into that pit, enter the tunnels, I have no doubt you will see ruined structures under the ice. You may see conduits that were used to transport the ancients via wind—"

"Wind?"

"Incredible wind generated by the heat of the magma," he said.

She made another face. "So now they were not just ancient humans, they had wings?"

"Sleds," he said. "Made of a substance similar to this."

Mikel reached into his pocket; it was time. He withdrew the *hortatur* mask he had used to help him breathe. He passed it to her.

"Lord Jesus," she said, slowing the truck as she stared. "Is that from—"

"It's Galderkhaani, yes."

Stopping the truck on a flat, smooth patch of compacted ice, Dr. Cummins stared at the ancient mask then started to reach for it but stopped.

"Are you sure it is safe to touch?" she asked. "Without gloves, I mean?"

He nodded. She took the mask, felt the texture between her thumb and index finger.

"You're a glaciologist, Dr. Cummins, I'm sure you've been around Arctic and Antarctic life," Mikel said. "Tell me, what animal does that come from?"

"It feels almost like seal," she said. "Walrus, perhaps."

"It's from a creature called a *shavula*, a kind of sea ram with fangs," he said.

"You know that how?" she asked. "From their writings?"

"There are libraries out there, down there," he said evasively. "Very comprehensive. I can read them."

"It's still oily," she said. "How is that possible? Did you treat it?"

"No," he said. "I don't know how it was treated—though it wasn't exposed to the elements for millennia, so that may change. Swiftly."

She returned the mask to Mikel and started up again. "Why didn't you tell all this to Dr. Bundy? He's rough around the hem but he's not here for his health. He has a right to know."

"That was not the time and place to explain," Mikel said. "There are time-sensitive reasons for going out there. And I didn't want him using it as a reason to delay. You know, sending it to the lab, waiting for results."

"What could be that 'time sensitive' about a dead civilization? Did you open a tomb? Are artifacts decaying?"

"It will be easier if I show you when we get there," Mikel replied.

They drove for a short period in silence. Then Dr. Cummins said, "When we saw that pillar of fire in the air, we thought we heard a voice. Strange words. So, that might have been Galderkhaani?"

"I am fairly certain it was," he replied.

"Spoken by—a spirit? A ghost?"

"Something like that," Mikel told her.

"Christ in his heaven," Dr. Cummins said. "That was the real reason Siem went back to collect you, that he was allowed to go back at all," the scientist went on. "He said that you were the only one who might be able to explain. But then you lost credibility with Eric Trout when you commandeered that vehicle. He decided you were— 'unhinged' was the word he used."

"Remarkably, I'm not."

"I mention that in light of what you said, about these ancients having had libraries, technology," Dr. Cummins said. "Is it possible that rather than being a spirit, the fire activated some kind of recording? Because it's not as strange as it might sound. The Greeks had all the materials they required to make voice recordings: clay, a stylus, funnels—only they never thought to do it."

"That's a smart supposition and there *are* recordings," Mikel admitted. "But this was a spirit. She pursued me underground. She tried to kill me."

Dr. Cummins was silent again. "Galderkhaan," she said. "Is that their word or yours?"

"Theirs," he replied. "From the words I saw and heard, I believe that *Galder* means an amount of some kind and that *khaan* means 'a city.' That was actually something my colleagues and I pieced together years ago."

"A collective of cities?"

"That seems to be the idea. It's fairly common in our world, isn't it? 'United' this or 'Confederation' of that. Unfortunately, there was a signing aspect to the spoken language to give it nuance, so the words alone don't tell the entire story."

"Fascinating," she said. "Like the click consonants in many African tongues."

"Exactly. But there is still a big piece of the puzzle I am missing," Mikel said.

"And that is?" she asked.

He was silent again.

"Are you thinking, Dr. Jasso, or am I going to have to pull each answer from you?" Dr. Cummins asked.

"Sorry," he said sincerely. "I was thinking. I'm trying to clarify ideas in my mind, which isn't easy. I'm not accustomed to discussing this away from the Group in New York, where everyone throws ideas into the ring. My confusion has to do with the Galderkhaani beliefs about the afterlife."

"Religion."

"Broadly," he agreed, "though I'm not sure they made a distinction between religion and everyday life. What I mean is, it wasn't so compartmentalized. Even the scientific class entertained a very strong belief in what we'd call the mystical."

"Like alchemists or druids," she said.

"I suppose that would be a good comparison," Mikel concurred. "Yes, quite apt."

"I grew up in Scotland, and it is steeped in those old beliefs, as you are probably aware," Dr. Cummins said. "As a child I first went to the mountains known as the Old Woman of the Moors, as their shape reminds some of a sleeping goddess. Every eighteen years, the full moon moves in such a way that a person standing with arms outstretched like Mr. Da Vinci's drawing would be perfectly framed by the moon. To those watching from one of the stone avenues constructed for that purpose, time and space vanishes and human and celestial body are one."

"An illusion of geometry," Mikel suggested.

"Now who is the doubter?" Dr. Cummins asked. "What you just said is quite true, but there's more. From that same vantage point, the course of the moon is such that it strokes the sides of the goddess Earth, rousing great energies. Everyone there feels it." She chuckled. "One reason I am out here with you, Dr. Jasso? Not because *you* are especially persuasive. The earth is, however. I went back home a year ago. Even with all my mental safeguards working on behalf of scientific explanations, I couldn't quantify the feeling I got inside. It was a kind of tickling in my belly that rose and fell from my skull to my toes. It made me smile long after the moon was gone. And I'll tell you this: I do not approach any peaks here, ice or stone, without feeling some of that sensation return. The geology, the cosmos, they *waken* something. Even in scientists." She gave him a quick look. "You too? Or are you more hard-nosed than that?"

"I was," he admitted as they thumped across a patch of snow that was rippled like speed bumps. "My grandmother's belief in spirits was absolute, but she was very old world."

"You say that as if 'new' is automatically better than 'old.' "

"The eyes are fresher, less steeped in accepted tradition than in proof." He looked in the direction of the pit. "I want, I *need* proof of what I experienced out there. I didn't become a scientist to disprove old ideas. Nothing would please me more than to know that what my grandmother felt was right."

"I understand that and I respect it," Dr. Cummins said. "Like you, I was set on this path by someone else."

"Who?"

"My uncle Timothy, who had a ranch in Kirkcudbright, Scotland.

The first time I saw a horse shyte, unicorns lost their magic for me. I need things that keep more than my curiosity alive. I am constantly searching for places that rekindle my sense of wonder."

Mikel replied thoughtfully, "This enterprise with Galderkhaan—it started that way. But the more relics my colleagues and I found, the more we learned of their language, it seemed as if they were shaping up to be a sad microcosm of all humanity: roughly one hundred thousand people who could not get along without dividing into factions. And I have since learned, from my excursion underground, that it wasn't just some*thing* that caused the Source to turn on its creators. There was a Dr. Frankenstein, someone who unleashed it."

"Mass homicide?"

"Unintentional, perhaps, but yes . . . the destruction of this entire civilization was spurred by sociopolitical, possibly romantic, fractures that would be all too familiar to any modern human."

Dr. Cummins considered this new information. "Entire," she said.

"I'm sorry?"

"You said it destroyed the entire civilization," Dr. Cummins said. "Are you sure?"

"What do you mean?"

"Ancient peoples were remarkably mobile across vast stretches of ocean," she said. "The Vikings, Kon-Tiki, even Columbus and Magellan . . ."

"That's true," Mikel said.

"Surely you and your colleagues have considered this."

"We have," he admitted.

Dr. Cummins regarded him. "Radio silence again," she said. "So you do have evidence of some diaspora."

"We have words and claims, not evidence," he told her. Once again, he didn't want to say any more. It was one thing to ruminate about a dead culture. It was another to confide in her that hostile agents were trying to finish a struggle they started millennia ago. That might be far, far more than she had bargained for.

The two fell silent as the truck purred across the ice. Mikel thought back to the conversation he had just had with Casey Skett, about the Group having an origin other than the one Flora had told him. This shift from seeking knowledge to seeking power was disturbing. It was fascinating, even compelling, certainly *logical* to think the Group had been founded by refugee Galderkhaani. It was frightening, however, to imagine these people, and Skett's people, still seeking to control the tiles. The stones were an incredible source of information. Yet they were also a source of great destructive power. Bringing just one back to New York had caused Arni's brain to liquefy. It had caused Mikel to hallucinate severely or, briefly, to time travel—he still didn't know which. In the lava tube to which they were returning, a wall of tiles enabled him to communicate with Galderkhaani *dead*—and for them to enter his mind from miles away. It had driven animals mad along lines of force that extended halfway around the globe.

Though he was headed back to the site as Casey Skett had commanded, Mikel wondered what kind of experiment the man had in mind . . . and whether he could actually go through with it. He did not *know* enough to bounce that off Dr. Cummins.

They crossed the partially drifted-over tracks of their previous transit, when they had been relocating the Halley VI modules from the compromised ice shelf. The rest of the ride continued to pass in silent reflection. For his part, Mikel was imagining a thriving civilization on the wastes across which they traveled. On ice? On clear plains? He didn't know. He pictured airships in the sky, vessels on the sea, animals long-since extinct like the one he'd seen below, the "guardian" of the chamber. It was not just an exponential Pompeii. In AD 79 when Vesuvius buried that port city, the vast bulk of the Roman Empire and its citizens, its diverse culture, survived. Galderkhaan and its people were obliterated. He did not know the degree to which any refugees may have maintained a pure form of the language, the arts, the faith, the technology.

But there is that magnificent library, he thought covetously. And there were ascended and transcended souls. To be able to talk to them, debrief them—it would be like being able to talk to the monotheistic pharaoh Akhenaten, who some archaeologists believe was one and the same with Moses, or Alexander the Great, or even just a vegetable vendor from Nero's Rome.

Mikel shivered, and not from the cold. Perhaps, he thought, right now, he was surrounded by ascended souls he could not see or hear. Regardless, the sadness of their loss was suddenly palpable, their trauma felt immediate as if it had just occurred. It was as real and as current as any he had ever known.

It may be that Pao and Rensat are watching, he thought. *Perhaps spirits have always been watching.*

Angels and devils. Many survivors of the cataclysm may have lost their roots over generations. The idea of Transcendence may have morphed, via Galderkhaani expatriates, into Valhalla, the Elysian Fields, heaven, and other versions of an afterlife. It could be that Candescents became the earliest gods.

"By coming here, we may be returning to God," he said.

"Sorry?"

"I was just thinking," Mikel said. "What if it's the tinsel that's fake, but the tree is real. What if all the trappings of religion were created to keep wandering minds engaged."

"I'm not following," Dr. Cummins said.

"I'm not sure I am either," Mikel admitted, smiling and once again falling silent.

Dr. Cummins slowed the truck and raised her goggles slightly. The insides of the lenses were misty and she wiped them with the side of her thumb. It could just be humidity. Or maybe she had felt something emotional here and shed a few tears. She said nothing as she replaced the dark glasses and urged the Toyota across the last, smooth leg of their journey.

As they neared the mouth of the round pit, Mikel saw that it was nearly perfectly round, about one hundred feet in diameter, with a shadow just below the lip that was as flat black as the snow was brilliant white. The edges had been melted unevenly by the flame then refrozen, creating the illusion of a small, circular waterfall stuck in time. The hairline fractures had also been filled in with melted ice and covered with windblown flecks. Dr. Cummins pressed on cautiously, both of them listening for any sound that could suggest the ice had weakened. The external thermometer mounted to the hood showed no discernable rise in temperature as they approached. There were no sudden dips in the ice field.

"I don't see any steam out there," Dr. Cummins said. "How deep were your tunnels?"

"The crevasse I descended was maybe a hundred feet," Mikel said. "I can't be sure. I fell some of the way."

"It was artificial?" she asked.

"A lava tube, as I assume this one is, since the fire was able to shoot through rock," Mikel said.

"We should go the rest of the way on foot," the glaciologist suggested. "Reconnoiter only. We can break out the gear when we know what we're looking at."

Mikel agreed, though at some point very soon he was going to have to tell her his assignment and contact Casey Skett and find out exactly why the man wanted him out here.

Dr. Cummins reported back to the communications center at Halley VI and after suiting up for the cold they hopped from the cab to the surface. The desolation was not as profound as it had been when Mikel first arrived in Antarctica. Dr. Cummins obviously felt it too: when she climbed from the cab she was not just looking at the pit, she was turning around.

Mikel walked over. "Anything wrong?" he asked over his muffler.

"I don't know," she admitted.

"But you feel something different from before."

The woman nodded.

Mikel didn't have to ask what that was. The Old Woman of the Moors was here—at least, her presence and mystery were.

Mikel moved first and Dr. Cummins followed. The crunch of the ice under their boots was muted by the drifted snow. Their toes kicked up little puffs that swirled in unseen eddies of air. The winds were calmer out here and everything else was quiet, save for something they noticed as they neared the pit: occasional, echoing raps.

"What's that?" Mikel asked, hesitating as he tried to make out the sound.

"Icicles falling," Dr. Cummins said. "It probably looks like a long white beard down there with the fast-frozen drips and runoff."

"The Old Woman has a companion," Mikel quipped.

Dr. Cummins flashed him a thumbs-up that relaxed them both. Mikel hadn't realized how on edge he was until then.

Walking almost shoulder to shoulder so that one could help the other in case of uncertain footing, they approached the pit with the same gingerly steps they would take approaching a fissure or crevasse. Along the opposite rim of the pit, Mikel saw only the fast-frozen ice, not ground. There wasn't a single visible crack in the deep cover here; it was like vanilla frosting laid on with a thick spatula.

"I've seen geothermal heat generate melting like this on the Amundsen Sea, but not here," Dr. Cummins said, leaning toward him as they trudged across the ice.

"That's quite a distance away."

"About two thousand kilometers," she said. "To be honest, we don't know the extent to which subaerial volcanism may be responsible for any of that. Even so, to have reached *this* far? That wasn't even part of the most ambitious thinking. Dr. Jasso, is it possible that your ancient civilization covered the entire continent to the western region? It was pretty icy there during the period you indicated."

"I don't believe so," he said. "From the research, I believe there were densely populated pockets across the continent. I would imagine that population, if not controlled, was strictly determined by the food supply."

"Obviously, they would have had fish, sea mammals, birds—"

"Possibly each other," he added. "I know nothing about their in-terment practices."

"That's an unpleasant thought, though you're right. I have heard about isolated pockets that practiced cannibalism along the Amazon."

"The Galderkhaani were big on jasmine," Mikel said. "Drank a lot of warm tea, I'd imagine."

"I like that better," Dr. Cummins said. "The practice, not that fla-vor of tea. Dr. Jasso?"

"Yes?"

"Am I whistling past a graveyard?" she asked.

"It's quite possible," he said. "I'm uneasy here too. I would be in-terested in going back through reports from this region, see if other researchers have experienced anything—" he stopped as he sought an appropriate word.

"Off? Ripe? Gray? Oppressive?" Dr. Cummins contributed.

"All of that," he said.

There was a high, warbling rush of sound. The two of them stopped at the same time. Dr. Cummins pulled her parka from one side and turned her ear toward the pit.

"That's not the wind," she said. "Did you hear anything like that below?"

Mikel shook his head. Whatever it was, the sound came from in-side the pit, soft and melodious, modulating slightly and echoing on its way up and down.

"It could be an ice flute," she suggested. "Wind through a hollow icicle—"

"That's not whistling," Mikel said. He had heard those in Norway, frozen "panpipes." Wind passing through a hollow tube of ice has a shriller quality. "That's humming."

"Can't be," Dr. Cummins said. "Can it?"

"I have learned to dismiss nothing where Galderkhaan is con-cerned."

Dr. Cummins shook her head as if to say, *I'm just not ready for that.*

They started walking again, cautiously, when the frozen water on the lip of the pit nearest them, the northeastern rim, began to darken. It was like watching bread turn moldy in time lapse: something unhealthy was moving toward them.

"Doctor?" Mikel asked.

"I don't know what it is, I've never seen anything like it," she said. "Let's go back to the truck."

She started to move but Mikel stayed where he was. He had an idea what it was . . . and what might stop it.

"Dr. Jasso?"

"Something may be trying to communicate."

"*That* is an optimistic take on a mass moving beneath the ice!"

The shadow rolled toward them unevenly, like an incoming tide, until Mikel could see for certain what it was made of.

"God*damn* him," Mikel said.

"What?"

"Get back in the truck."

"What is it?"

"Please *go!*" Mikel yelled. "They're being controlled by a tile in New York!"

Dr. Cummins did not need to be told again. She backed away then ran as fast as her boot-heavy feet could take her.

Snatching off his glove, the archaeologist grabbed his cell phone from the pocket of his parka and punched a button.

CHAPTER 10

In New York, at the subdued headquarters of the Group, the call came as expected.

Downstairs in the laboratory, Casey Skett winked at Flora, who was seated in a folding chair, her hands tightly knit on her lap. Adrienne Dowman was on the other side of him, in an old, thickly cushioned chair, sitting supernaturally still and just staring. Skett had one hand on the keypad controls of the acoustic levitation device. He had his eight-inch knife in the other. He slipped the blade into a sheath attached to the back of his belt. "I can get to it quickly," he cautioned Flora.

"I have no doubt," she replied.

Skett answered the phone. "Hello, Dr. Jasso. I'm glad to see you made it."

"I said I would!" he yelled. "Now call them off! You didn't have to do this!"

"I was testing the acoustic suspension," he said. "Consider it a dry run and also a little bit of insurance.

"They are *Belgica Antarctica*, flightless midges. On average, only a sixth of an inch long . . . but there are a lot of them, eh? They were awakened from hibernation by a frisson of ancient Galderkhaani power, following the arc from here to there."

"I know the mechanism, damn you, Skett. Cut it. *Now!*"

"But they're harmless," Skett assured him. "Unless they gum up your engine or crawl up your pant legs, nibbling and nesting. Which they will do, seeking the warmth they've been deprived of."

"I swear to you—"

"What, Dr. Jasso? *What* will you do?" Skett's tone lost its affected bonhomie. "I know—perhaps you'll keep in touch with me instead of hopping about on your own, leaving me blind?"

"Yes, fine. We just got here by truck and were reconnoitering the pit."

"We?"

"Myself and Dr. Victoria Cummins."

"The glaciologist?"

"That's right! Now *cut* the link!"

"How did you get there?" Skett asked.

"Toyota Tacoma."

"Excellent," Skett said. "Very good. Makes things easier."

Skett was facing the monitor that controlled the acoustic levitation waves. He punched the numbers up. In front of him, the stone Mikel had recovered from the Falklands was crushed by sound, its energies dampened.

"Back the truck away roughly ten meters," Skett said. He glanced at a laptop on the laboratory table. "The insects won't come any closer as a group . . . the line vectors off there. Unless I amp up the power."

Mikel's voice was muffled, no doubt shouting instructions to his companion. The scientist was definitely outside the truck; Skett could hear the wind's raspy brush against the audio.

After a moment Mikel came back on the line. "Is that why Flora screamed, Skett?" Mikel asked. "You were flexing your long-distance muscles?"

"Poor dear overreacted," Skett said. "I think she thought that allowing the tile to power up, you would be attacked by penguins or whales."

"How did you know I *wouldn't* be?"

"You're well enough inland," Skett replied. "There are two tiles—I brought one to the party, you see. Two tiles, two separate but proximate lines of power, one weak, one stronger—the stronger one being the one I presently control. Sections of the coastline may be covered with penguin feathers thanks to the other . . . a whale or two might have butted a ship . . . and I think I heard some dogs baying on this end. But that's all. The arcs from here to there are very precise. You will notice, I think, that the insects left their nesting ground and lined up pretty much in a southwesterly direction, well, westerly to you, since south has little meaning where you are. Are they disbursing?"

Mikel was silent for a moment. "If you could call being buried by icy snow disbursing."

"Don't worry about them," Skett said. "Most will get away. They are very, very hardy. They will dig down and hibernate. It is remarkable though, isn't it? The fact that the slightest variation in the acoustic modulation being employed here can impact a life-form at the end of the earth. It's a shame Arni didn't know that, eh?"

"We've all had a very steep learning curve," Mikel replied. "All right, Skett, it's cold where I am. What am I doing here?"

"You're going down into the pit."

There was a brief silence. "With a broken wrist?"

"I didn't say you were going to climb," Skett said. "Good God, I'm not a lunatic. The Tacoma must have a winch and you can rig a sling. In any case, you *are* going into the pit."

"And once I'm there?" Mikel asked.

"You will send me video of whatever is there as you see it."

"That's not going to happen," Mikel said.

"Oh?"

"That one's not me being obstinate, Skett. I could barely get a signal the last time I was there. I'll record images and send them later."

Skett considered that. "As insurance for you, no doubt?"

"That too," Mikel said. "If anything happens to me, to any of us, you get nothing."

"That's not true, you know," Skett said. "All it means is that I'll have to send someone else, and that will mean a delay. And Flora will be dead: I will kill her and burn her with my various rodents and pigeons. Anyway," Skett went on, "I don't think you'll be uncooperative."

"You're sure of that?"

"I am," Skett said. "You can stonewall and posture all you want, Dr. Jasso, but you want to probe the knowledge of that civilization. Why else would you be in the South Pole? Why did you risk death?"

Skett had a point. Mikel did not answer.

"To do all that before you freeze, you will need my help," Skett went on.

"Skett, you *do* understand what you're playing with?"

Skett snickered. "Do *you* understand who you're talking to? Dr. Jasso, I've spent decades studying this subject . . . waiting for global warming to catch up to my needs, to show me what hacked satellites and outpost communications could not, to reveal Galderkhaan. I have waited patiently for this moment. I need eyes on—*now*, if you please."

There was another short silence on Mikel's end. Skett's careful eyes slid toward Flora. He was accustomed to watching everything from the shadows: studying the reactions of people on the street to the dead animals he collected for the city, watching how other animals responded to death, even watching how people responded to their own death, like Yokane and the others he had been forced to murder for his people. He knew fear and defeat, compliance and docility, when he saw it. All those qualities were present in Flora Davies. It hadn't been necessary to restrain her: as long as he controlled the acoustic monitor, he controlled the two tiles and their fearful power—even the near-dormant artifact in the freezer. Flora knew what his colleague Eilifir Benediktsson and the team in Connecticut knew. They had all seen what those unbridled forces did to poor, fumbling Arni Haugan in this very room . . . and to Caitlin O'Hara in the park. The reason she hadn't perished was not known to Skett. That too was something he needed to uncover.

All in its time, he told himself.

Flora knew all of that too. She sat quite still-not because she feared for her life, but because she did not want to distract Skett needlessly. Not with the forces at his fingertips. And as heartless as it was, she too was curious. Adrienne was already in the thrall of the stone in the laboratory; Flora had noticed her fingertips stiffen when Skett boosted the power slightly. They were relaxed now. She suspected that Adrienne was the target of the experiment on this end. She had no idea what he was expecting on the other end.

"How is it going out there, Dr. Jasso?" Skett demanded.

"The truck is getting into position."

Skett glanced at his watch. "You have another minute. One. That's how long it should take."

Mikel went silent and Skett saw Flora glaring at him.

"Oh, poor Flora, sidelined and denied her place in the modern Galderkhaani pantheon."

"It's nothing like that," she said. "All I ever wanted to do was learn, to work with the tiles. You want to control them."

"Like love and marriage, you can't have one without the other," Skett said.

"It's your mind-set that is objectionable," she said. "All these years, these centuries of exploration and struggle, and this is how it finishes. With a prize in the hands of some Technologist."

"Not 'some,'" Skett said. "'The.' He is *the* senior surviving Technologist. His name is Antoa."

"And what are you?" Flora asked. "A hireling."

"You cannot humiliate me, if that is your intent," Skett said.

She snickered. "You still have blood on the side of your hand . . . like a butcher."

"It's honorable blood, blood spit from the mouth of Yokane, the blood of a Priest," he said.

"Lunatic hatreds," she sneered.

"Which *you* have helped to perpetuate."

"Not true!" she said. "I rejected the overtures of Priests, of those like Yokane. I knew they existed but I refused to communicate with them. I only served one cause: knowledge."

"But you took their funding," Skett said. "You had to know."

"I didn't know and I would have stopped, at once, had anyone interfered," Flora said. "Whatever was arranged was set up long before my grandparents were born. And never did I kill, or advocate killing." She raised a chin toward the tile. "Mikel was very careful about obtaining that. Stealth and thievery, not murder."

"What about Arni? What about two decades ago, Dr. Meyers, who was killed in Hong Kong trying to buy an artifact from the Triad."

"Unfortunate," she admitted. "We all know this is dangerous work. I'm not naïve, Skett. We've robbed museums, private collections. People have gone to prison."

"Not you, though. You are careful and pragmatic, and I salute that. But you also have no right to judge me." Skett squatted to face her, held the side of his bloody hand to her cheek. "In the old days, I'm told, before 'civilization' came to Galderkhaan, human blood was a means of communication, of writing, of art."

"Of sacrifice."

"That too," he admitted. "There was barbarism. The adolescence of an ancient people."

"Galderkhaan banished it," Flora said.

"Did they?" Skett said. "Even after violence was outlawed, bloodletting continued under the aegis of the Priests. Blood caused words to grow, quite literally."

"That's not been proven."

"We have writings that verify it," he said. "They describe how the mosses and molds that sprouted from paintings executed in blood gave rise to the accents, the hand movements, of the Galderkhaani. The ancients believed that the Candescents were speaking to them . . . through blood."

"Divination has always embraced strange, ultimately disproved customs," she said.

"Questioned, yes. Disproved? Never quite that. Mosses grew differently, more eloquently, on certain stones. These stones. The ones that vibrated. If they were not special, why would we all have sought them these many centuries?"

"Not because we believed that a god was trying to talk to us through fungus sprouting naturally from biological material," Flora said. "We were looking for deeper secrets that were locked in the stones, in matter that we believe dates to the dawn of the universe."

"Then we should agree on what is about to transpire," Skett said. "That is what I am looking for—more proof of all those 'we believes.'"

"Skett?" a voice said in his phone.

"Here," Skett replied.

"We're ready to move on this," Mikel informed him. "Do you know anything about that—hold on. Dr. Cummins, do you hear that?"

Skett heard a mumbled response.

"Mikel, what is it?" Skett demanded.

"I hear a sort of cooing. Definitely not a geologic sound," Mikel said. "Skett, the thing that created this pit—could that entity still be down there?"

"It's possible. What do you know about that?"

Mikel didn't answer. Skett hadn't expected him to. Always and still the careful Group agent.

"We're setting up a rope," Mikel said. "I'm going to keep this line open. If I need information, you will give it to me."

"Of course," Skett replied. "We both want the same thing. To understand."

"I don't believe you," Mikel told him. "If you wanted to pool our resources, you would have done it long before this."

"As would have Flora and her people."

"Then you're all stupid," Mikel said.

"Save the editorializing, highwayman. You brought something to a city of more than eight million without vetting it, without quarantine. That, Dr. Jasso, was stupid. It caused death. Not just Arni, but Andreas Campbell, a mailman down the street. Maybe others. All *I'm* asking you to do is observe and report. Innocent stuff. Now, do you want to stand there and freeze or will you do what you went to the South Pole to accomplish—just for a different chief executive?"

"I've already agreed," Mikel said. "Let's get on with it."

Skett was standing again, looking at the stone. It didn't seem to have changed, nor had the digital numbers gone up or down on the monitor. Peripherally, he saw sudden anxiety on Flora's face. It wasn't just for Mikel Jasso: she was also no doubt starting to be concerned about her stone and the future of the Group. For all her faults, Flora had always been about the work.

Maybe that's why she's so good at this job, Skett thought. *Her agenda is unbiased toward Priest or Technologist.*

"I'm ready to make my descent," Mikel said at last. "For the record—and I hope you're keeping one—there is some kind of humming down there. It sounds almost like cooing of some kind. My companion hears it too."

"Human?"

"Difficult to say."

Skett motioned his head at Flora. She followed where he was pointing, saw a tablet on the table. It was the same one Arni had been using when his brain liquefied. She used it to turn on the audio recorder, to open a new file.

"I'm recording now," Skett said. "I want to know everything."

"You will," Mikel replied. "Assuming that even the audio signal can get out."

There was a low, smooth grinding sound—the winch on the truck, Skett assumed—and Mikel was quiet for another long moment. The Technologist agent noticed Flora's breath quicken slightly. For Mikel, or for what the Technologists might be on the verge of acquiring?

Finally, the voice of the archaeologist came over the phone once more: "Beginning my descent."

CHAPTER 11

Mother?"

Standor Qala craned her head to watch as Vilu raised his cheek from her shoulder. The boy tapped both index fingers against his temples. There was a blossoming look of wonder in the child's face, like a baby discovering its toes for the first time.

Beside Qala, Bayarma was looking around with frank confusion. "Where—where is this?" she asked in Galderkhaani.

"Mother?" the young boy said again, in English.

"Vilu, are you all right?" Qala asked.

The boy continued tapping the area in front of his ears and smiling strangely. He was not looking at either woman but rather staring off at nothing in particular.

"Vilu!" Qala said.

The boy looked at the *Standor*. "I can hear you," he replied in effortless Galderkhaani.

"Then why didn't you answer?"

"I am. I said, 'I can hear you!' "

"Where am I and who are you *both*?" Bayarma asked. Her eyes moved to the side of the gondola. A small gasp puffed from between her lips. "I am *aloft*?!"

"You are aboard my airship," Qala answered, frowning as her eyes shifted to the woman. "Apparently, high-cloud madness has touched the two of you. *You* claimed to be from another time and place," she told Bayarma, "and you," she continued, looking at the boy, "suddenly fell unconscious in the street where Lasha and this woman found you."

"I don't remember," the boy responded. Vilu looked at the other woman. His hands moved from near his ears, made little gestures the next time he spoke. He didn't seem to notice what he was doing. "I thought—I thought that you were my mother," he told Bayarma, then looked around. "But you aren't. Where is she? Where am *I*?" His eyes returned to Qala. "And why are you dressed like that? Halloween was weeks ago."

Only when he said that one word, "Halloween," in English, did the boy become frightened.

Vilu began to breathe rapidly, his hands became fists, and he looked around, unsure what to do or say next. He squirmed and pushed against the broad shoulders of the *Standor*. She held him firmly.

"Boy, relax yourself," Qala told him. "You're onboard the pride of Galderkhaan—"

"I can't, I—I want to be *home*! This . . . this is not a good place."

"It's a fine place, boy," the *Standor* insisted. She stood him on the taut wicker floor of the gondola. "Youngster, you are behaving very strangely. We are going to go see the physician."

Vilu stood there unsteadily on the gently swaying deck. He looked past the officer's legs at the gangplank. "A doctor. My mother is a doctor," he thought aloud. "I heard her talking about a place, about Galderkhaan."

"You are there," Qala said.

Vilu shook his head. "No. I am dreaming."

"You are quite awake—"

"*I can't be here!*" the boy shouted. "Something is supposed to happen."

"A celebration," Qala said.

Vilu looked around, as if trying to remember the something. "Why can I hear everything so clearly?" he asked.

"Perhaps you struck your head, but that is past," Qala said.

"No, no!" Vilu insisted, his voice rising. "I can *hear*! How is that possible? Where are my hearing aids?"

Once again, the *Standor* did not know what the boy was talking about, did not even understand the words. She turned to Bayarma, hoping to get some insight. But the Aankhaan woman seemed equally confused. Around them, great fabric hoses were being uncoiled and carried to the top of the column, to replenish the air volume with the rising heat.

"We're on an *airship*!" Bayarma marveled, looking up at the great envelope. "How did I *get* here?"

"You had a fit in the water courtyard, you came to help look after the boy," Qala said.

"I remember none of it!" She looked around. "I've never been so high!"

"Are you frightened?" Qala asked.

"No—not of this ship. I always wondered what it would be like."

"How did you come to Falkhaan?" Qala asked.

"I left my birth mother and birth daughter and came by river to Dijokhaan, then the rest of the way by foot."

"And the reason for your journey?"

"I was selected by my caste, by lot," Bayarma said. "I was bringing tokens blessed by Aankhaan Priests and others along the route. I had just left the amulets with the Priest Avat. I was going to say words over one of my ancestors and meet others for the celebration when—I was here."

Qala looked from Bayarma to Vilu. "Two curious cases," she announced. "One bit of passing madness—that I've seen. It is the close timing and proximity of these two that has me concerned. The strange words and ideas. And the *violence*. Bayarma, you were fighting with Lasha, the water guardian."

"Fighting? I have never fought with anyone, *Standor!*"

"That is why you are *both* going to see the physician," Qala said. "Come."

Hoisting the boy back on her shoulder, the *Standor* took Bayarma's hand and started along the side of the enclosed cabin toward a door in the back. Despite the unexplained mental state of her two guests, Bayarma's hand felt strong and right in her own. They separated when the space between the central cabin structure and the outer wall of the gondola grew somewhat narrow, so Bayarma had to walk slightly behind.

The large door panel was made of the same fabric as the envelope of the airbag, the skin of the *shavula*, in this case sun-dried and taut. The frame was made of knotted seaweed, also baked in the sun. Like the rest of the structural materials, the door was designed to be as strong but as lightweight as possible.

Qala pressed a palm to the door. It wasn't bolted, meaning there were no patients and the physician was not meditating. The *Standor* entered. As they did, Vilu reached out and rapped the doorjamb, hard, then listened as if awaiting a response. When none came, his fingers clutched the *Standor* tighter.

The physician was sitting in a low-hanging mesh sling that hung from an overhead beam. Qala had to duck to avoid the beam; the roof was so low she could barely stand upright. The physician was reading a scroll and looked up.

"*Standor*, we need to take on more fish oil for the health of the children in Aankhaan," the youthful-looking man said. He slapped the scroll with the back of one hand. "This ridiculous manifest is less than half of what I requested."

"We needed room for the explosive dyes, Zell."

"Did you hear what you just said, *Standor?*" Zell said. "Entertainment over medicine?"

"It wasn't my decision," Qala said. "The Great Council commanded."

"Because the citizenry must have a colorful celebration," the physician said, gesturing angrily with his free hand. "*That* is more important?"

"Take your complaint to the Council," Qala said. "I have patients for you."

With a deft shrug of his wide shoulders, the physician extricated himself from the confines of the sling. The short but powerfully built man wore a blue tunic and skirt with a white sash pulled tightly from left shoulder to right hip, identifying him as a physician. His shoulder-length blond hair hung freely, framing a round face with wide-set eyes. His flesh was ruddy from hours spent in the rigging of the airship, where there were pots that grew medicinal herbs. Behind him were racks of narrow clay containers, over forty in all, that were painted a variety of colors denoting their contents. They were held in place by leathery bands that protected them during turbulence.

The physician contemptuously tossed the scroll to the floor as his eyes focused on the boy and the civilian woman.

"What did you do to them, *Standor*?" Zell asked. "They look quite terrified."

"This woman is named Bayarma," Qala said. "She was in a physical struggle with the water guardian and has no memory of that or the time it took to walk from the town—"

"I had just left the company of a Priest and now I'm here!" she exclaimed.

"That will teach you to mingle with Priests," the physician muttered.

"—and she was talking strangely the entire time," Qala said.

"About?" Zell asked.

"Being from another time," she said. "And she occasionally used very odd words."

Zell seemed intrigued. "Did she speak of the past?"

Qala shook her head. "She told me she is from the future."

That seemed to take the physician by surprise. "So it's not Candescent Yearning," he said.

"I don't believe so," Qala replied.

"What is that?" Bayarma asked.

"The conviction that one is an all-knowing god," Zell said casually. He looked away from Bayarma and stepped up to the boy. "And what about you?"

The boy buried the lower half of his face in Qala's shoulder. He did not speak.

"Vilu fainted shortly after Bayarma and the guardian fought," Qala said. "And now the woman seems all right but the boy is speaking oddly. He claims he was unable to hear, and now he can."

"I can," the boy raised his mouth and pouted. "And . . . my name is not Vilu."

"Oh?" said the physician. "What is it?"

"Jacob," the boy said. "Jacob O'Hara."

"Jay-cup-oh-ha-rayaah," the *Standor* said thoughtfully. "Oh-ha-ray-aah was part of the woman's name as well."

"A shared delusion or something you overheard?" Zell wondered. "What was the rest of the other name?"

"The first part of it was Caty-laahn? Cayta-laahn? That's how it sounded."

"Caitlin," Jacob said easily. "Caitlin O'Hara."

"Yes," Qala said at once. "That's exactly it. Very impressive, Vilu."

"I am *not* Vilu. Caitlin O'Hara, *Dr.* Caitlin O'Hara—she's my mother," the boy replied, his eyes shifting to Bayarma.

"Dahk-tar?" Zell said.

"*Doctor*, like they say you are, but she helps people with mental illness," the boy said.

"These occurrences were in the same location?" Zell asked.

"At a pool. But Lasha, the water guardian, was unaffected. So were others who gathered around. So was I, for that matter."

"My mother *was* here," the boy insisted. He pointed a slender finger at Bayarma. "She was her."

"But she isn't now," Zell said.

The boy shook his head once.

"Are *you* from the future?" Zell asked the boy.

"I am from New York," he replied. "Not from Galderkhaan. I was reading about Nemo and a ship like this . . . then I slept . . . I think I am still asleep."

Zell regarded Bayarma. "And you are *not* his mother."

"No. As I said, my allotted birth child, Bayarmii, is with her grandmother in Aankhaan."

Zell motioned for Qala to put the boy down in a hammock that hung high in the middle of the room. The *Standor* obliged. Vilu fought for a moment then dropped of his own weight when the *Standor* bent. The boy quickly gathered himself in a ball in the center.

"Did you two happen to eat from the same barrel of fish, drink from the same cistern?" the physician asked.

"You sound like the water guardian Lasha," Qala said.

"There is truth in folk wisdom," the physician said. He raised his brows inquisitively. "Well, Bayarma?"

"I had fish and cake this morning, but how am I to know?" Bayarma said. "I never saw the boy before now."

Zell ran the side of his thumb absently along his sash. "Boy, you say your name is Jay-cupo-oh-ha-rah-ah. I have never heard such a name, and I have been many places in Galderkhaan."

"Have you been to New York?"

"I have not heard of such a place," Zell admitted.

"He kept touching around his ears," the *Standor* said. "Here." She touched her temples to indicate the spot. "Could that account for the strange words?"

"I did that because I could hear!" the boy said, trying to sit up in the swaying hammock. "I couldn't before. Are you people even *listening* to me?"

"Cayta-laahn had a similar streak of disrespect," Qala observed.

The boy threw himself back down on the mesh in frustration. Zell selected a bottle from the shelf. He shook it, unscrewed the top, and stepped over to the hammock. He moved the coral plug back and forth under the boy's nostrils.

"Oh!" the youngster said and immediately opened his eyes wide.

Zell bent over him and leaned close to his ear. "I would like to speak with the core voice."

The boy hesitated. Zell gave him a second whiff of the contents of the jar. The boy's brows shot up and he stared ahead. For a time, only the creaking of the gondola and the breathing of the two observers could be heard. Bayarma grabbed the *Standor*'s arm. That too felt good.

"Who are you?" Zell asked.

"Vilu of Falkhaan," the boy replied.

"Who is with you, Vilu?"

"A . . . a spirit."

Bayarma held Qala's arm tighter; whatever had happened to the boy, was inside the boy, most likely had affected her as well.

"Who is this spirit?" Zell asked, moving his hands carefully to repeat what the boy had said. Just asking the question sent a chill through the cabin. The word Vilu had used was not *mazh*, an ascended soul. He had said *jatma*, a noncorporeal being. The term was derived from *maat*, a Candescent.

"I do not know him," Vilu replied. "He scares me. He is confused."

Zell walked back and selected another bottle. He ran the stopper under the boy's nose. This time Vilu relaxed.

"I would like to talk to the *jatma*," Zell said.

There was a long pause, the quiet broken only by shouts of the crew from outside the thick walls, and the groaning of the balloon overhead.

"I . . . am . . . here," the boy finally said in a different voice. "I do not want to be."

"How did you get here?"

"I do not know. I just went to sleep."

"Where?"

"In my room, in my bed. I was drawing . . . a . . . comic."

The boy's small hands moved tentatively, trying to find counterparts in the Galderkhaani vernacular for what he was trying to say. Suddenly, Vilu's body became agitated. The *Standor* started toward him but Zell held up a hand.

"What is happening?" Zell asked.

"Someone else—hello?"

"Is it your mother?"

"No," the boy said. "*Hello? Can you help me?*"

The little body began to tremble as if it were cold. Zell pulled a blanket from a rack, threw it over him, shook his head at Qala when she tried to approach again.

"Describe what you're seeing," Zell said.

"A circle . . . of . . . light. A ring. There are things moving in it." The boy began to wince. His eyes narrowed, fluttered. "Blinding—"

"What kinds of things are in the ring?"

"Things! *Creatures!* Get me away from here!" the boy yelled. "Please! Mother, please!"

"Why are you afraid of the things? Is your mother there?"

"I don't know! Get me *out* of here! Get me someplace! I don't know where I am . . . the way out! *Please!*"

"Zell, please—" Qala said.

"Boy, I must know if it is the ring or the . . . or being *lost* that frightens you?"

"Lost!" he cried.

Vilu started to sob.

"Stop this," Qala said. "At once, Zell."

Zell returned at once to the first bottle and brought Vilu out of the trancelike state. The boy blinked several times. A few lingering tears rolled from his eyes. He used the edge of the blanket to wipe them away.

"I can see now," the boy said, blinking hard and looking around. "But I am still here . . . in Galderkhaan."

"You are not Vilu, then?" Zell asked.

"I told you who I am!" the boy protested.

"So you did," the physician said, smiling. "But you are safe now," he said. He was still holding the vials so he touched the young boy's cheek with his own, then stood facing Bayarma. He did not say anything. He just watched her.

"What is it?" Qala asked.

"Hold her," Zell said.

The woman was just standing there, regarding Zell with a strange, vacant expression. She did not react when Qala put strong fingers around her upper arms.

"What is it?" the *Standor* asked Zell.

"The open vials," Zell answered.

"You did this on purpose?"

"Of course. I did not want her to suspect."

"Will she be all right?"

"She is not all right *now*," Zell pointed out. "And we can't help either of them without an examination."

"But you'll stop it if—"

"Yes, yes," Zell said, mildly annoyed. "All I have to do is replace the stoppers and she'll come back."

"You're sure."

"Remove the flame and water ceases to boil," Zell said. "Nature is constant."

Qala knew Zell well enough to know that he liked to push his patients, but it was always with a goal of healing, and then learning how to heal others, so the *Standor* didn't protest. Bayarma continued to look at him without seeing him. Then her brows lowered as if she were concentrating. Her breath came more quickly.

Zell came a little closer, leaned toward her ear. "What are you feeling?" he asked her.

"There . . . is something . . . still within my . . . my . . ." she said.

"Your what?" Zell said.

"My soul," she replied.

"Zell, what's happening?" the *Standor* asked.

"A miracle," Zell told his superior. "These two unrelated Galderkhaani somehow have the same—it isn't a delusion, *Standor*. They share some kind of alien energy, the same internal entanglement, though the power in Bayarma is extremely faint." Zell switched the vials to one hand and put his other arm around Bayarma's waist. "Take the boy, please, *Standor*."

Carefully releasing Bayarma to Zell, Qala walked to the hammock and opened her arms to Vilu. The boy hesitated, then went willingly and held her tight. Zell led Bayarma to the hammock and lay her down. He took the second vial and moved it closer.

Almost at once, Bayarma tensed and a sense of unrest filled the room. It was nothing that Qala could isolate, no physical change in her ship, no sudden movement by the two visitors. But it was there.

"You feel it too?" Zell asked the *Standor*.

"It's like a storm coming toward us," Qala said softly.

"Exactly what I was thinking," the physician remarked. "Out at sea and moving toward land, causing unrest in the air."

"But there are no warning horns," Qala said.

"Not as such, no," Zell agreed.

Shouldering Vilu, the *Standor* went to the door and looked out, over the outer wall of the airship. She squinted toward the sea, past the great flutes suspended parallel to the bottom of the airbag, tubes that whistled loudly when storm winds blew through them. She did not see what she expected. Seabirds were clustering in a linear formation toward the vessel. *Thyodularasi* were breaking the surface in an increasingly synchronous movement from the shore toward the horizon. Farther out, the fish had stopped leaping.

When she looked back in the cabin, Qala saw Bayarma breathing more heavily and beginning to perspire. The physician was watching her.

"The *jatma* is not present in this one, not anymore," Zell said. "Just a shadow, some kind of tenuous fiber triggered by the compounds."

"I don't understand," Qala said.

"As we watch the alien energies, they are watching us."

That sent a fresh chill through the *Standor*.

He used the first vial to restore Bayarma to equilibrium. At once, her breath came more naturally and she began to relax. Then he took both vials away and stood back.

"Are you all right?" Zell asked her.

The young woman blinked. "I think so . . . now," she replied. He handed her a vial from the shelf and instructed her to drink it.

"What is it?" she asked.

"A sleep agent," he said. "You have been through a small ordeal. You should recuperate."

She obliged and lay back. He took the vial from her and walked over to Qala.

"The future," he said in an almost reverent voice.

"What about it?" Qala asked.

Zell looked from Vilu to Bayarma. "Is it . . . *possible*? There is only one power that can erase time, and not all of us believe in it."

"*Standor* Qala!"

Qala ducked her head back out the door. It was her second-in-command, *Femora* Loi. The man, whose calm demeanor was an anchor for the crew, seemed uncharacteristically agitated.

"Yes, *Femora*?" Qala said.

"Please come at once," he said. "You have to see."

Qala glanced back at the room. The physician nodded briskly and Qala left. She strode along the side of the ship, following the man toward the plank that led to the column. The hoses lay across the deck and were inflated, carrying hot air into the bags. But there were no rippling stretches of air to suggest a leak, no pockets of heat. That wasn't what was creating the warmth.

The *Standor* saw what was happening even before she reached the plank. The top of the column was a few heads higher, but she could see a very faint nimbus around the rim. Her chest tightened.

Qala was not a deeply devotional soul. She had no interest in the squabbles between the Priests and Technologists as long as they remained philosophical debates. She had no strong opinion about the Candescents, the race of gods that were said to have created the Galderkhaani. She certainly did not believe that their spirits resided in the tiles that were a part of every grounded structure in Galderkhaan. Those tiles, ribboned with metals that somehow formed in veins underground, had strange magnetic properties, properties that captured and replayed images and sounds—but those were naturally explained, like the reflections in water or the reverberations of bells. As Zell had said, nature is constant.

But to Qala's knowledge, the strange, powerful tiles had never done this.

Reaching the top of the ramp, followed by Loi and the eyes of those working on the hoses, Qala saw a misty glow just within the top of the column. It reminded her of the kind of halo that formed around the sun before a rainstorm—diaphanous, elusive, slightly prismatic. She came closer, looked at the tiles on the opposite side of the column. Through the haze she could see they were dull but uniformly lit.

"A reflection of fires from below?" Loi speculated.

"The illumination is too consistent," Qala said. "Double the loading crew, *Femora*. I want to be away from here as soon as possible."

"Are you afraid for the column, *Standor*?" Loi asked with concern. "I have lovers and children here—"

"No," she replied with a reassuring smile. "I want to see if this is happening in other columns along the route."

CHAPTER 12

It was a small library, unassuming as libraries went in Galderkhaan. There were a few more olivine tiles, but not so many that anyone would suspect their true nature.

These tiles, built in the Technologist complex beside the *motu-varkas*, were designed to control the winds that were not only generated by the magma deep below Galderkhaan: forced through tunnels constructed by the Technologists, the same winds held the magma down and back, one elemental force controlling the other. The heat of the lava actually strengthened the ferocity and power of the winds that contained it.

The Source was corrupt. The Source drew on energies that caused mountains to rumble and flame. It caused the ground to split and consume villages whole. It created great waves that smashed the coastline, killing the creatures of the sea and the citizens who lived there. Freed, it would not allow Galderkhaani to contain it.

The Council did not want to hear that. The Council was comprised of aged men and women who were eager to achieve immortality. There was evidence for an existence after this one, and they wanted to access it *now*. If the Technologists were wrong, then there was still time to support the approach of the Priests, the *cazh*. They did not understand why both methods should not be explored.

"The Candescents found merit in the fires beneath the land," the Chief Councilor had said, reciting the decision of her fellow members. "Why should we, then, shun these forces?"

Most of the seven Councilors were Azha's lovers. The Source hearings that preceded and followed the trial of *Femora* Azha lacked the objectivity of that grim matter. It was incomprehensible that the social issue of "violence" should receive a fairer, saner hearing than the potentially catastrophic matter of tapping and unleashing the flames and heat from below. Even the ice engineers, who cleared swaths of terrain for settlement, were afraid to use heat from the towers. The risen pools of magma were used solely to warm water through careful release of heat, great stone doors and vents, operated by pulleys, being employed to control the wind.

The monstrosity beyond the library? It had been expanded and enlarged without sufficient study. Models suggested this and drawings suggested that. Nothing had been proven. Technologists *thought* the olivine tiles would allow them to control the various mechanisms they were constructing.

That was not only dangerous, it was lunatic.

Which was why Vol had made love to a clutch of Technologists, one of whom had allowed him to come to this chamber just "to see" the refurbished *motu-varkas*. The Priest had no interest in the man who had given him access or the détente he said interested him.

The Priest felt extremely guilty having used love and lovemaking, and his sacred poetry, to seduce his way into the library. He felt far worse about that than he did about the necessary deaths that were liable to result from this.

Vol was consumed with just one idea, an idea that *Femora* Azha had gotten right. Before the networks were connected, Vol wanted to turn on the Source at its very core. He was willing to sacrifice himself and the others in the tower to prove that such containment was not possible.

He had already shut the library tiles so his actions would not be recorded; it was an easy matter to clandestinely replace his own tile for one of those crafted by the Technologists. He had simply gone to one wall, replaced a Technologist tile with one to which he had transferred his own thoughts and plans, and no one would notice that a massive trapdoor would not shut until it was too late. The magma would be agitated by the opening of other lava tubes and the *motuvarkas* would spit death into the immediate vicinity.

Vol did not want this to reflect badly on any fellow Priests, like his beloved Rensat, or even the moderate Pao. What happened here would look like an accident. The power to destroy Galderkhaan—by accident or, more dangerously, by power-hungry Technologists—would be eliminated. And the true course of Ascension, Transcendence, and Candescence would be pursued by the Priests.

Already, the attention of the Technologists in the library was drawn to odd stirrings from below the ground. They would check the olivine tiles inside the tower first. That would take them quite some time. They would not find his tile in the library, they would fail to remove it in time; it was outwardly benign and too well integrated into the system. If necessary, he would prevent them from doing so by releasing its latent energy.

Vol had full control of a system that, once tripped, had no other way of being shut down. Henceforth, the Night of Miracles would be remembered for much more than the folklorish creation of the Galderkhaani. By tonight, the Source and its Technologist acolytes would be a memory. And instead of being slaves of the towers, the olivine tiles would finally be turned over for study by those who wanted to release, not control, their ancient, dormant energies—the Priests of Galderkhaan.

CHAPTER THIRTEEN

For Caitlin, the vision had the character of a sharp, sudden relapse.

She was medically sedated and yet she was very conscious in her dreamless state. She was floating again, as she'd been in Washington Square Park. She was rootless, drifting, no point of orientation, only darkness. The image was in her mind, not in her eyes, but Caitlin knew that she was *not* dreaming. She was not hallucinating from whatever drug was pulsing through her veins because there was a solid realism to what she *did* see.

It was a ring of light. It didn't grow, it simply appeared, like a lightning bolt that erupted but did not fade. Yet the more she looked at it, she could see that it was not simply a ring: it was more like an ouroboros, a tail-devouring snake. Present in countless cultures, interpreted and reinterpreted in classic psychotherapy, a true human archetype.

Why is it here, in my mind?

She tried to ask it, but the serpentine form did not want to be accessed. The circle just floated in its own soupy white light, set against the blackness, unable to be addressed or touched . . . yet obviously willing to be seen.

Willing, Caitlin thought suddenly. She felt—she *knew*—that the serpent had consciousness.

The light snake seemed solid so it surprised her, the more she stared, to see components within its brilliant glow. They were difficult to see, darting within the light like microbes on a slide.

The snake was similar in size to the serpent she had seen in the vision in Haiti, though that had been a darker creature in every sense of the word: black, choking, destructive. She had touched that one and was knocked back by a powerful force.

What about this one? Can I touch it?

Caitlin thought about extending a hand and suddenly she possessed one. It *was* hers, slightly luminous in the dark, aglow with . . . life? There was no bracelet on the wrist; the skin wasn't sun-bronzed. Her fingers stretched toward the light—

No!

She froze inside. It occurred to her that this might be a near-death experience and to go toward the light might mean the end of her life. But there was no retreat either. She could not turn about. And then her options lessened even further—

She was moving toward the ring, as though she were on ice and possessed frictionless, effortless motion with no way to stop. The facets within the form of the ring itself were more visible now, each comprised of writhing lines of light, with more and more lines within those. There were so many elongated particles of luminescence that she found herself becoming overwhelmed, frightened. She was afraid of being consumed, of vanishing, of being subsumed by *something* that lacked physicality but somehow had gravity.

Caitlin was jerked toward it and her eyes snapped open.

She was breathing heavily and staring at the ceiling of the hospital room. She felt warm but was not perspiring. Her breathing immediately began to slow, and her racing heart rate returned to normal. She moved her fingers and toes, could feel them all.

The experience had had every quality of a panic attack. An *uncon-*

scious state panic attack. The idea was something she had never even encountered in the literature.

Caitlin heard the instruments humming around her, adjusted to the strangely unexpected presence of substance, of weight, of material things. She looked to the right, over the rails alongside the bed. The door was shut. The chair was empty. Her mother was probably in the commissary or else on the phone. Perhaps she was taking a nap somewhere. No doubt she had been told that her daughter would sleep for hours more.

Caitlin looked at her arm. The IV drip in her hand was giving infusion therapy, probably a cocktail that included a sedative. She had to stop the flow. She hesitated; there was an occlusion alarm.

Just get the damn thing out, she told herself.

She removed the tape from just below the knuckles of her left hand, jerked out the needle, and jabbed it in her pillow so the formula would continue to flow. The alarm barely had time to chirp. There was no immediate response from the staff. She did not want to sleep or be examined. No nurse, no doctor could find what was wrong with her.

No doctor . . . in this *era,* she thought suddenly, strangely.

And they would miss what was very right with her: that she was somehow, miraculously, present again in the real world after having spent waking time in Galderkhaan.

Caitlin looked around. There was no window, no clock; she had no idea what time it was. What about her clothes, her belongings? When she had gone down in Washington Square Park she only had what she was wearing and her phone. She looked at the nightstand, didn't see her phone, saw a small closet. That was to be her first destination.

She snickered—at herself, at the irony of the metaphysical world in which she had been spending so much time. She could travel millennia by pointing two fingers at the ground. She could go God knows where in an unconscious vision. Could she cover two yards in a hospital room without falling?

Caitlin tried to sit by sliding up a little on the bed. She used her elbows for propulsion, moved just a careful few inches and her head responded with a swirl of dark light and a painful jolt. She stopped. She put her tongue against the roof of her mouth to prevent herself from hyperventilating and breathed deeply. She closed her eyes.

Do it slowly, dammit.

This time she placed her palms on the bars and moved back tentatively. Her head swam, but only a little. She waited a moment, moved back a little more. She managed to get herself into an upright sitting position. She waited there, then felt for the latch to release "the cage." She found it, pressed, and lowered the aluminum side so it wouldn't clang on the mattress frame. She just now noticed that she was wearing her own pajamas.

Mom, she thought sweetly.

Caitlin allowed herself another moment. She felt like Jacob must feel when he played games on his bed, especially with the lights out, hoping she didn't hear. As she thought of him a smile briefly turned her mouth; it was followed by a choke. If any boy on the planet could get his footing in Galderkhaan, it was little Captain Nemo himself. Still, she had to get to him and pushed, again, on the sturdy mattress.

As Caitlin slowly swung her legs over the side of the bed, the door opened and a visibly tired Nancy O'Hara shuffled in carrying a plastic tray from the commissary. The woman froze when she saw her daughter. Caitlin was just beginning to pull off the pajamas Nancy had brought.

"What are you doing?" the older woman demanded.

"I've got to get out of here."

Nancy turned to look down the hall. "I'm calling the doctor."

"Mother, *no*—don't!" Caitlin said.

"You're only half-awake, you don't know what you're doing!"

"I *do* know, just—*please*. Listen to me."

Nancy half turned back into the room. She scowled. "You took the IV out of your hand!" she said, just noticing. "Caitlin, I'm getting him now."

"I did do that, but you have to *listen!*" Caitlin said. "I truly know what I'm doing."

"How can you?" Nancy asked. "You've been drugged! Before that, you were unconscious in a park."

"Mom, just come in, shut the door, and let's talk."

"Why? So you can convince me to let you do something you shouldn't be doing? I won't allow it."

"Okay, fine," Caitlin said, holding up her hands. She pulled back on her pajama top. "I don't want to stress you. I appreciate you being here. I assume Dad is with Jacob?"

Nancy nodded, calming slightly. "Your friend Anita is there too, resting."

"Thank you," Caitlin said. "I don't know where my clothes are, anyway."

Nancy softened further. "On a tray under the bed and they're a disaster," she said.

Caitlin sat there looking at her mother. "You know, you wouldn't believe from me, from my clothes, that the last few weeks have actually been pretty astonishing. How is Jacob?"

"All right," Nancy said. "He's resting too."

"What time is it? What *day* is it?"

"Tomorrow for you, about four o'clock." She added, "In the afternoon." Her expression continued to lose its edge as she came forward. "Caitlin, what happened? Did you have some kind of seizure?"

"Is that what the doctors said?"

"They don't know what to think, exactly."

"I'm not surprised. It was more like a hypnotic episode—it's a long story but there's nothing wrong with me. Nothing physical. Nothing I need to be *here* for."

"Ohhhh . . . I know what you're doing, Caitlin."

"I'm sorry?"

"I wouldn't let you out angry so you're trying to smooch me up. It won't work. You're going to let Dr. Yang decide what should be done, and that includes when you leave."

"He doesn't know me and I don't know him," Caitlin protested.

"You don't know everything," Nancy said.

"Excuse me?"

"Dr. Yang actually knows about your work," Nancy said with a hint of pride. "He says he's read the articles you wrote in the *Journal of Pediatric Health Care* about children and the trauma of tribal warfare."

Caitlin's defiance, which had been threatening to resurface, deflated just a little. "Mother, I'm flattered and touched and I'm not trying to be difficult, I'm truly not. But you have to trust me to handle my own trauma."

"You take too many chances, Caitlin."

"Honestly, Mom? I've already taken them. Right now I'm only trying to clean up the loose ends."

"Does this have to do with all those trips you took recently?" Nancy asked. "To Haiti, to Iran of all places . . . ?"

"They're part of it. Couldn't be helped."

Nancy shook her head. "You're so impatient. Impatient to *know* and to know *now*. You always have been."

"Not like my steady, ready sister."

"I'm not *comparing* you," Nancy insisted.

"Sure you are. You just ticked off the two big things that Abby is not."

"Abby has her flaws," Nancy said. "You have a very open mind. She's Ms. Know-it-All."

Nancy was right about that. Caitlin kept her mouth shut and looked down. She began moving her fingers a little, extending them down, then out, trying to find the tile or the point in the past from which she had departed. It was gone. All of it.

Nancy did not notice what her daughter was doing. She moved toward Caitlin and began to sob a little as she approached.

"I *did* speak with Abby on the way in," Nancy said.

"Ah."

"She told me not to let you do exactly what you're doing—take charge of your own health care. She meant it with love and concern."

"I'm sure that's how she meant it," Caitlin replied. She looked up. Her mother seemed very, very tired. Caitlin felt guilty about that, but also grateful. Whether it was running off to disasters around the globe or being a single mother, she did challenge her mother's traditional beliefs over and over, especially compared to her very traditional younger sister, a surgeon who was married with two children and living in Santa Monica.

Nancy nodded and wiped her eyes with a finger. "I'm sorry, but we were asleep and got a call from your friend Ben that something had happened to you—he didn't say what, only that you were in the hospital. It wasn't until we got here that I was able to talk to someone who would understand."

"I'm so sorry for that," Caitlin said quietly.

"Forgive me if I'm trying to keep you with us, *safe*. Not just for your father and me but for your son."

"I know."

"What—*what* were you doing in the park at that hour? Had you gone to see a patient? Were you on a date?"

Caitlin couldn't help but smile at that. Her mother had actually sounded hopeful. "Not exactly."

"I remember that boy—man, I mean. Ben. He was with you last night—"

"Ships passing," Caitlin said.

"Just last night, you mean?"

"I don't know," Caitlin answered honestly. "Listen, we can talk about this later, Mom, okay? I don't mean to take charge, but my brain is starting to function clearly again and there are a few things I have to know. I'm at Lenox Hill, right?"

Nancy nodded once.

"Okay—you said Jacob is sleeping. Do you know for how long?"

"Since early this morning, according to Anita," Nancy admitted, sniffling briefly but stopping herself. "Is he involved in whatever is going on?"

"He is, which, frankly, is why I have to get out of here."

Nancy tried, and failed, to stifle a little gasp.

"Mom, just hear me out. The trance that hit me in the park? He got caught by some of it as well—"

"How is that possible? What were you doing?"

"Helping patients, and I succeeded. Please—let me ask the questions? They're really important."

"All right."

"You said Dad's with him. And Anita. What about Ben? My . . . my friend."

"No. But he's been checking in all day, with both of us."

Caitlin quietly thanked Anita, her father, Ben, and God, in that order. The last—coming from an agnostic—indicated to Caitlin just how far her spirituality had evolved in a very short time.

"Did Anita say anything about Jacob's condition?" Caitlin asked.

"She said that his vitals were fine and we agreed, ultimately, that you wouldn't want him to go to the hospital. Your father wasn't happy with that, but she said that she's a doctor and had seen this before."

"She's absolutely right." She saw it with Caitlin, in fact.

"Your father was doing what *he* thought was best—"

"I know. I'm just saying that Anita knows the situation, made the right call. And I'm very grateful Dad went along with her. Okay," Caitlin went on, quickly prioritizing. "I want to talk to Anita but first you have to do me a favor."

Nancy hesitated. "What?"

"Text Barbara Melchior. My therapist. Her number's on my phone."

Nancy looked toward the closet then back to Caitlin. "You'll stay where you are?"

Caitlin crossed her heart. "I will not push you in and lock the door like when I was ten."

"I don't believe you. Get into bed and lift up the rail."

"Jesus, Mom—"

"In the bed and lift it."

Caitlin knew the tone of voice: Nancy O'Hara wasn't moving until Caitlin did as she asked. Caitlin acquiesced. It was either that or bum-rushing her to get the phone. She sat cross-legged in the middle of the bed, away from the damp pillow. She pulled up the rail. The bars locked upright with finality. Nancy hesitated, her eyes ranging along the IV tube. She gasped when she saw where it ended.

"In the pillow?" Nancy exclaimed.

"I'm not putting that back in, so don't even ask," Caitlin said. "I need my wits."

Nancy shook her head. "What am I even doing here?"

"Helping me," Caitlin said. "Mom, I'm always out on a ledge, I know it. That's why I *need* you."

Nancy's shoulders had tensed. They relaxed. Exhaling loudly, she went to the closet and retrieved her daughter's phone from the top shelf. She looked at it.

"I have no idea how to work this," she said, stepping forward and thrusting the smartphone at her daughter. Nancy was the very image, then, of when Jacob was younger, broke a toy, and handed it to his mother to fix.

Caitlin took the phone and texted Barbara. The exchange was brief. Caitlin did not explain why she was in the hospital, only that she needed her psychiatrist . . . and friend. Barbara promised to come over at five thirty, after her last appointment. Caitlin thanked her then called Anita.

"Honey, it is *good* to hear your voice!" Anita exclaimed.

"Sorry to wake you, if I did."

"You didn't," Anita said. "Who can sleep? Besides you, I mean."

Caitlin laughed. Nancy seemed surprised. It felt good.

"First, a huge *thank-you*," Caitlin said.

"You're welcome. I never take sick days, was overdue. More important, how are *you*?"

"I truly do not know how to answer that," Caitlin said. "Physically, fine. But tell me about Jacob."

"Relying on just the medical evidence, he's manifesting a form of hyper-sopor. I would have taken him to the emergency room except that there are no obviously actionable symptoms, he did not have any trauma, and the only food he had was what he hadn't finished yesterday. His tendon reflexes are normal, there's no fever, resting heartbeat and respiration are consistent with clinical lethargy, it's not drug-induced, obviously, and I wanted to talk to you first. Anyway, a relative would have had to sign off on further evaluation."

"That is absolutely what I would have done," Caitlin told her. "Has he moved, said anything?"

"Moved—he was half-awake, rapping on the wall, then back asleep. That was about—dawn, I guess. Since then, very little. Opened his mouth slowly as if he was cracking his jaw. Eye movement. Not like REM, only sporadic and definitely deliberate."

"Like lucid dreaming?"

After considering that for a moment Anita said, "Yes, that's actually what it's like. As if he's awake and consciously, purposefully looking at something. But with his eyes closed."

"Bless you again for not moving him," Caitlin said. "It's a form of trance, like the one I experienced."

"I figured, but hold on, Caitlin—there's more," Anita said. "You had visitors."

"Who?"

Anita said quietly so Caitlin's father wouldn't hear, "From Haiti. A Vodou priestess and her son."

Caitlin felt a sudden boiling in her gut. "Go on."

Anita told her about Madame Langlois and the snake, both of which surprised Caitlin but also comforted her in a strange way: the Galderkhaani Priest Yokane was dead and the transcended spirit of the Galderkhaani Azha was gone. Caitlin was glad to have someone around who understood. And there was another snake: a physical manifestation, unlike the others. That was information, even if she did not yet know what to make of it.

"Did Madame Langlois say anything about the serpent?" Caitlin asked.

Nancy frowned, deeply. Caitlin waved her hand as if the question were irrelevant.

"Nothing that made it any less creepy," Anita said. "A conjurer's trick, I suppose, though she kept referring to the snake with a plural pronoun—'they.' "

Then she told her how the Vodou-summoned snake was made up of smaller parts, just like the snake in her own recent vision. That too was fascinating . . . but elusive.

"I don't assume they are still there," Caitlin said. "I can't see my father allowing that."

"No," Anita said. "Ben found somewhere to put the madame and her son, though he didn't tell me where."

Caitlin quickly scrolled through her e-mails, saw nothing from Ben. He was probably afraid someone else might look at it. She worked hard to remain calm. She had to fight the pressing urge to be with Jacob, to see the Haitians, to get back to Flora Davies, to find out why all the stones on the planet seemed to have gone quiet, to return to Galderkhaan *somehow*. Instead, she took an uncharacteristically small, single step:

"Ben is at work?" Caitlin asked.

"Yes. He called here at least a half-dozen times asking if I'd heard from you, making sure Jacob was still the same."

Just talking about him brought a sudden, welcome equilibrium, as if she'd downloaded all the cautions and safeguards and different points of view that were lodged in his sane British brain. Her mother was a mother, loving and concerned with a strong vein of *I know better*, but Ben had been a comrade in all this . . . in so many things going back to their university years.

Caitlin heard dripping then, saw that her pillow was getting soggy and had started to overflow. Caitlin hadn't expected to be here still, and reluctantly shut the flow. A few moments later a nurse entered.

"I gotta go," Caitlin said to Anita and ended the call after thanking her again.

The young nurse frowned when he too heard the dripping and looked at the bed.

"Dr. O'Hara—"

"It—came out," Caitlin told him.

"Did it?"

"Well . . . clearly."

"I see."

"And as you can also see, I'm okay now," Caitlin went on. "Except that I need a fresh pillow."

The nurse scowled. He summoned an orderly and a fresh pillow was brought in. Dr. Yang followed briskly with a look that was half-concern, half-disapproval.

The physician made quick work of his patient, finding nothing in her eyes, blood pressure, or chest to alarm him. He agreed not to replace the IV if Caitlin promised to stay in bed. Nancy O'Hara assured him that she would.

"If we weren't understaffed—" he began.

"I'd help, if you'd let me," Caitlin said. She was serious.

"Thanks, no. Management prefers when their doctors aren't also patients."

"Phuket and the Philippines weren't so picky," Caitlin muttered to his back. Sometimes, American health care—and liability—just got to her.

The physician left, along with the nurse, the orderly, and Caitlin's considerably medicated pillow.

Nancy sat heavily and gratefully in the chair. "This is your life, isn't it? Urgent, urgent, urgent."

" 'Fraid so."

"I'm too tired to keep up," Nancy said. "I only slept for three hours last night. I'm going to shut my eyes." She fixed those eyes on her daughter. "You *will* stay there?"

"I will," Caitlin said. She wiggled her smartphone. "Barbara will be here in an hour or so. I'm just going to send e-mails while there's still life in the battery."

Her mother nodded agreeably, folded her hands on her waist, and settled back. Caitlin looked at her a moment longer. She understood the woman's concerns for her daughter because Caitlin shared them for her own child. She could not let on *how* concerned she was. If Jacob were in Galderkhaan—spiritually, at least—she only hoped *Standor* Qala had believed what she told her, and that the commander's physician was a man of curiosity and caution who would do nothing rash or extreme. Caitlin prayed—to a dead man in a dead civilization—to try to understand rather than undo what had occurred. Restoring Vilu by some dramatic, potentially traumatic means could cost Jacob his soul.

Once again, Caitlin had to prioritize as she did in Phuket and other devastated regions around the globe. Jacob had slipped into the past while she was there—possibly drawn by her through some spiritual mechanism she did not understand. There had been a few moments of overlap, of transition. Perhaps it was a variation of what had happened with Maanik, some version of the *cazh*, their powerful bond pulling his spirit to where she was.

But there was a problem, Caitlin thought. With Maanik, Gaelle, and Atash, the souls from the past tried to drag them *into* the past. Had Caitlin's longing to be with Jacob been strong enough to unwittingly create a *cazh*? Had it failed after a moment or two because it had been subconscious, without the ritual that helped the souls to focus? Had Madame Langlois or her snake done something that prevented them from bonding?

You're just spitballing, Caitlin told herself. Not that there was anything wrong with that, if she had the time. She did not. Hopefully Barbara could get some answers through hypnosis.

In the meantime, she had to contact Ben and find out what he may have learned from the Haitian mother and son. After the serpentine vision she had experienced in Haiti, and again in her dream, she was particularly interested in the snake Anita had mentioned. That was now too prevalent to be a coincidence.

Jung believed in synchronicity and so do I, she thought.

In this case, she had to.

Jacob's safety might well depend on it.

She wrote to Ben: *I'm awake. Thanks for all. Barbara coming for hypnosis. Anything?*

It took several battery-sapping minutes for Ben to text back: *I arranged for Technologists to take Haitians to CT HQ. Don't ask. Plus new twist. Halley VI reports there was massive fireball yesterday. Vibrations under ice, suspected drilling. Brit ambassador told Security Council that Royal Navy and RAF sending assets south. Suspect Russia of military ops out of Vostok Station.*

Caitlin wrote back: *What will UK do?*

Ben answered: *Land troops. Investigate.*

Caitlin wrote: *Flora has a man there.*

Ben texted back: *Will tell US reps. Gotta go. Love you.*

Oddly, the last comment didn't bother her like it used to. Maybe she wanted it—or maybe she was troubled by this new development and desperately needed a partner. She actually felt violated by all the attention from London, as though her private world were about to be invaded.

Which it was.

The tiles might be active down there, energy that was being picked up at Halley or by satellite but wasn't giving her "juice." That was worrisome enough. But the thought that the military, any military, might obtain the power of the Source was more frightening still.

Sneaking out of bed to get her lunch tray, Caitlin ate—something she hadn't done for too long. Then she lay back on her fresh pillow, tried to clear her head, and awaited Barbara Melchior's arrival.

CHAPTER 14

Lowered by the growling winch of the truck, showered by chips of ice and dead bugs that were being cut from the lip over which he'd been suspended, Mikel Jasso descended slowly into the pit. His goggles were around his chin, his eyes struggling to adjust to the darkness. As the rope-sling was lowered into the pit, twisting slightly from side to side, the archaeologist had time to think. And as he thought, one phrase kept running through his tired, overworked brain:

One day, Dr. Jasso, your rope will fray. One day the hastily crafted sling or raft or ladder will fail you.

Mikel was one of those who believed it was better to die in the saddle than on the sidelines, but that came with an acute awareness that the thick of things was never the safest place to be.

From his early childhood in Pamplona, through his years in Harvard and his adventures with the Group, Mikel had relished any and all physical challenges, especially those that logic told him were beyond his means. Going underground, into the ruins of Galderkhaan . . . soaring through a wind tunnel on a sled made of millennia-old animal hide . . . that was madness. Communing with the souls of the dead was not exactly reckless, but believing in them lacked the kind of empirical science in which he was schooled. But in every instance, the rewards had been vast. There was rarely a middle ground when it came to risk-taking in his field: either you squandered years or risked your life, but that was how you located King Tut. Or Amelia Earhart's airplane.

Or Galderkhaan.

But now he was sitting in this makeshift support, descending into a dark pit that had been newly cut by a flaming—what? An eternally burning soul, a soul that might still be down there, angry as hell and looking for lost Galderkhaani souls?—doing all this with a broken wrist; *that* was new, even for Mikel.

Fortunately, he thought, curiosity still slightly—very slightly—trumped fear. He wanted to know more about the phenomenon, and also what Casey Skett had planned.

When light from the outer world no longer reached him, Mikel pulled a flashlight from the shoulder bag slung over his bad arm. He threw a cone of white light against the wall to his right. Here and there midges still clung to the stone walls, walls that revealed dark stone beneath serpentine, fast-frozen mounds of ice. Dr. Cummins had reported that the remainder of the insects, those which hadn't frozen where they last stood, had wandered aimlessly from the truck, a strange column of brownish black crawling along the ice as if they were disoriented, no longer stuck between the two powerful tiles. Like the other animals Mikel had witnessed or been told about, some herding quality in their brain—an atavistic version of *cazh?*—had been revved by the tiles.

Which is probably why the Technologists thought the tiles were all that was required to join souls, Mikel thought with sudden clarity.

Physically, the pit itself was a chimeric thing. On closer inspection, not only ice but what looked like shale had been flash-molten and quickly hardened, like melted ice cream. Here and there were large stone bubbles where air had been released then quickly trapped by fast-hardened rock. Ice, melted from above, was frozen in sheets across large areas. They reminded him of a Japanese waterfall by Hokusai, thick rivulets of water stiff at the end of the floes, slender and reaching. He angled the flashlight down. Below was flat, silent darkness, save for what appeared to be a large, inexplicable bulb of opalescent white that sat at some distance below. It reminded him of a pearl seen through seawater. It rested in the center of the darkness, with fuzzy edges that blended slowly into the blackness. The deeper Mikel went, the pit became wider and less light fell on the surrounding walls. Yet the milky hue remained constant, glowing, growing slightly in diameter but not luminosity as he descended.

The cooing that Mikel and Dr. Cummins heard had ceased as soon as he began his descent. He still didn't know what it had been. The only constant sounds were the distant drone and squeak of the winch, the jostling of the shoulder bag he carried, and the wind that rose and fell in volume as it swept across the opening or rushed down at him with sudden, brief enthusiasm. Those sounds and Mikel's heartbeat and breath created quite a strange symphony. His cold-weather gear kept that sound close to his body, the drumming in his ears in tune with the physical sensation of blood pumping to his extremities. He would occasionally report what he was seeing to Skett, though the man on the other end made no comment and asked no questions. Mikel was certain he was there, however: there was a very dull, low hum from the phone, just as there had been when they spoke back at Halley VI. No doubt Skett was focused on the experiment, not on communication. Now and then Mikel would also check in with Dr. Cummins over the radio that was hooked to the cable just above his head. When she spoke—letting him know how far he had descended— she had to shout, since the winch was complaining, loudly, as it fought the icy cold.

For a place that was alive with surreal imagery and borrowed sound, the pit itself was not like a living cave with active water dripping or flowing and a feeling of flora, fauna, and biota all about. The place seemed—it *was*—quite still and dead. There did not even seem to be any Galderkhaani spirits in residence: Pao, Rensat, Enzo, and Jina had all had a palpable presence, a spiritual substance that registered as chill or warmth or low pressure or flame. They were immaterial but the ripples they created were real.

Not here.

And yet Mikel felt certain he was not alone. At first he suspected it was the natural fear of the unknown, where imagined dangers caused people to hallucinate spirits or predators, to self-generate hysteria. Then he began to suspect that the pit could be like the lava tube he had entered before, with an adjacent channel or tunnel that contained something alive. For all he knew, there could be tiles below him or somewhere else nearby.

Mikel got his answer after about five minutes of the slow unraveling of the cable. The ivory-like glow below him was no longer just a globe: there was a shape, a mass below it. Perhaps it had always been there, just not visible from so high up. At first glance it reminded him of Michelangelo's *Pietà* but seen from above, the covered head of Mary rising from her shoulders. But the shroud was not fabric: as he neared he saw that it was long hair hanging in graceful waves over the figure's shoulders.

At about one hundred and fifty feet down, the glow of the flashlight finally illuminated a solid floor below him with what looked to be opposing cave mouths on the eastern and western sides of the pit. They looked exactly like the Galderkhaani tunnels he had navigated previously. And then he heard it: the tunnels beyond the two mouths were filled with fierce winds, Aeolian fury like that which had dashed him against a rock wall, heat-generated fury that the Galderkhaani rode as a sort of rapid-transit system. This network consisted of ancient lava tubes that had been enlarged and expanded by the Galderkhaani. No doubt the earliest Galderkhaani towns and cities arose around the caldera of some ancient volcano, around hot springs, located in clearings carved by natural forces from the ancient ice sheets. Mikel believed that these natural channels were later connected by the Technologists, expanded as the civilization grew.

Smokestack-like columns had been constructed throughout the ancient civilization, no doubt to allow the heat to vent, to prevent a cataclysm like Vesuvius or Krakatoa.

Mikel was nearly at the bottom of the pit when he saw that the figure in white was in a sitting position just above the ground. He could see that it was a woman and she was looking north. He wondered if this were another spirit or a recording of some kind, projected by the olivine tiles. There was a tranquility about the figure, something that didn't fit with the others he had met. Thinking back to his first reaction—a pearl underwater—he realized it reminded him of classical views of mermaids: their long hair floating around them, their skin pale and fair, their attention on the sea and not those who would intrude from above.

Another archetype with roots in Galderkhaan? he wondered.

Whatever it was, the being did not acknowledge his presence, even when he rapped his flashlight on the utility bag. He thought he saw the chest moving slowly beneath what looked like a toga. The clothing was after the style of Rensat's. It had to be an ascended spirit.

Mikel instructed Dr. Cummins to stop the winch. The rope-sling jerked to a twisting stop in the darkness, just a few yards above the figure. Now all that Mikel heard were his own breathing and heartbeat. He felt the condensation of his breath on the thick fabric of his muffler. He pulled it down, smelled his own musk rising from it.

Mikel reported everything he saw to Skett. There was a long silence before Skett's voice cut through the hum of the phone.

"Can you see anything else? Anything around her?" he demanded.

"Nothing. But—the light isn't radiant. It looks as if she's pasted on the darkness, within a faint nimbus."

"Where are her hands?"

Mikel had to lean out to see over his hanging legs. "Her arms are straight at her sides. It's difficult to tell—there aren't really any shadows, just contours. Also, though I can't see through her, there doesn't appear to be any substance."

"That is perfect," Skett said, almost gleefully. "There will be."

His tone alarmed Mikel more than the apparition did. He tried to imagine what could possibly be exciting the Technologist so much. The figure was not frozen in stasis; it was moving, slightly, like a sunbather.

And then it occurred to him: this figure was different because it wasn't actually there, now. Pao had been there. Rensat, Enzo . . . those ancient souls had been there. This figure: it was still back in Galderkhaan!

"Skett, you're hooked into *time*, aren't you? Into the past?"

"Nicely done," Skett said. "Yes, I am, through Flora's lab assistant. The tile did just what the Technologists said it would: it bonded the two people—not souls, *people*—through time."

"You're going to pull this one forward?"

"That would be quite an achievement, wouldn't it?" Skett said.

"Is this real?" Dr. Cummins said, listening in through the radio.

"Very," Mikel replied.

"All right, Mikel," Skett said. "I'm going to loosen the hold of the acoustic levitation waves on this end. Please record and describe everything that happens down there."

"I'm above her," Mikel said. "Do you want me to go lower, to be facing her?" He was suddenly excited by the prospect of being the first person to be face-to-face with a living, ancient Galderkhaani.

"Absolutely not. I don't want you harmed."

"Harmed how?"

"We have no precedent for this, do we? We don't know what will happen."

Mikel didn't think Skett was worried about him: he wanted Mikel's report and video. The archaeologist turned the phone toward the figure below.

"Are you receiving?" Mikel asked, his voice echoing throughout the pit.

"No," Skett said. "In fact, I can barely hear you now. You'll have to shout, please, when you describe what is happening."

Skett said something to Flora then told Mikel that they were beginning. Then Mikel used the radio to inform Dr. Cummins to have the winch ready to haul him out.

"Why?" she asked. "Is something happening?"

"Nothing yet," he said. "You heard everything. Just be ready."

"I heard, but I didn't understand," Dr. Cummins said. "What exactly is being done?"

"The olivine tile that corralled those bugs is being ramped up with a slightly different target," he said. "The forty-thousand-year-old figure on the floor of the pit."

"Then I *did* hear correctly," she marveled.

"Yes."

"But the figure is not in a pit *then*," Dr. Cummins said.

"No. It could be sitting on a seashore, in a field—I don't know. Only the figures are linked, in New York and in Galderkhaan."

As they spoke, the figure below began to change. Though she didn't move, the apparition took on hints of color. The hair darkened toward black, the skin grew slightly ruddy, the folds of a blue toga began to appear on the previously colorless fabric that draped the torso.

"What's happening?" Skett asked.

"She's starting to show detail—hair, skin, clothes!" Mikel yelled into the phone. "I can't say for sure whether it's substance, but it's definitely looking more like a Galderkhaani woman."

Skett said something else to Flora that Mikel couldn't hear. Moments later, the figure took on even more detail. Her legs were bare, her skin smooth, and she appeared to be in her twenties; he couldn't be sure from this angle.

Suddenly, the folds of her clothes and her hair seemed to come alive, raised and lofted as if by a breeze. Then her hair and garment was whipped to her right as if hit with a blast of wind. The howling increased, reverberating up the stone walls of the pit.

"Skett, she's reacting to something coming at her from the west!" Mikel yelled.

He heard indistinct but agitated conversation on the other end.

"Skett!" Mikel shouted into the phone. "What's going on?"

If the man replied, Mikel couldn't hear him. The roar of the wind was almost painful now. Yet the wind itself did not rise: it was blowing from tunnel to tunnel below him.

The woman's toga and hair moved like seaweed in a tidal pool, horizontally beside her, the ends whipping around as the wind increased—wind Mikel himself could not feel. The air in the pit remained cold, static.

"Skett?" Mikel repeated.

"Giving . . . tile . . . more . . . freedom," he heard Skett enunciate carefully, over protests from Flora, her cautioning tone clear even if her words were not.

"Skett, slow down!" Mikel shouted back. "This is getting very real very fast!"

"Dr. Jasso?" Dr. Cummins yelled.

"I'm all right!" he shouted into the radio.

Mikel looked down. He blinked hard, not convinced that he was seeing correctly. In front of the woman the blackness seemed to glow with a blue blush. The color took on more prominence and then Mikel saw what looked like white streaks, black streaks—

White caps, sea creatures, he suddenly realized. *The woman is sitting at the edge of the ocean. The cooing is—sea creatures.*

Just then, Mikel was distracted by something new: smoke, rising from the toga's folds. Licks of red began to appear through the fabric along the shoulders, the waist, down the spine. The same thing must be happening on Skett's end, which was probably why Flora was agitated.

"Skett, she's starting to burn!" Mikel shouted. "The tile is killing her!"

"*In the past!*" Skett screamed with almost giddy triumph.

"Did you hear me? You're killing someone *there!*"

"She's already dead!" Skett yelled. "The Technologists are *right*—you can transcend with the tiles! You don't need prayer!"

Mikel realized that the rising smoke was not real. Like the apparition, it belonged to another time. But something else was real: a band of glowing rock at the base of the pit. There was a golden hue to the band: tiles buried beneath the once-molten rock. The tile in New York and the tiles buried here had bonded through time to open a portal and connect to a woman in *this* time. There was a tower below this pit.

"Dr. Cummins, pull me up. There are tiles down here and they're becoming active!"

"Hang on!" she said.

The winch began to groan and the rope jerked up.

"Skett, is the same thing happening to Adrienne up there?" Mikel shouted as loud as he could. He waited a moment, until he was higher, then repeated the question.

"Of course! The two women are transcending together!"

"Skett—"

"I'm *freeing* them, damn you! The tile wasn't going to release them—*I* didn't do this. You did, you brought the tile back!"

"No, Skett. We could have found another way!"

"We have transcended time! We can do it again! You *used* to be a scientist, Jasso! Understanding power like this is worth a life!"

"I'm going back to the truck, Skett—"

"No! Keep recording, damn you!"

"I am," Mikel said. "But you haven't proved Transcendence at all. All you've done is reached back in time to burn a woman to death."

"She's been dead for forty millennia," Skett replied.

"Something that *you* caused, Skett."

Mikel watched as smoke rolled back from the folds of the toga and insubstantial flames began to consume the fabric, blackened the fringes of her hair, caused her arms to rise from their prayerful position and extend outward. Fire began to chew at the flesh of her upper arms, formed an ugly orange ruff around her throat, turned red skin to a brown, then black sheet of chapped flesh. Blood turned to steam and pieces of skin drifted off, ugly particles of ash riding the smoke.

Finally, the youthful face turned upward. The mouth was pulled wide in a high scream as her cheekbones broke through charred flesh. Her eyes burst and poured from their sockets like runny eggs. Her teeth seemed to grow and grimace as her lips and mouth burned away. The cry of pain ended as fire turned her saliva to burning vapor and made speech impossible.

That was when Mikel realized that all the shrieks were not just coming from below. Some were rising from the phone.

"Goddamn you," Mikel said, snarling into the phone. "Damn you to hell!"

Mikel looked away as the figure below him turned to ash and fell in on itself. He heard Flora's voice over the phone, then screaming as Skett shouted and probably threatened her—or worse, because after that everything was quiet. Below, the circle of tiles dulled and the winds diminished. Perhaps Skett had finally turned the tile "off" in New York.

Mikel took a moment to calm himself. His flesh was chilled from cooling perspiration. The sling had pinched under his thighs and his upper legs were numb. He adjusted his position to encourage circulation. Then he bent back toward the phone.

"Skett," Mikel said, his voice loud in the sudden quiet. There was no answer. Mikel turned his face toward the radio. "Did you hear any of that?" he asked Dr. Cummins.

"I heard *all* of it, Dr. Jasso," she replied. "I can't believe it."

"It happened," Mikel replied.

"But—*how*? There couldn't really have been someone down there with you."

Mikel was too emotionally exhausted to answer.

"It could be a leaking pocket of ethylene gas . . . a hallucination. That would also explain what you thought you saw previously, what some of us thought we heard coming from the pillar of fire."

"It could be but it isn't," Mikel insisted. "I have video."

"We'll have to review that data," she said. "I saw nothing burning up here. Not like last time."

"It wasn't the same," Mikel said. "This happened forty thousand years ago."

"But triggered now."

"That's right."

The archaeologist was still looking down when something abruptly changed below.

With a unity that he had not yet seen in his interactions with Galderkhaan, the tiles below reclaimed some of the luster they had had a few moments before.

"Christ, what now?" Mikel asked. "Skett, are you doing something with the tile?"

There was no answer.

"Dr. Jasso?" the glaciologist asked.

"Get me out of here," Mikel said. "We have an emergency!"

CHAPTER 15

Barbara Melchior arrived at the hospital at five forty-five, which was fortunate: even though Caitlin kept herself busy, lying in bed nearly caused the psychiatrist to lose her mind. Her phone was nearly dead, but she used the charge she had left to read about Antarctic geography. She was looking for reconstructions of the continent as it would have looked some forty thousand years ago. If she were able to go back, even briefly, she wanted to have some idea about where she was and where she needed to be. Anything with ice cover could be ruled out.

Barbara swept into the room with more than her usual panache: it was the satisfaction of a New Yorker having beaten the system.

"The travel gods were with me," the psychiatrist said as she entered. "A cab was discharging at my doorstep in rush hour and the traffic was actually moving."

She hung her coat on a hanger behind the door as she noticed Nancy O'Hara, who had been drowsing in the armchair.

"Oh—sorry if I woke you," Barbara said, grimacing.

"It's all right," Nancy said. She put her hands on the armrests and pushed off slowly. "I should leave you two alone anyway."

"It was good to see you again," Barbara said.

"And you," Nancy said. "I wish you both luck. I'll be in the waiting area."

"You can go home if you like, Mom," Caitlin said. "Get some actual rest in a real bed. I'll be fine."

"I'll wait to hear that from Dr. Yang," Nancy said, shutting the door behind her.

Barbara looked at her patient. "Peter Yang?"

"The same," Caitlin said. "You know him?"

"Read his full-throated defense of atypical antipsychotics and the treatment of schizophrenia," she said. "I don't like it when GPs play in my sandbox." Barbara came forward. She continued to regard Caitlin. "You look like you've been in a war zone."

"That bad? I haven't looked."

"Yeah," Barbara said. "You want a brush?"

"No thanks. But you do have an iPhone 6, right?"

"Yeah—"

"You happen to have your power cord?" Caitlin asked, holding out her hand. "My phone is kaput."

Barbara fetched the cable from her shoulder bag and plugged Caitlin's phone into a wall socket.

"There needs to be a study about this," Barbara said.

"About what?"

"Why I always feel physically healthier when my dead phone starts to charge."

"There have been lots of studies about it," Caitlin said. "It's called dependent personality disorder."

"It's more than that," Barbara said. "I mean, why should energy in a device make us feel *physically* charged?"

Caitlin did not answer that. She could have.

"So," Barbara said looking down at her friend. "Small talk duties— check. Why am I really here?"

"Regression," Caitlin said. "I have to go back. I think Jacob is stuck in the past and there's military activity brewing in the South Pole."

"And that's your problem how?"

"If they find or destroy or start messing with the relics under the ice, my conduit there may be damaged," Caitlin said. "I have to try and connect, somehow. Regression may jump-start me. Nothing else is working."

Barbara had pulled over Nancy's chair and sat in it. "Caitlin . . ."

"Barbara, it's not in my head and it's not a dream," Caitlin told her. "I was there. Now Jacob is stuck there while his body is semicatatonic in the apartment."

"In the *apartment*? Caitlin!"

"Don't," Caitlin said. "Anita Carter is with him. Doctors cannot help. I can."

"Honey, I cannot go along with that."

"Do you think I'd risk his life if I weren't *sure*?" Caitlin asked. Their voices were rising; Caitlin brought it down. "Barbara, tell me—what would his pediatrician do? You know the drill: blood tests, check his thyroid, see if he hit his head."

"It wouldn't hurt to begin that process, Caitlin."

"But none of that is what's wrong with him! His spirit may be stuck forty freakin' millennia from here! How is Synthroid going to help that? I want him as quiet and "the same" as is possible, not drugged, not away from his bed. At least now I know generally where he is and *how* he is."

Barbara considered that. The psychiatrist was always a voice of caution and devil's advocacy, but she respected her colleague/patient and was not an entirely hard sell. Caitlin knew Barbara was open to the idea of an astral "pool" of experiences, the possibility of tapping into the energies of those who came before us. If she weren't sold, at least the door was open. But Barbara also was not one to humor her patients' delusions. To her, this straddled both those possibilities.

"Barbara?" Caitlin said, reaching for her hand. "I know what I'm doing. It worked for my other patients in similar circumstances. But I need your help."

Barbara threw up her free hand and shook her head. "I've said my piece. He's not my patient, you are."

"Thank you."

"And since you are, I want to go on record as saying that regression is a tool to give me information as your therapist—not for you to jump to convenient conclusions."

"The two are not mutually exclusive."

"They are not. But that is for me to decide," Barbara said.

"With an open mind," Caitlin pointed out.

Barbara's mouth twisted. "Are you done last-wording me, Dr. O'Hara?"

Caitlin nodded.

"All right, then." Barbara fixed her dark eyes on Caitlin. "So. Your usual self-hypnosis technique . . . did not work?"

Caitlin made a face. The way she said "technique" made it sound like "trick." "It helped me to blow up Washington Square Park."

The dark eyes opened wider. "You're saying that was you?"

"It was, full of the same kind of power I had the first time I went back," Caitlin told her. "But since then, something is blocking me from accessing the past. Either the host body back then is closed or dead, or it could be that the tiles are shut down. I don't know. I had a dream—or a vision, something—about a snake or snakes in a ringlike shape. I have no context for that either, except that it's similar to what I saw during a trance in Haiti."

"Symbol of trouble? Phallus? Death?"

"No idea," Caitlin said. "None. That's why I need help. Consider the alternative."

"What's that?"

Caitlin whipped her hands to her sides, over the railings. "I'm gonna keep throwing my two fingers out, trying to plug into the ether, until they dislocate."

Caitlin stopped suddenly, her left hand fully extended.

"What is it?" Barbara asked.

"I thought—I thought there was something there," she said. Caitlin wriggled her extended fingers. "It's weak but . . . there's something, some energy."

"You still want to do this?" Barbara asked.

Caitlin hesitated a moment longer then lowered her arms. "Yes. I do."

Deciding there was no point in debating further, Barbara told Caitlin to lie back comfortably.

"Thank you," Caitlin said as she snuggled back into the crisp polyurethane.

"You want me to record the session?"

"Yes, please."

Barbara pushed the record button on her phone and placed it on the nightstand. She shut the light off, then lifted the chair and moved in even closer, so she could bend nearer to Caitlin's ear. Her smooth, low voice would be Caitlin's only connection to this world. That would leave her free to give up all other tethers, to float in her subconscious. The only light came from the monitors at Caitlin's bedside and a sliver that slashed across the floor beneath the door.

Caitlin shut her eyes and forced herself to relax.

"All right, Caitlin. You're going to answer each question with the first thing that comes to your mind," Barbara said. "Do you understand?"

"I understand."

"Where are you?"

"In a hospital room."

"In your mind's eye, look up," Barbara instructed. "What do you see?"

"The ceiling."

"What do you see beyond it?"

"A room above me."

"Who's in the room?"

"A . . . a very sick . . . woman."

"What's her name?"

"Jessica."

"What's wrong with her?"

"Car accident."

"Where?"

"FDR."

"What is she thinking?"

Caitlin's voice caught, choked. "How . . . how good her life has been."

"Why?"

"Because she's had love."

"Whose?"

"Her husband's. Her children's."

"What does she see in her head?"

"Her family. Her parents. And . . ." Caitlin smiled. "Summer camp."

"What is there that makes her happy?"

Caitlin continued to smile. "First love. First kiss."

"Where are they in the camp?"

"At a dark lake."

"What's the lake called?"

"Garbage . . . beach."

"Why?"

"Counselors . . . drink . . . there . . . make out . . ."

Caitlin's monotone and hesitation showed that she was beginning to disassociate from her own life. Barbara wanted to push her further; that was where control lay and guidance could be achieved.

"Do you see them?"

Caitlin smiled. "No . . . I hear them. Sex. Smell them . . . toking . . ."

"Are you contact-high?"

The smile broadened. "A little." She giggled. "A lot. Whoo! Haven't . . . been . . . high . . . since . . . since . . ."

"I want you to go back further," Barbara gently coaxed her. "You're floating now, in your life."

"Gee, Abby . . . is . . . so . . . pretty."

"Your sister."

"Baby. Baby . . . sister."

"Go back further."

Caitlin had been smiling lightly. The smile left. "Stupid . . . pogo . . . stick . . ."

"Further. You're no longer Caitlin."

Caitlin seemed to sink into the bed; it was really a long, slow exhale. Her arms rose in unison then dropped.

"What just happened?" Barbara asked.

"China . . . chi gong exercise . . . village . . ."

"Go back again and keep going. Don't stop until you are with Jacob."

"Polar bears . . . Northern Lights . . . an iron forge . . . wooden boats . . . warriors . . ."

Caitlin's expression brightened, then tensed. This was followed by a slight side-to-side motion of her head.

"I am here . . . but I cannot find my son," she said, her voice rising. "I cannot see Jacob!"

"Stay calm," Barbara said.

"He should . . . be here . . . I should . . . *feel* him."

"Be patient," Barbara said gently.

"No!"

"What is it?"

"Galderkhaan . . . fading!"

Barbara laid her fingers on Caitlin's wrist. Her pulse was speeding. "Caitlin, you must stay calm. If you panic, you'll break the trance."

Barbara left her fingers where they were. After a long moment she heard a moan. It came from Caitlin but did not belong to her. It was much, much deeper than her normal voice. At the same time, Caitlin's pulse steadied. Then it slowed. Barbara jumped. Caitlin was staring at the ceiling.

"Caitlin, can you hear me?"

The woman continued to stare. Barbara tapped her wrist. She was striking an acupressure point designed to stimulate the blood flow without removing her from the trance.

"Caitlin?"

The woman did not respond. She continued to stare, unblinking. Her breathing was slow and deep. Then she began to shiver. Barbara continued tapping her wrist with two fingers.

"I'm going to bring you out," Barbara said. "Close your eyes."

Barbara reached out to shut her patient's eyes but hesitated; it was as if she was going to close the eyes of a dead person. Instead, she held a finger in front of her eyes.

"Caitlin, it's time for you to come back. I want you to look at my finger."

Suddenly, Caitlin's arms rose slowly from her sides as if they were weightless. Barbara quickly withdrew her finger, not wanting to interfere with the ideomotor reflex. It was action independent of the hypnotist, often the key to deeply buried conflicts. Barbara watched as her companion's arms formed a circle above her torso and just hovered there.

"They're here," Caitlin said in a low monotone. "I am with them."

"Who?" Barbara asked.

"The luminous circle . . . the gold snake."

"Is this the same snake you saw before? In your vision?"

Caitlin nodded. "They . . . they are real," she said. "They want me to . . . come."

"You will not go," Barbara said.

"I must. They . . . want to endure."

"You are to stay here," Barbara said more insistently.

Caitlin was suddenly not herself. It happened in a series of subtle ways as her arms formed the circle: her voice flattened, eyes deadened, respiration grew low.

Barbara grabbed her cell phone and shined the flashlight briefly in Caitlin's eyes. Her pupils were fully dilated yet they barely responded.

"Caitlin, where is the circle?" Barbara asked.

"In awful darkness!" she said. "This is not . . . death! It is absolute destruction! But—my god, it's not the end!"

"Yes, it is," Barbara said. She pushed Caitlin's arms down, thrust her finger back in front of her eyes. "Look at me!" Barbara shouted. "I'm going to count to three and you will come back with me to the hospital room."

"Can . . . can . . ."

"Yes, you *can*!" Barbara agreed.

The psychiatrist began to count. When she was finished, Caitlin exhaled loudly then relaxed. She was still staring, though her eyes were not as wide, her pupils no longer fully dilated.

"Where are you, Caitlin?" Barbara demanded.

The woman blinked at her. "I'm here. I'm with you," she replied.

"So you see me?"

"Yes. Of course."

"Did you see the light I shined in your eyes?"

Caitlin hesitated. Barbara turned the light back on. This time Caitlin winced when it struck her pupils.

"You didn't react when I did that half a minute ago," Barbara said as she turned off the record button.

"What was happening? What was I saying?" Caitlin asked.

"I'll play it back for you in a minute," Barbara said. She herself needed a moment to try and figure out what had just transpired. "You just lie there. Don't even think about trying to get up."

Caitlin did as she was told. "I don't understand where I ended up," Caitlin said. "I was in Galderkhaan, then it was gone. Not destroyed, just . . . gone. I can't remember how it happened."

"You were retreating," Barbara said. "You went back very fast, very far."

"I didn't see Jacob when I passed through Galderkhaan," Caitlin said. Tears began to form in her eyes. "I know that much. I couldn't even feel him."

"Do you know why?" Barbara asked. "It's what I've been trying to tell you, Caitlin. Jacob is *here*. He's in New York, in your apartment."

Caitlin wiped the tears. She was confused, she was angry, and she had no idea what to do next. Maybe Anita and Barbara *were* right. Maybe everything she did going forward would just muck things up even more.

"Whatever you just experienced, Caitlin, we both know you didn't leave the room. We've had this discussion. Real or not, everything you think you experienced was in your head, where it is subject to person- alization, corruption, subjectivity, a *host* of unreliable markers. Even with racial memories—which are bona fide genetic triggers, quantifi- able biological imprinting—those ancient codes inside us may still be using the mind to tell a *story*."

Caitlin shook her head slowly. "I don't believe that. Just because we can't understand it, that doesn't mean what's in my head is false. After the incident in the park I *was* in Galderkhaan!"

"And after the tornado, Dorothy was in Oz," Barbara said.

Caitlin grew angry. "I know the difference, dammit!"

"Do you? Because there's also a rational explanation for everything you said when you were under, and you know what it is."

"What? Delusion? *Grandiose* delusion?"

"It fits, doesn't it? Inflated sense of self, relationship with a deity— called to the side of God. You just said as much in the session. How many point-to-point correlations do you need?" Barbara moved closer. "You know I believe in energies that exist apart from the body. But Caitlin—you've used that idea, that belief, to concoct a psychodrama."

Caitlin looked at Barbara with an expression that was profoundly sad and something else Barbara had not seen, ever: fear.

"That's not what's happening," Caitlin said. "Anita has seen things . . . Ben."

"They saw shadows, they heard your words, your—what, acting out?"

"I cured those kids, Barbara!"

"By getting into their psychoses," she said. "It was a masterful job of psychiatry. And then it was done."

"You're wrong."

"We all want to support you, Caitlin. You say you destroyed the park. The FDNY says it was underground water and gas lines."

"Which I broke."

Barbara sat back. "I'm not going to continue arguing this with you. There's no point. What you do in the hospital is between you and Dr. Yang. But as much as I find this topic personally fascinating, this approach is not doing you or Jacob any good."

"Uh huh. And your recommendation?"

"Rest, girl. Those kids a few weeks ago—the situation between India and Pakistan boiling around you? That took a toll."

Caitlin pouted. It was the only way she could stop herself from screaming.

"How about I do this?" she said, rising. "I'll send you the recording of the session. Listen to it. Have Ben come over and listen with you. If there's somewhere, some way, you're convinced I've whiffed, call me. In the meantime, just do me one favor. Please reconsider what you're doing with your son."

"Sure."

"I mean that, Caitlin."

"I know. And I'll think about it. I will." She looked at her friend. "I may not agree with you, but you know how much I respect you." Caitlin managed a half-smile. "And that's the last word."

Barbara gave her a squeeze on the shoulder. Collecting her phone cable, she sent the audio file then left with a little smile and a small wave.

Alone in the hospital room, Caitlin O'Hara knew then that her life would never be the same: to her, *Standor* Qala, Vilu, Bayarma, Yokane, and Azha seemed more real to her than anyone in her life, other than her son.

Which meant that either she was truly delusional . . . or two worlds were on the verge of colliding.

CHAPTER 16

Flora Davies gazed at the spot where Adrienne Dowman had been sitting.

All that remained of the young woman was a diploma on the wall and a stiff, blackened corpse on the floor. Strips of burned flesh hung from her bones with red, raw muscle peeking out from beneath. The odor was sinful.

Throughout the experiment, the laboratory associate had sat supernaturally still even as flames started to appear under her clothes. Then, in a flash, a ferocious blaze erupted, consuming her body from sole to scalp. As though entranced, she had not moved, had not cried out, had not even twitched. She just sat there as her flesh bubbled away, as her hair flew off in short-lived flamelets, as her eyes and the insides of her nostrils liquefied and ran down the white bones of her face—the entire process concealed more and more by noxious, oily smoke. It only took seconds for the ruddy fire to finish its job before dissipating.

The laboratory sprinklers had come on as the young scholar burned. The water not only doused the flames, it caused her body to collapse with a soggy crunch by its added weight. The shower also short-circuited the electronics.

The acoustic levitation hookup died. The olivine tile fell to the platform with a *thunk*.

As water rained down, Skett cried out an oath over and over, louder and louder. Flora forced herself not to think about Adrienne. It was the stone that had connected her with a Galderkhaani. There was no way to break the connection other than by learning to control the tile.

But Skett hadn't expected an inferno, Flora thought. *The Technologists never had sufficient respect for the tiles.*

Almost at once, smoke detectors throughout the Fifth Avenue mansion went wild. An automated call went out to the New York Fire Department. Flora did not concern herself with that. Her three-person office staff was used to crises; this was one more. The ungoverned tile was her immediate concern.

She jumped from the seat where Skett had placed her and slapped on a large industrial-size fan whose location she knew by feel. Choking in the ash-filled air, she pulled a towel from a rack by the industrial-size lab sink, wet it in the spray from the overhead nozzles, and wrapped it around her mouth and nose. She shut the sprinklers from a panel above the sink then approached Casey Skett. He was coughing and leaning over heavily by a laptop on the lab table, pinned there by the opaque smoke.

Simultaneously, Flora's wall-mounted landline beeped. It was her personal aide, Erika. The Group director picked up, after nearly slipping on the water-slickened floor.

"Ms. Davies, are you all right?"

"Yes," Flora told her aide. "Shut the alarms and call the neighbors. Apologize for the incident, but assure them there's no danger. Then call the fire department—tell them it was a smoke condition, nothing more."

"I'll call the FDNY first," she said.

"I would hold off on that one," Skett said, coughing hard as he turned toward her.

"Wait, Erika." Flora regarded Skett with open contempt. "Why?"

"Let them come, you're going to need them," he said. "And tell her to leave the building. Quickly."

Flora told Erika to hold off on calling the fire department and just to go outside. She could alert neighbors in person.

"If I need anything, I'll call your cell," Flora said. Hanging up, her eyes continued to burn into Skett. "Explain yourself. What else have you done?"

"Me? Nothing. We've *both* done this, Flora."

"We've done *what*? And no lectures, please."

"This tile," he cocked his head toward the olivine stone. "It's going to rip this place to sawdust."

"It didn't do that *before* we had the acoustic control," she said. "Why should it now?"

Skett wiped his face with his sleeve. "Figure it out, dammit."

"No, you're going to talk," she said.

"What's your leverage?" he asked. He wiggled the phone. "This is drenched and dead. Jasso's cut off."

"The computer is, and has been, recording everything that has taken place in this room. The recording is being stored offsite. If this place comes down, if I die, that data will automatically be reviewed."

He looked over at the laptop. "That's soaked too."

"It's waterproof."

Skett's eyes narrowed in challenge. "You're bluffing."

"Not my style," Flora assured him. "The Technologists really *don't* know much about technology, do they? Everything in here is custom-built. Did you really think I submitted to you because of a knife? I let you run this because how else was I to find out who you really are, who you work for, and what you and your Technologist employers know?"

"Paranoia will always trump planning," Skett said. He pushed back his wet hair and happened to glance at the charred body that, just moments before, had been a living woman. "And I always thought *I* was low on compassion!"

"Spare the psych profile," Flora said. "She was beyond help before we started this. We're wasting time. The fire department is only a few blocks away. What else do you know that you're not telling me?"

He looked over at the tile. It was still vibrating and beginning to glow again. "That stone is now fully reconnected to the tiles in the South Pole, and it is probably getting a bump from the one in the freezer," Skett told her.

"That one is dormant."

"Is it?" he said.

"They don't *function* in subzero. That's why Galderkhaan was quiet for forty thousand years, until the ice began to melt."

"You're wrong, Flora," Skett said. "They were *quiet* until Jasso found the other tile and Arni turned it on! Now none of the tiles are sleeping. You linked them all—or someone did."

That revelation hit Flora with a shock so hard she actually wobbled. *Caitlin O'Hara did that.* The Group director did not like where this was headed.

"Your dead assistant here was linked with someone in the past," Skett went on. "We knew that. But instead of being able to communicate with that person through her, which is what I was trying to do, instead of waking them both up, the tile here went ballistic and those two transcended against their will."

Flora nodded. "And that connection between the tiles is still open," she said, catching up to Skett.

"Very much so," Skett said, regarding the tile with growing concern. "Open and growing, only now the power won't be a simple, 'Hi, how are you?' connection as when Arni turned it on. It won't be rats massing or intestinal bugs eating a mail carrier from the inside out or insects gathering at the South Pole. Mikel Jasso is standing beside a still-open doorway to Galderkhaan. I thought we could control that through this woman and her partner—"

"But the tiles are working on their own now," Flora said. "Fueled by the Source?"

"I don't know," Skett admitted. "I sincerely pray they are not. There isn't an acoustic monitor this side of the universe that can contain that."

Flora eyed Adrienne's body. Sirens blaring sounded closer. There would be an investigation; that was unavoidable now.

"I'm going to get a cooler," Flora said. "Without the tiles, this will be a forensics nightmare."

She saw Skett shaking his head.

"What, dammit?" Flora asked, approaching him through the thinning tester of smoke. "Why not?"

"A cooler is not going to work," he said. "Not anymore." He cocked a thumb toward the hallway, toward the storage room. "Listen."

Flora reluctantly obliged him. There was a deep hum, like a long, low note on a bass cello.

"The other tile," Flora said.

"Already active and getting livelier," Skett said.

"It *shouldn't* be!" Flora said.

"It's drawing more and more power from this one and, I suspect, breaking its icy bonds. The freezer won't contain it much longer, and a frigid little container certainly won't stop *this* one." He indicated the tile in the laboratory.

"There *has* to be a point of equilibrium," she said. "Dammit, the tiles didn't go chewing up Galderkhaan every time somebody used one!"

"No, but they were all—synched somehow. Honestly, Flora? I don't know what the tiles can do. Until I held this specimen, I'd never seen one. But we had better continue this from a distance."

Then the Group director looked around. "No. I'm staying."

"What are you going to do?"

"Stop this." Flora began typing on the computer.

The tile was beginning to shake harder, creating a high-pitched sound that was beginning to pierce her skull. Several yards away, Skett too was beginning to wince. He edged into the hall.

"What are you trying to do?" he yelled at her.

"No one should control a power this monstrous," she said.

Covering his ears, Skett returned to the laboratory. He looked over Flora's shoulder, saw that she had opened a program that accessed Mikel's phone.

"No!" he said. "We have worked too hard to reach this point! *All* of us have!"

"So did Galderkhaan," Flora said, "and look where it got them."

Skett reached for the woman and pulled her from the laptop. The woman pulled herself from his one-armed grab, turned toward a drawer in the lab table, and yanked it open. She withdrew a scalpel and spun back toward her unwanted guest.

"Get out!" she said, just as Skett drove his own blade hard into her chest, plunging the silver blade to the hilt, through her heart.

"Mikel, destroy the tiles!" she cried out as she slid off the knife and hit the floor, dead.

"Flora?" a voice shouted thinly on the other end. *"Flora!"*

Skett swore. He didn't know if Jasso would figure out what had happened, couldn't stay here to find out, and Skett wasn't sure what he'd tell the archaeologist in any case. Jasso probably wasn't carrying explosives on the vehicle and he would have a hell of a time obtaining them if he went back to the outpost.

What do you need them for? Bundy or one of the others would ask.

To destroy an archaeological find, Jasso would reply.

It would never happen.

Confidently slipping the blade back into its sheath and stealing a quick glance at the wildly shaking tile, he killed the connection to Mikel, closed Flora's laptop, and tucked it under his arm. He glanced back at her.

"Sorry," he said. "I no longer need you—just this to access your offsite storage."

Then he turned and hurried back into the hallway. The olivine stone in the laboratory was a lost cause, already too active. Yokane probably kept it near her for that reason: it would immediately become alert if another stone were in close proximity. He'd collect the other. With luck, his exit should time out perfectly.

Behind him, the tools in the table drawer began to shake loudly and then the lab table began to hop around; a moment later the walls themselves began to undulate like sails in a typhoon. Below them, the remains of Flora Davies began to liquefy. First the brain and other internal organs; then, as the unchecked vibration of the stone increased, the rest of her cellular structure came apart. Within moments, the woman was a pool of biological material spilled across the laboratory floor. There was no longer a knife wound, or anything to point to homicide. The floor itself was quaking, spreading the material thin and wide.

Skett followed the steady pulse of the original tile. He went down a flight of stairs to a sub-basement where the Group maintained a row of subzero freezers. He had been down here before: this was where the door to the alley was located, the alley through which he'd transported Arni's body as well as other biological mishaps over the years.

Skett waited anxiously. He stood there, his skin vibrating as the air around him began to quiver. The old beams in the mansion shook and screamed and the structural matter of the century-old building also began to tremble faster and faster and then groan, loudly. He heard crashing above and then a pop that wasn't so much a loud noise as a dull punch in his ears. It was followed by a massive shockwave that slapped him from above and behind him—the location of the laboratory.

Hopefully, that was the tile reaching some kind of critical mass, releasing its energy before going quiet—

The tile in the freezer instantly calmed once its link to the southern tiles had gone silent. As the building above him fell to dust, Skett grabbed the tile and ran for the door. Behind him, large stone and wood pieces disintegrated as they dropped, the ceiling vanished completely, and millions of tiny pieces of laboratory fell into the sub-basement, the upper floors crashing on top of that, all of them creating a pile that rose nearly half a story above a shocked Fifth Avenue.

Observers wondered aloud if it had been weakened by the flooding and fires from the night before. The fire department arrived and pushed back everyone who was recording the event on cell phones. The police department sealed the block, in the event it was a crime scene.

Within that rubble, the olivine tile was quiet now. The collapse of the edifice had caused the orientation to be lost. It would take a boost to raise its energy sufficiently to find the others, to reestablish a connection with the collective. Until then, the now-subdued energy within resumed its waiting patiently, as it had done for an eternity. As it would do for an eternity more if it had to.

The power inside the tile wasn't conscious but it was sentient. It wasn't artificial but it wasn't alive. It was a result. A result that was invulnerable to time, impervious to destruction, merely waiting as it had always waited.

But before it went entirely quiet again, the olivine tile briefly experienced a flash of power, someone reaching for it from nearby . . . someone whose energy it recognized from the night before . . .

Someone who would certainly seek it again, for she had been hungry.

CHAPTER 17

As a child, Qala had lived in the deep, lush valley of western Codurazh. There, a river carried jasmine to and from the processing farm operated by her several guardians. With soil rich in nutrients from ancient volcanism and long periods of shelter from icy winds provided by the surrounding mountains, it was there that the tea leaves and jasmine plants, along with other medicinal herbs, were born. Floated to the airships in Falkhaan, they were taken aloft to be nourished by the moisture in the clouds, to grow healthy and large in the pure, plentiful, even brazen sunshine. Like the airship personnel themselves, they thrived beyond the smoke of the magma towers, beyond the foggy dampness of coastal mornings. When they were ripe, the leaves were returned to Codurazhkhaan to be blended into tea or bottled for therapeutic and aromatic uses. From there, the river carried the finished product everywhere along its route, from the western coast to the eastern ice boundaries.

Because she grew up surrounded by high peaks—including the majestic Zetora, legendary home of the first Galderkhaani—it had always been Qala's ambition to soar above them. She occasionally saw the largest of the airships pass high overhead, and when the flier recruitment boat came along the river, this girl still shy of womanhood implored *Femora* Ninma to allow her to apply. The old commander later told Qala that what he saw in her then was not just desire and poise. It was awe. He believed that one who flew on an airship should never lose a feeling of wonder for the skies—and whatever lay beyond.

"What *does* lie beyond, do you think?" the youthful Qala had once asked during training.

Ninma had answered, "Some say it is the true home of the Candescents, but I don't know. And there is some beauty in not knowing."

"How do you mean?" Qala asked.

Ninma had smiled warmly. "Your young thoughts are as valid as my old ones, possibly even more so. Ideas should always remain fresh. And," he began, then stopped.

"Yes, *Femora*?"

He had looked at Qala then and said, "And I hope we never find out. That would make someone right and someone wrong."

"Isn't knowledge worth that?" Qala had asked.

"Questions are always more valuable than answers," Ninma had replied. "I suppose if answers encourage new questions, they are valid. But this one? I do not think any of the major participants would receive the truth kindly, or willingly."

By "major participants" Ninma meant the Priests and Technologists. Even as a child, Qala recognized the rising dislike and mistrust between the two groups that supposedly served the general well-being of Galderkhaan.

The importance of questions was one of the most valuable lessons Qala had ever learned: always to seek, to ask, to look, and then to look beyond—if possible through different eyes, younger eyes, older eyes. In that way, Qala had always maintained her balance. To stop and "gloat" about being correct was the stagnating act of a future imbecile.

Sitting with the physician as he spoke with Vilu, Qala could not help but remember dear Ninma and her own years apprenticing on larger and larger airships. Because she spent so much time on the ground in

Falkhaan, Qala had formed a special bond with Vilu and had always understood and even encouraged the boy's enthusiasm for flight. He was only slightly younger than she had been when she left the valley, and every bit as obsessed. In the many coastal cities she had visited, Qala discovered that those Galderkhaani who plied the seas felt a similar respect and love for that vastness: What was below, they wondered? What was beyond? It used to perplex Qala that a sailor or flier could feel the same humble love for two very different mysteries, two different places, above and below. Yet a Priest had once asked her, during a long, moody night flight: "How strange is it that among people we can have many loves, each special and deep in its own way? Yet for fliers and sailors, affection can only be for one or the other, the sea or the air?"

Qala had no answer for that. She felt, though, that those two worlds were in many ways the same: the mysteries of one reflected the mysteries of the other. Answers to one showed the way to answers in the other. The Galderkhaani called this concept *Raque*, and it was one of the oldest concepts in the civilization: the idea that there was a sublime and perfect balance in the differences of all things, one-to-one and many-to-many.

It was not known whether it was the ancient concept of *Raque* that gave rise to the legends of the Candescents, or the other way around. The *Anata-Raque*, who later became the Priests, believed that if there was life in the sea, there must be life in the skies, beyond the highest clouds, beyond the hovering phosphorescence. The future Technologists, the *Eija-Raque*, felt that because all things come from above, including the waters that made the seas, a great power they named Tawazh had to have been the primal cause.

The great debate had begun, but there was one thing the early Galderkhaani believed. Before they had mastered flight, the thunder that occasionally rose from Zetora convinced them that the Candescents actually dwelt there. The mountain that glowed, the peak that rumbled with life from time to time, the cliffs that gave Galderkhaan their first *Yua*, the olivine tiles that spoke to those who were the first

Technologists—there was no other conceivable cause. The *Anata-Raque* and the *Eija-Raque* agreed on that, and that only. No one then, or now, addressed the mammoth flaw in the split between the groups: believing that all things came from above, the Technologists nonetheless tapped power from inside the world to create the Source. While the Priests, believing in balance, embraced the idea that there was a hierarchy to Candescence.

Qala was not a devoted student of such matters, certainly not like the Priests and their followers, who believed in deeply reflective prayer as a means to understand the Candescents; or the Technologists and their acolytes, who believed in the *Yua* as the medium for direct communication.

Torn by conflicts, no longer asking questions of each other, neither group had proved anything. The *zembo*, the nighttime lights far above even the highest airship, were still as mysterious as ever. The world after death was still unknown. And the bottom of the sea was stubbornly elusive.

Qala herself did believe that there is life above, even though those who had tried to reach it failed. Their balloons ripped or exploded and the fliers perished, just like those who attempted to use weighted, airtight conveyances to journey deep below the waters. She believed it because the spots of light hovered and watched with a friendly familiarity, in the way sand or stone, fire or molten rock, did not. Something must be behind them. Sometimes the lights flashed by, like leaves dropping from trees. Perhaps they too became extinguished.

Because the *zembo* could not be seized, like fish, Qala held that the lives and secrets of the Candescents were meant to be contemplated, not examined. One could surmise a great deal from the remains of sea creatures. Not the lights. Not even the largest one, the *zembo-jutan*, gave up its secrets—other than its sex, for its shape changed like that of a woman with child as it birthed and rebirthed the *zembo* every time darkness arrived.

The lights were meant to be considered in solitude or talked about in a group but, in the end, the majesty of their abodes was probably unknowable.

And yet, the things this boy was saying, like the sentiments Bayarma had spoken, were unlike anything Qala had ever heard. *Raque* described a realm where there was "above" and "below." It did not address a time that was "now" and "then."

Yet if balance is universal and constant . . . such contrasting worlds should exist, Qala thought. She wished Ninma had spent more time addressing the frustrating aspect of questions, as well as their merits.

Qala had returned to the physician's cabin after witnessing the discomfort of the sky. By the time Zell was finished talking with the boy, Qala had been informed that the airship was nearly ready to depart. The physician joined Qala outside the cabin while Bayarma remained inside, the boy curling beside her in the hammock.

Pressed by the *galdani*, Qala told him everything Bayarma had said to her as they walked toward the column.

"I do not know what to make of him, or her, or *them*," the physician admitted.

"I don't believe that," Qala said. "You always have an idea, or at least an opinion."

Zell shook his head. "I always have a sense of the truth behind something, whether the ailment is mental or physical. Not here. I cannot say whether this is something profound, a fabrication worked out by these two, or a mad shared fantasy."

"Your instincts are—" Qala pressed.

"Failing me," Zell admitted with a shrug of his bony shoulders. "What have these two to gain by such a tale? Yet how could they share a delusion? Which leaves only the one option, that this is a miracle for the Night of Miracles." He leaned closer so none of the crew would hear. "But that would compel me to believe in beings I am not convinced exist!"

"I was thinking that too," Qala said. "Yet there is also the timing, the way one appeared as the other left."

"What about it?"

Qala answered carefully, thoughtfully, because she knew that her explanation brought her in line with the doubts Zell had just expressed.

"It is as though the winds of *Raque* were blowing, informing us that our view of balance is too narrow," she said.

Zell fired her a look. "That's not what I would expect from my *Standor*, whose cabin is full of maps and more maps because, as we know, the ground is fickle, unbalanced, uneven, and unstable—as strong an argument against *Raque* as one can find."

"I know," Qala agreed. "But if what Bayarma said is true, that someone from the future was speaking through her, then her sudden departure as this other boy arrived means that that balance was being preserved through time, from future to past, past to future."

That idea caused Zell to sigh. He leaned forward on the smooth wooden rail. "I had that thought too," the *galdani* admitted. "It is the cleanest, simplest explanation. So why do I find it the most difficult to accept?"

"Because it makes sense and it opens a frightening, humbling possibility," Qala replied. "Several, in fact."

"Balance is a reality and an absolute," Zell said.

"Correct. If true, it means that the past is known so the future must be knowable. It also means that since there is life in the sea, there must be life in the skies."

"And the reverse, though, must also be true," Zell said. He gestured above with a wave of his hand. "Beings in the skies? We have never seen life on high, other than birds—and they eventually come to ground, alive or dead," Zell continued, returning to a favorite argument against celestial beings. "Hypothetical beings would perish and fall, as creatures of the deep sea perish and rise. We would see them. We *must*."

"Only if balance applies to things of substance," Qala said. "The past is no longer real, but we know it exists."

"Ah, the old Priestly argument," Zell replied.

"Yes, but there is logic that would not turn the head of a Technologist in disgust: What if, because there is physical life in the water, the *Raque must* be insubstantial life in the air?"

Zell grinned. "And *I* am supposed to be the esoteric one, Qala, sniffing potions and smoke to see what is inside the minds of others." The physician looked out across the landscape. It possessed a dark and brooding quality that had come on suddenly. "It is a strange day," he remarked.

"Very."

"I notice the tower is putting out more heat and light than usual," Zell said.

"I want to get above it as soon as possible, try to determine the levels of molten rock, the status of the tiles," Qala said. She peered toward the mountainous horizon. "I also want to see if this is unique. There appears to be light beyond the peaks."

Zell nodded. "Celebrations for the Night of Miracles, no doubt."

"Perhaps."

The physician sighed again. "We know so little—about the molten rock, about the tiles. Yet we use them as if we own them."

"Didn't the *Drudaya* teach that we should welcome all strangers, for how else would we get to know them?" Zell asked.

"Strangers don't spit flaming rock at villages from time to time," Qala said.

"True enough. And a consortium of Priests and Technologists don't band together to try and resolve differences based on *Raque*," Zell said. "Maybe the *Drudaya* were wrong, after all. It has been said that Priests dream the way and Technologists figure out how to get there. Balance does not always mean cooperation. Sometimes it arises from rivalry."

Qala nodded. "Fortunately, I just fly an airship. The only ones who ask what I think are crew members and the occasional child who is infatuated with flight."

Femora Loi approached quickly. "We are ready to depart, *Standor*."

"Thank you," Qala said. "Hold a moment." The *Standor* regarded Zell. "A last chance: What do we do with our guests? They will be your responsibility."

"The boy cannot be returned and the woman wishes to go to Aankhaan," the physician said. "What else is there to do but take them?"

Qala turned back to Loi. "Give word to the tower agent that the boy, Vilu, accompanies us for medical reasons," the *Standor* said. "Have them send a messenger to the water guardian Lasha. Tell him to let the custodians of the boy's home know that he is in the personal care of *Galdani* Zell."

"At once."

"I also want to circle the tower to have a look at the pool inside, see if we can see some reason for the rising heat. You have wing command, *Femora*."

Loi's quick, delighted smile said he was surprised by the last part of the order. "All will be done," Loi said smartly, then departed.

The physician was studying Qala with interest. "So. Finally."

"You're referring to Loi?"

"You know very well that I'm not," Zell said. "He is well trained and perfectly suited to handle this run."

Qala grinned.

Zell continued to gaze at Qala. "You realize what this means?"

"I do," Qala said. "And that's all right. Children are more of a nuisance than *thyodularasi*. But this boy *has* something."

"Something you recognize. And are prepared to nurture. Because you cannot give him back. That would crush him."

"I understand, and I am not just doing this for the boy but for the future of the fleet."

"There is no truth in what you just said," Zell remarked. "None."

"I am not interested in bearing or parenting," Qala insisted.

"Yet if he doesn't recover his wits, you may find him your responsibility regardless," Zell pointed out.

"I know," Qala replied. "But we get ahead of ourselves. First, you must heal him so we know if we have Vilu, or whatever he called himself."

"Jay-cupo-oh-ha-rayaah," Zell said. "Which is another puzzle. To suffer from mental illness, yet have such a precise, repeatable name . . . the two of them." The physician gripped the rail as the airship lurched from its moorings. "Which is what we came out here to discuss, before philosophy got in the way—again," Zell told her. "I do not want to use herbs to try and shock away whatever illness has come over Vilu."

"Why?"

"The presence—whatever it is, whether real or imagined—must not be subjugated, it must be removed."

"All right. Why?"

"Because you said yourself, a foreign soul was present in Bayarma, even though the normal Galderkhaani woman is 'here' now. She could seem normal for a time and then that other personality may return. In both of them it must be found, isolated, and removed."

"How?" Qala asked.

Zell leaned on the chest-high railing and looked out at the city. In the distance, they heard the plank stowed on the deck, the ropes around and below the bag groaning as the inflated envelope bore the entire weight of the gondola.

"I'll tell you in a moment," Zell said. "I want to make sure I understand—you did nothing to the woman to cause Bayarma to revert from or to her present state?"

"Nothing," Qala assured him. "We were talking and it suddenly happened after we walked on a Path of Ancestors," she said, glancing in the direction of the roadway. "Perhaps that had some effect?"

"Old bones and sinew? I doubt it, unless the ascended souls were still present, which I also doubt." He shook his head. "I've walked that road many times and never felt anything there."

"We don't have to explore that now," Qala said. "It affects those who wish to be affected."

"Who imagine too much," Zell said. "But yes, for another time. Right now, we have two, possibly four, lost and conflated beings."

Both felt the sudden, gentle shift aloft and toward the stern as the airship fully surrendered itself to the sky and its winds. The gondola rocked gently from side to side as the ropes that held it to the bag settled with taut familiarity that was controlled by the personnel of the wing commander. There was a familiar rustling sound as the proud wings unfurled to catch the wind. Qala had not experienced departure from the side of the carriage since she was a young *usa-femora*. Typically she was in the forward cabin. Watching the landscape shift sideways, instead of flying into it, made her smile. As soon as the flight settled, she would go aft to look down into the tower.

"You were saying, Zell?" Qala said.

"Eh?"

"About the boy," Qala coaxed. "What will you try to reach this other—person?"

"I want to attempt *nuat, Standor*."

Disapproval clouded Qala's open features. "Even the Technologists disapprove of that and they invented it."

"Discovered," Zell gently corrected his superior.

"The distinction won't matter to one whose mind . . . *melts!*"

"The result of over-exuberance, not careful application."

"No, Zell. Not the boy."

"It *can* be moderated," Zell insisted.

"The stones *cannot* be controlled outside a ring, you know that," Qala replied. "They seek, they reach out with . . . with fists, not fingers. And if one is in the way—"

"That is Priestly fear-mongering," Zell said dismissively. "If properly applied, it is said it can chase bad humors from any mind."

"You've done it?"

"No."

"Then that is my answer."

"I see," Zell said. "Is it more dangerous than having someone else's spirit inhabit your body?"

"I don't know," Qala admitted. "It's possible we all do, I suppose."

"Yes, of course. You're referring to that woman Ula who had her own small airship and flew from town to town displaying the seven or eight voices in her head?" Zell shook his head angrily. "I saw her when I was a boy. It was an act."

"Others say it was not."

"They're wrong," Zell said.

"Even so, 'One charlatan does not a theory discredit,' " Qala said.

"That must be one of Vol's sayings. He's a poet, a naysayer for anything that has actual evidence to support it. He conveniently moves on whenever anyone proves him to be a fabulist."

" 'The Priests dream,' " Qala mused. "And it's not just Vol's idea, that a form of *cazh* can link living and ascended. Perhaps certain stimuli are the triggers." She cocked her head toward the physician's cabin. "I say again, those two were in the same courtyard. I can't shake the feeling that something there might have done it. Lasha blamed it on bad fish."

"That's stupid."

"I agree, but there could be some other medium. They may have interacted with the same *thyodularasi* who actually pulled me to where the boy had fallen."

"So *its* mind merged with theirs?" Zell said mockingly.

"I don't know. It may have brought something from the sea, a new scent, something that confused their minds," Qala said.

"Indeed it could have," Zell said. "The sea is always throwing out surprises. But—and I'm sorry to repeat myself—"

"No, you're not sorry. You like hearing yourself speak."

"I am orating," Zell insisted with a knowing smirk. "But the only way to learn more is from the only material we have at hand. That means our two subjects."

Qala exhaled slowly. She looked out at Galderkhaan. The vista was both shrinking and expanding: the smaller Falkhaan became, the greater their view of the surrounding lands. There were icy foothills and then the distant peaks of Qala's native valley. One could no longer make out the features of the people but the underbellies of the clouds became more detailed, their movements subtler, swifter in their detail. Qala saw the shadow of her vessel shifting and diminishing over the landscape the higher they went.

"I'm going to have to think about this while I have a look at the tower," Qala said. "Until I do, my answer stands. Give me other options."

"Well, I *can* use my compounds to try and communicate with these beings, but language might be an impediment if, as we've seen, the other souls do not speak Galderkhaani. But, *Standor*, I don't know what risks we face there either. If the boy goes away again, he may not return. That is why I return to the more radical—"

"No."

"Qala, unlike the route we fly, the route we take with those two is uncharted—"

"Which is why we move with caution," the *Standor* said. She regarded Zell. "Do you understand?"

"I understand," Zell grumped.

"Thank you." Qala smiled a little as she shook her head at the persistent physician, then went to take readings of the molten rock and tile luminescence, which were measured using an optical gauge. Filters fashioned from different colors recorded changes from the last readings.

Zell watched her go then turned with sudden urgency toward his cabin.

Qala was right but she was also wrong. And the *galdani* had very little time to decide which it was.

CHAPTER 18

Ben was already on his way to the hospital when he phoned Nancy O'Hara. He didn't know if Caitlin was napping or sedated again, and not wanting to disturb her, he felt it best to communicate through her mother. He told the woman he would be there in minutes and asked her if Caitlin was awake.

"She is," her mother said. "But she is in her room meeting with Barbara—"

"I see," Ben said. "When you can, please tell Cai that I just got an emergency notification from NYC on my phone. Tell her that the Group mansion has apparently imploded."

"The who?"

"Just tell her to check the news. It'll probably be on local TV," Ben said.

"All right," Nancy said. "As long as it won't upset her."

"She needs to know," Ben assured her and hung up. He didn't want to get into any explanations. It was the reason he was hurrying. This could be sabotage, part of a larger struggle, or it could be something they were monkeying with in the laboratory. Or both. One thing he had learned working at the United Nations is that crises rarely had one underlying cause.

Ben arrived at Lenox Hill within minutes. He went right to Caitlin's floor where he was met by Dr. Yang.

"Doctor, I hear our patient is up," Ben said, offering his hand.

"I just saw Mrs. O'Hara who told me you were coming," the physician said. "Dr. Melchior just left. Why does Dr. O'Hara now require a linguist?"

"No, it's not that—I'm her closest friend," Ben replied.

"And that is the capacity in which you're here?" Dr. Yang asked.

"Yes. Yes, why else?"

"I am not entirely sure," the doctor confessed.

Dr. Yang wasn't happy with so many nonfamily visitors turning the room into a convention center. But he respected Caitlin O'Hara and while escorting Ben to her bedside, Caitlin assured him there were larger safety issues than her own in play.

"But you cannot elaborate," Dr. Yang said. "Confidentiality."

"Yes."

"Which does not extend to this young man."

"It does," Caitlin said. "I need his support."

Dr. Yang looked at Nancy O'Hara, who didn't seem sure whether she should stay or go. Then he regarded her daughter.

"This is a professional courtesy," he informed Caitlin before giving them a half-hour with Ben. "Please do not take advantage of that, unless you wish to go back to sleep, Dr. O'Hara."

"I understand," Caitlin had assured him. "If we run over, though—"

"Half an hour," he repeated firmly. "I have other patients and no time to monitor this. Are we clear?"

"We are," Caitlin said. "Thank you."

The bed had been raised and Caitlin was sitting up. Ben looked over at Nancy, who was standing beside the night table. She seemed to be using her body to block the TV remote.

"Did you watch?" Ben asked.

"She did not," Nancy said.

"Watch what?" Caitlin asked.

"Wow. This is important," Ben insisted. "Didn't you *tell* her?"

"I did not."

"Tell me what?" Caitlin said. "What are you both talking about?"

Over Nancy's harsh stare, Ben took out his phone and read the alert: "Subject: Notify NYC—NYU vicinity explosion. The New York City Departments of Fire and Police have jointly issued an advisory that the quarantined area around Washington Square Park has been expanded three blocks north along Fifth Avenue due to the unexplained collapse of a structure, in its entirety, at the corner of Ninth Street and Fifth Avenue. The area five blocks north between Sixth Avenue and Broadway have also been closed to vehicular traffic to allow emergency vehicles to access the site. Con Edison is also on-site checking for gas leaks. No time has been set for a lifting of these restrictions. For more information or to view this message in American Sign Language . . . etc."

"Christ," Caitlin said.

"Yeah," Ben replied.

"Nothing about casualties?" Caitlin asked.

Ben shook his head.

"I don't think we should concern ourselves with this," Nancy said to Caitlin. "As we were just discussing, you have decisions to make regarding your situation and that of your son."

"What decisions?" Ben asked as he eased into the empty chair.

"Family decisions," Nancy said.

"Ben *is* family," Caitlin said sharply. "Would you give us a few minutes, please, mother? Please?"

Nancy left without a word, without looking at either her daughter or Ben.

"Jeez, I'm really, really sorry," Ben said.

"Don't be. You and I have to talk. I'm . . . shit, I don't know what I am! I was starting to doubt myself, but the situation at the Group mansion changes things."

"You were doubting yourself?" Ben said with genuine surprise.

"It happens, yeah. Especially because people I love and respect are telling me what I'm doing with Jacob is wrong."

"Back up," Ben said. "How'd you get to that point?"

"Barbara did a regression, but . . . it wasn't like anything else I've experienced. I didn't settle anywhere, not in past life experiences or in Galderkhaan. I felt like a goddamn stone skipping across a pond. When I finally did stop I was in—you ready for it?"

"Big old thing or scary new one?"

"New," she said, "which is why I'm questioning my perceptions. Being in another body, back then . . . that's something I can get my arms around."

"Yeah, I'm still not there yet, Cai."

"I know," she said with a hint of impatience, "and let's table that. This other journey—was new, different. I was in this golden, talking light. At least, that's what it seemed to be."

"Talking . . . how?"

"Not with words but with—this is going to sound crazy—with si-lence."

"You're right. That's obviously not possible."

"True, true. Except that—you know the way that black is the ab-sorption of all color? This seemed to be the absorption of all sound, collected in a place and in a way I couldn't access it. I felt that some-thing was out there."

Ben nodded. "I see. Sort of like—" he stopped.

"What?"

"I was going to say it's the same way you had to ease into commu-nication with ascended and transcended souls," Ben said. "You had to learn to understand them, change your way of listening. The last ones, they had to reach you through Jacob."

Inside, Caitlin blessed him for his academic detachment and ab-sence of judgment. He began to restore her faith in herself.

"All that is true, though this was beyond anything I've experienced since we started, which is why I need more information—to know I'm not making this up, acting out on a subconscious level."

"You know, of course, what you're describing."

"I do, but people who 'head toward the light' in near-death experiences don't get there by regressing, by missing their train stop—in this case Galderkhaan, where I was trying to go. I saw it, tried to find Jacob, and it was gone before I could stop myself."

Ben huddled closer to her. "What do you want me to do?" he asked, placing a reassuring hand on her shoulder. "Apart from compliment you on your lovely PJs?"

Caitlin didn't smile. That's how he knew this was very, very serious. She looked into his eyes.

"More than anyone, except for my son—who I think knew it before any of us, now that I think back on it—you are willing to allow that what's happening may be real," Caitlin said. "Or at least, I think, you're closer to believing it. I need to find a way to get to Jacob. Anita told me about the snake."

"What about it?"

"It seemed to seek him out," Caitlin said.

"Maybe," Ben said. "*Big* maybe. I have no explanation for that beyond 'conjurer's trick,' " Ben said.

"Oh, come on—"

"Egyptian magicians created similar images thousands of years ago. "

"Is that what you really think that was?"

"Honestly, Cai, I *was* with a Vodou priestess from Haiti—"

"Which, given the history of that region, should give her added credibility."

"Well, it didn't . . . maybe because she was so damned recalcitrant. She and her statue of a son. I'm not saying it isn't possible," he added to forestall debate, "and she did feel your energy on the roof . . . she said."

"Did she say where she felt it, or how?"

Ben thought for a moment. "She pointed toward the East Village area. With a cigar."

Caitlin made a fist and shook it. "That's exactly where I sent it," she said. "How would she know if it wasn't real, if she weren't legit?"

"As I said, I have no answer, Cai. Just a sort of open mind about her."

"All right, let's put her aside for a moment," Caitlin said. "There's something else. Even before I knew about the Group mansion, the tiles went dormant. To me, anyway."

"Suggesting what?"

"I was controlling the lines of power between here and there," she said. "Between the two stones here and the tiles that are in Antarctica. Something happened to change the arc, to cut me out of the loop."

"Something at the mansion?"

"Has to be," Caitlin said. "Flora had one tile in cold storage, I *felt* that, and the other in some kind of acoustic levitation setup. Remove me from the middle and they would have hooked directly into each other. If they were strong enough to whip me back to Galderkhaan and strand me there—if they could tear a hole in time—imagine what they could do to an old mansion."

Ben sat back. "That is a very, very big leap."

"Give me some alternative—" And then Caitlin stiffened, like a dog hearing a car approaching. She turned to the door, a glazed look in her eyes.

"Cai?" Ben said.

"It's out there," she answered.

"What is?"

"Yokane's stone," Caitlin replied. The first two fingers of her right hand rose, circled, pointed. "I felt it before, when Barbara was here. I'm feeling it again. It's *out* there."

"Where?" Ben asked.

Caitlin let her fingers drift; like a divining rod, Ben thought.

"North," she said. "It's stable, just as it was with Yokane. It's no longer communicating with any other stones."

"So the other one was destroyed?" Ben asked.

"I don't know. I don't see how. It survived the pressure on the bottom of the ocean." Caitlin lowered the bars of her bed. "I'm getting out of here," she announced.

Ben leaned toward her, arms extended. "Cai, hold on—"

She brushed them aside and swung her legs from the bed. "A patient has the right to self-determination and autonomy," she said. "I'm leaving. I have to follow that stone. It's the only way back to Jacob. I would love your help, but I'll do this alone if I have to."

"I said hold on!" Ben snapped.

"Why?"

"Because this may not be necessary," Ben said. "Rushing I mean."

Caitlin regarded him. He had a *there's something I didn't tell you* tone in his voice. "What is it?" she asked.

"Let me make a call," he said.

"To?"

He braced himself. "The Technologist I met outside your apartment this morning."

Caitlin's rising frustration came to a sudden, icy stop. "How was that not your lead item, Ben? Freakin' *how?*"

"In the General Assembly they call that a battering ram," he answered. "You don't use it unless all else fails. It can cause collateral splintering."

"Such as?"

"The Technologists and the Priests are apparently still at war and the Group was caught in the crossfire," Ben said. "Both have obviously been watching you. If you go blundering into—"

"Make your call," Caitlin interrupted. "Now. I have to get to that stone, connect with the others in the South, and save my son."

"A few minutes ago you weren't certain that was the way to go."

"Technologists at my threshold just made me certain," she said. "Damn you, Ben. You should have told me!"

"I'm sorry," he said. "It's been a long effin' night and day and journey for me too."

Caitlin did not reply. She didn't seem to have any words left in her. She looked at Ben. After a moment she touched his cheek in apology, then climbed from the bed and pulled her battle-scarred wardrobe from the tray under the bed.

After a long, unhappy breath Ben called Eilifir Benediktsson.

CHAPTER 19

Mikel Jasso pulled the muffler from over his mouth. He didn't bother with the radio.

"I need fuel!" he yelled at Dr. Cummins.

She rolled down the window. "I don't understand."

"I need petrol—gas—all that we can spare."

The glaciologist looked down at him as he neared the driver's side of the truck. "To do what? We may need those reserves to go farther or go back."

"This is more important," Mikel said, breathless as he reached the cab.

"Than getting back?"

"We can radio for help if it comes to that," he panted. He jerked a thumb toward the pit. "We have to melt the ice around that, flood the hole, and let it freeze."

Dr. Cummins's eyes reflected shock. "You want to cover up the very thing we came out here to study?"

"I do," Mikel replied. "Quickly."

"*Why?*" she asked. "Is it deteriorating or are you afraid of something else?"

"The latter," Mikel said. "Something happened in New York, something that may set these things loose. As far as I know, cold is the only thing that can stop them."

"Dr. Jasso, you've quite lost me. 'Loose'?"

Mikel motioned for her to follow as he started toward the back of the truck. She thumped down onto the ice.

"I'm not sure what I mean myself," he admitted. "These stones obliterate time and distance. I've only experienced their ability to create or re-create images, but not to destroy, as I just saw."

"I'm not even sure what you saw," Dr. Cummins said, perplexed.

"A forty-thousand-year-old girl and a woman in New York burned to death simultaneously," he said. "The linked tiles appear to be the cause. We opened a portal. My superior there was screaming for me to shut them down and she is not a screamer. We have to dial this back, quickly."

Mikel had already begun hauling the spare cans of gas from the back. Dr. Cummins joined him. Her movements were mechanical. She was still trying hard to understand what he was saying.

"You didn't anticipate any of this?" Dr. Cummins asked.

"I didn't *know* about any of this," he said. "Look, we'll do this, then take stock of where we are. We can always remove the ice to get back in there."

"I have to notify Halley," she said as Mikel began waddling ahead with two of the heavy cans. "They may not approve of you setting fire to the ice."

"No, this has *got* to be done," he said over his shoulder. "Quickly. We are not in a good place if those tiles become active. For all I know the entire ice shelf may be in danger, to Halley and beyond."

The woman took two cans and looked over at the pit as she followed Mikel. She shook her head. "I don't see anything that—"

There was a rumble that caused the fuel in the cans to slosh audibly. Dr. Cummins stopped suddenly. So did Mikel.

"You felt that, right?" he asked.

The ground continued to vibrate slightly, as if a subwoofer were turned on nearby.

"That could just be recracking caused by our truck, our activities here," the glaciologist said.

A low hum rose up through the ice. The piled, windblown shavings jiggled like metal filings on a snare drum.

"*That* could be an echo from somewhere else," she said. "Those can move every which way for several minutes."

"It's coming from the pit," Mikel said as he hurried ahead, half walking, half stumbling. He stopped about ten yards from the edge. The ice particles and dead bugs continued to vibrate and move in response to the hum.

Mikel unscrewed the cap of one of the two containers. He pushed it on its side then opened the second one and did the same. The overhang of ice was the greatest here, on the western side.

"Mikel, wait!" Dr. Cummins said as she reached his side. "Shouldn't we wait a few minutes, just to see?"

"I'm afraid to," he admitted. "Very afraid." He ran back to get the last two cans.

His urgency was enough to spur Dr. Cummins on. "Where do you want these?" she asked.

"Make it about twenty yards to the north, half as close," Mikel said, shouting back after watching the way the petrol flowed. "We've got a downward slope of about five degrees here . . . it's straighter there."

Dr. Cummins acknowledged with a big nod then hurried off. She did her work quickly as the ground continued to vibrate. They could both see little ripples in the slightly yellowish fuel that pooled on the ice.

Mikel poured gas on the south side. When they were finished, they carried the containers back to the truck and Mikel got a flare pistol and cartridge from the equipment locker in the rear.

"Back the Toyota away," Mikel told her. "We don't want to risk igniting the gas in the truck."

"Way ahead of you," she said, getting back into the cab. "You watch yourself—stay low, the heat will rise as it rolls out."

Even as she spoke, the ground began to shake more violently. It wasn't sound. Mikel couldn't be sure what it was, whether it was the tiles themselves, the fracturing result of the tiles, or both. As she backed the truck up, he crouched with a knee on the ground well away from the gas and to the west. The wind was blowing east so there wouldn't be any superheated fumes.

The gun was a single-shot twelve-gauge pistol. Mikel loaded it and, checking that the Toyota was a safe distance off, he fired at the edge of the nearest pool. The gas went up with a soft whoosh, the six-foot-high flames following the flow of the gas and bending immediately in the direction of the wind. After just a few seconds the surface of the ice began to pock and large chunks began to crack, sink, and melt, pouring streams of water and gas toward the pit. The heat and hot water melted more ice and soon large slabs of ice were snapping and sliding toward the edge and over the side, sending a spray of water and flaming fuel into the air. They came back down like the hail of Jehovah.

Mikel rose and backed away, toward the truck. He was surprised to find the vibration continuing to increase, actually shaking loose more and more of the weakened ice.

"Dr. Jasso, hurry!" Dr. Cummins cried, leaning out the door of the truck.

He nodded and ran toward her. The smell of the burning gas was strong, despite the wind blowing away from him. Within moments steam was rising from the pit as water met fire. The heat caused ice on all sides to break away, and he could hear the ice splitting and popping inside, cracking like rifle shots, a symphony of destruction. The long flutes fell with eerie whistling sounds until they knifed into the slush at the bottom.

Or are those ascended spirits, Mikel could not help but wonder, *the dead somehow trapped in the tiles?*

Suddenly, the vibration stopped. Mikel wasn't expecting that to happen until the water froze. Had the water itself quieted the tiles?

He stopped a few steps shy of the truck and turned, waited, looked across the smoking, malodorous expanse.

No, he thought with a chill that managed to run up his spine even in this cold. *The vibration hasn't stopped. It's just gotten lower and more stable.*

Something caught his eye to his right, far away, an area free of smoke, on the western horizon where blue sky met the ice. He raised his goggles and peered toward it where he saw a faint glow. Just then he noticed—through the smoke and flame—that the pit he had just inundated was also domed with a hazy yellow light.

"Dr. Jasso?" Dr. Cummins was leaning from the truck.

Mikel was looking at the distant glow. The light here and the light there appeared to be the same color.

Christ, he thought with awful horror. *Is this column* talking *to another buried column?*

"Dr. Jasso!" he heard Dr. Cummins yell.

He turned around, toward her, saw her pointing with agitation to the area behind the truck, to the east. There was another dim light on the horizon. This one was in the direction where he had seen the airship crack free of the ice before sinking just days ago.

Mikel started back toward the cab. "It has to be," he muttered.

"What?" she asked.

"The towers of the ancient Source network are waking," he said. "They're . . . talking to one another."

"Because of the fire?"

"I—I don't think so," he said. "This has to be what Flora was afraid of! We appear to be too late."

"I've got Halley on the radio; they aren't reading anything, no geologic activity except the thermal signature you created."

"It isn't seismic and I don't think it's the magma," Mikel replied as he reached the cab. "Hell, it may not even be just now."

"What?"

"I opened a path to the past," he said. "But I'm sure it's the olivine tiles. They're awake, they're linked, and they're communicating."

"How is that possible? Magnetically? Electronically? How else would stones 'talk'?"

"I don't know," he said. "When I was below, they were sharing information. Maybe they share the same data pool or—"

He stopped.

"What is it?" Dr. Cummins asked.

"Not a pool," he said. "Living images."

"Again?"

"I assumed that what I saw were images. What if they weren't . . . aren't. These tiles may not be storage systems—they could be *windows!*"

"Powered by what?" she asked.

"We're at the pole—magnetism?"

She checked her analog compass, saw no deviations, went to check the digital device, and the Toyota fell instantly, ominously quiet.

"Did you do that?" Mikel asked.

"No. I did not."

There was a palpable feeling of something dreadful in the vast ice fields around them. It was more than the vibration, more than the faint glow. It was a sense of something enormous.

"Big drop in air pressure," Dr. Cummins said.

"Yeah. Like something drained it away."

The winds died and there was only the cricketing sound of the surface ice snapping.

"Dr. Jasso, talk to me," the woman said. "Spitball. Give me something to think about." Dr. Cummins's voice was without fear or reproach. But there was concern in her movements as she tried to restart the vehicle, then went from button to button trying to activate something . . . anything. "Nothing," she said. "This vehicle is dead."

Mikel turned back to the pit. The melted ice was still dripping down. There was no steam now, so no heat. The radiance was definitely something other than dying flame. He looked across the horizon. The silence seemed almost to have weight. It was as if someone—something—were approaching. It was not something moldy and gray and dead like the spirits he'd seen below, nor a flaming demon like Enzo. This was—

An explosion of life was all that came to mind. Something was rolling across the Antarctic expanse, possibly across time itself, filling the empty spaces with something tangible yet still elusive.

"Dr. Jasso?" Dr. Cummins said quietly.

He looked back at her, saw her pointing ahead, near the pit. He turned wordlessly.

Something was moving. It was something hazy and indistinct, like sea spray, but moving along a very narrow path, as if it were inside a tunnel. It unrolled toward them; at least, it was coming in their direction. Mikel could not be sure that they or the truck was a destination.

Nonetheless, Dr. Cummins popped the door and got out. "I don't like this," she said.

"I don't either, but it's here," he replied.

He watched as the misty droplets that comprised the shape darkened.

"Smoke from the pit?" Dr. Cummins asked, stepping to one side. "Is the fire still burning?"

The object seemed to widen, to expand, to include her new position. She did not bother to move again.

"I don't think it's smoke," Mikel said, stepping toward it.

"Dr. Jasso, what are you doing?"

"It's going to reach us eventually," he said, and sniffed. "I don't smell anything. If it were from magma or a fire, there should be some kind of noxious content."

"And if it's not? You talked about *something* burning below."

"She didn't smoke," he said.

Mikel was about forty yards from the pit with the forward end of the mist about half that distance away. He stopped and studied the new phenomenon. As the shape moved, he saw that the ice softened beneath it: a slick gloss covered the surface wherever it moved.

"There's something sentient in that, isn't there?" Dr. Cummins asked.

"Why do you say that?"

"Didn't you see it move when I did?"

"Any number of things could cause that," Mikel said. "My guess is it's moving toward the distant light. You happened to block it."

"What makes you think *that*?" Dr. Cummins asked.

"Because there's another one forming on the other side of the pit," Mikel replied.

Dr. Cummins spun her head in that direction. "They're both heading toward the distant glows."

"And I'm willing to bet there are clouds heading from there to meet them."

"Christ, what have we opened here?" Dr. Cummins asked. It was the first time she had lost her scientific detachment.

"Not us," he said. "We were just the witnesses."

Dr. Cummins got back in the cab of the truck and tried the engine, then the radio, then the computer. Everything stayed dead. The mist was still moving forward, a slowly surging, narrow wave. About five feet in diameter the shape was becoming round, like a pipe, yet it undulated forward almost like a worm. It continued to darken but the sunlight played against it oddly: amid the charcoal gray that comprised it were pinpoint facets of light, rippling like sun on the ocean.

Mikel resumed his slow walk toward the shape. He heard his boots crunch, then he did not. He looked down and noticed that the ice was now liquefying ahead of the object. Maybe that was just residual heat from the fire he'd set . . . or, he wondered, could those tiny facets of light be producing their own heat?

The front of the "smoke" was now ten feet away. Despite what Mikel had said to Dr. Cummins, he too had the sense that there was something conscious inside, something doing more than just blindly, instinctively seeking something.

"Dr. Jasso!"

The woman had cracked the door and was leaning out. Mikel turned at the glaciologist's cry. It was far more alarmed than before. He turned, squinted, thrust his goggles back in front of his eyes.

And then, finally, he was afraid.

Each trail of smoke suddenly exploded with light, as though skin had been shed and a radiance released. The glittering facets remained, diamonds amid the golden glow, causing even more melting across the surface of the ice.

His legs weak, his boots failing to find traction, Mikel half walked, half slid across the ice back to the truck. However, he did not hurry. There was no reason and there was no need. Fear was replaced by fascination, which was replaced by certainty.

Mikel Jasso knew he was meant to see this.

CHAPTER 20

Zell was a difficult, quarrelsome man.

He knew it. His lovers had always said so, even when he was young and just starting out on his chosen path. His first had been a woman who made adornments from bird feathers and sold them in the market. Though he was fascinated with the dyes Palu created, he didn't understand why anyone would wear such things.

"They are lively," she said.

"They are dead," Zell had pointed out. "And who wants an ascended bird, if such there is, to come pecking at them?"

His last had been Atak, a man who made charts of the designs in the olivine tiles, claiming that the serpentine patterns had prophetic meaning. He expounded on those in scroll after scroll. Zell didn't understand how Atak could only study the surface when the bulk of the design was within.

"For the same reason vessels remain on the surface of the sea," he had replied. "It is what we were meant to see."

"Meant? By whom?" Zell had asked.

"By the Candescents," Atak had affirmed.

"Why would they want to keep us stupid?" Zell had queried with attitude.

Lovers and friends and birth partners made no sense, so Zell had given up having them. Minerals and leaves, oils and waters, blood and lava—these behaved rationally, predictably, even when combined. Their uses could be understood, repeated, and the results were enlightening. The natural world made sense to him, and Zell had no reservations about saying so.

His patients frequently resented his brusqueness, his incessant probing, and his argumentative nature, which is why he moved to a situation where there was no choice in the selection of a *galdani*. Even *Standor* Qala occasionally had to walk away from him when he grew "insistent," which was her diplomatic way of saying "stubborn as a *flendro*." Zell had always considered that a ridiculous analogy, since he was physically quite different from the burly mountain bulls that were harnessed to liberate fresh lands from beneath ancient ice.

But whatever else could be said about him, Zell was undeniably a master of empathetic energy. He believed that this talent was really what put people off: he tore easily through what they themselves knew—or had to suspect—was weak, merely comfortable reasoning. That was why they got so angry at him.

From his early childhood, he was able to care for sick lake birds in Bulcaz, not far from the eastern perimeter of the habitable lands. Zell dwelt with a small community of ice monitors, who studied the expansion and retreat of the great sheets that covered the continent; there wasn't much for a young boy to do other than slide down ice sheets or otherwise amuse himself. Zell selected birds, since he envied their ability to leave the region, which they did with some regularity. The youth wasn't able to join *with* the birds mentally; his skill was not the equivalent of some proto-*cazh* that made two souls one, a Priestly idea he heard about from the airship crews that supplied the region.

Through the birds, however, Zell got a strong sense of what was wrong with them, where their bodies were hurting. He later understood that it was what the Priests called *ilkhmelz*: the capacity to feel another's pain so acutely that it could be isolated. There was no dancing and waving of hands as in the ancient days. It was a quiet process, almost prayerful. Leaving Bulcaz on an airship, he was introduced to others who followed the profession of *galdani*.

Yet even they had limitations, relying solely on a mind-spirit connection. Zell used his own mixtures of cold-weather leaves and minerals, some heated, some chilled, some lotions, some ingested. He refined these by endless experimentation and a great many bird deaths, until he was finally able to heal more creatures than he killed. And soon he was healing all of them, even the aged.

There was a contradiction in that, of course, for as soon as the birds were well one of the humans in Bulcaz would kill and roast them or put them in a soup. But sometimes, Zell was able to sneak one away, to give it at least a chance for life.

A chance for life, he thought as he returned to the cabin after the unsatisfactory chat with *Standor* Qala. That was all most *galdani*, most physicians, could offer. When he settled down to study healing arts in Aankhaan, he found he had the same skill with humans that he possessed with birds. The big difference was that humans were less cooperative, since those in pain could not have their wings pinned. Where birds surrendered, humans fought. After earning a reputation for belligerence in Aankhaan—and healing one of *Standor* Qala's essential crew members of persistent airsickness—Zell took to the skies.

Except to collect ingredients for his cures, the physician never left the ship. Qala once suggested that perhaps Zell had meshed too well with the birds; perhaps there was some truth in that. Zell was always happiest when he was aloft.

Yet of all the patients he had treated in his career, the *galdani* had never met anyone as perplexing as this boy in his care. There was no explanation Zell could think of to account for how, clearly, two beings inhabited one body. The explanation had to be found, not just for Vilu but also for Zell: where there were two, there would likely be more. Qala's concerns and reservations could not be permitted to interfere.

Bayarma had fallen asleep quickly and deeply in his hammock. Vilu was just lying by her side, clutching her toga. Zell drew shut a curtain made of tightly woven vines to give that little corner of his cabin privacy and darkness. The curtain was only drawn during emergency work: in case anyone entered, they would know to leave quietly.

Zell bent in a corner where he kept raw minerals in crates. Beneath these were blankets made of heavy *flendro* hide. The covers were used for patients with chills and also helped to buffer the more fragile stones during turbulent flight.

Within the covers, its hum muted by the thick skins, was an olivine tile that had been given to him by Palu. It had been gifted before private ownership of the stones had been banned by a rare, joint act of the Priests and Technologists. Any outstanding tiles were supposed to have been turned in.

Zell had retained this one because, unlike Atak, he was not content to misunderstand its qualities. He studied it when he was alone, tried to bond with it, understood that there was great power within . . . power that he did not understand. Once, however, he had used it to examine the mind of a patient who had been struck by a whipping sail. With it, he was able to see the man's thoughts. This arcane process, known to the Priests as *nuat*, had been deemed illegal because of the danger it presented to the patient—minds had liquefied, it was said—and the temptation toward corruption it offered the user. The *Drudaya*, a group of rogue Priests and Technologists who made a habit of this practice, had been banned.

Zell had no use for fear, he had no tolerance for rules, and he was a healer with two sick patients who defied standard treatment. *Nuat* offered them "a chance for life."

The tile seemed to be vibrating with more than its usual quiet hum.

"Responding to my patients?" Zell asked the stone, turning quickly to see if there was any reaction from the boy.

There was, and it was not the kind of mildly curious response he had been expecting. Vilu was crawling toward him across the hammock. Crawling purposefully, not like a boy child but like a predatory animal. The boy was moving awkwardly but only because he was only using one arm. The other arm, the left, was pointed directly at Zell, the first two fingers rigid in his direction.

Bayarma was still asleep, under the influence of the sedative.

"What is it, Vilu?" Zell asked, moving forward.

The boy didn't answer. Zell realized that the youngster was not looking at him or pointing at him: the tile was the object of Vilu's attention. Zell stopped. He noticed that the tile was vibrating strangely now, not only causing a mild tremor in his hand but also getting heavier. Zell bent with it.

The boy swung from the hammock, dropped to his knees, and crept forward, the two fingers never wavering. Zell realized, then, that the tile wasn't getting heavier. It was *moving* toward the ground, the way some of his heavy stones pulled at each other when placed nearby.

"Vilu, talk to me," Zell instructed. He was now kneeling as well, facing the boy. The two were just an arm's length away. "What are you feeling?"

"Fire," Vilu said.

"Inside you?" Zell asked.

"No," he replied. He looked at Zell for the first time. "Inside the stone. Inside you."

The *galdani* was startled by that, but almost at once he realized the boy was right. The olivine tile was vibrating so rapidly that it was beginning to generate heat, warmth that ran up his arm, into his shoulder, and up his neck. It moved so quickly that it felt like flowing water.

Zell released the tile but the respite was only momentary: it was glowing now and the heat became radiant. The dome of yellow light enveloped him, forcing him back on his palms.

On the other side of the light, Vilu had stopped moving but was still pointing his fingers. He did not seem to feel any heat: rather, he appeared to be undergoing some kind of rapture. His breathing was quickened, his eyes were wide, his mouth was pulled back in an expression that was somewhere between pain and euphoria.

Nuat *should not be working so quickly, so decisively*, the physician thought. *Something has happened to the tile.*

As perspiration pushed through the pores of his face and neck, Zell recalled what Qala had said about the tower and the rising heat.

It's not the fiery rock that's causing it, Zell realized. *It's the tiles within. Something has caused them to become very active.*

The reason probably wasn't Vilu or Bayarma. The tower was warming up before they arrived. But they might be part of whatever phenomenon was causing this.

The physician grabbed the covers from behind him and threw it on the tile. The glow was dampened but only briefly. The hide began to crackle as the underside was dried, baked.

Zell rose and quickly jumped over it, scooping Vilu in his arms. He pushed through the curtain and out the door, setting the boy on the gondola.

"Remain here," Zell said.

Vilu began to extend his fingers back toward the tile.

"No!" Zell shouted, slapping his arm down. "Do not point!"

The incident drew the attention of *Standor* Qala, who was standing forward of the cabin as the airship gained lift over the sea and turned to pass above the *simu-varkas*.

"Zell, what happened?" Qala asked, rushing forward.

Instead of answering, the physician ran back into the cabin and pushed through the vine curtain. The area around the hammock was filled with a nearly transparent white luminescence, not blinding but hot and causing Bayarma to gasp for breath as she slept. Zell reached her and bundled her to his chest, turning his back to the tile to protect her from its heat.

Qala met him at the door, where Zell pushed the woman into her arms.

"The tiles, something is affecting them!" Zell said before jumping back inside. "These two must have felt it first!"

While Qala processed that information—ignoring the obvious fact that the physician had disobeyed her orders—Zell tore at the curtain, ripping it from its woven hangers. He dropped it on the bundle of covers that was already atop the tile. Then he swept all of them, including the olivine tile, into his arms.

He shrieked like the wind from the mountains as invisible fire ripped through his eye sockets into his brain. Zell managed to turn and fling himself at the door, moving past Qala with such ferocious determination that the *Standor* wasn't able to stop him. Along with several crew members who had run over to care for Vilu and Bayarma, Qala watched with horror as the physician hit the rail with such force that it cracked and spilled him over the side. Qala bolted after him, too late to do more than watch as Zell, the hides, and the tile tumbled through the crisp morning sky toward the distant waters.

The stone tile was burning fiercely. It did not melt, it simply flamed. And as it fell something inexplicable occurred: while *Galdani* Zell plunged beneath the waves, the olivine tile changed direction and was pulled on a course parallel to the ground, toward the tower. It hit near the bottom with force that created a thunderclap that could be heard on the airship.

Qala knelt beside Vilu and Bayarma, who were unconscious. Then she turned to *Usa-Femora* Inai, who had dropped from the rigging directly above.

"Tell *Femora* Loi to disregard previous instructions," the *Standor* said. "I want height, as much as he can give me without leaving this spot."

"At once, *Standor*."

Qala rose and called over two crew members to bring their guests to the sleeping cabin. Then she strode forward to look at the tower. The glow was more pronounced now, as was the heat.

Zell had not been prone to random ideas and indiscriminate theory. He had pinned the blame for this, his dying words, on the tiles.

The elusive storm Qala had been sensing was here. And the only ones who could possibly explain it were two souls inhabiting bodies that were not their own.

PART THREE

CHAPTER 21

Interstate 95 is a wide, sterile highway that slashes through Connecticut like a scar. The treeless, industrial commercial expanse made Caitlin long for the humanity of Galderkhaan. The more she thought about it, the more she realized that in the brief time she was there she felt a kind of comfort and camaraderie she had rarely felt in New York, Phuket, Haiti, or anywhere else she'd been—at least, not since her student days with Ben, when the world was fresh with new ideas, when the only responsibility was to learn and engage, when it was still theoretically possible to be and do whatever they could imagine.

Falkhaan had been a campus, with possibilities for intellectual, spiritual, and interactive growth in every direction—including up.

Caitlin and Ben rode in the rental car mostly in silence. Ben had picked up the Prius while Caitlin checked herself out of the hospital. Except for Nancy O'Hara's protests, leaving the hospital was easy enough. Dr. Yang voiced strong disapproval but had no power to compel her to stay. Her mother was angry and insisted she go back to her room; Caitlin was calm but insisted she would be in better hands somewhere else. She didn't say where that somewhere was or whose hands were out there. Her refusal to answer those questions added to

Nancy's frustration. When Ben pulled up, Caitlin put her mother in a cab and that was that.

Along the way, Ben tried several times to ignite a conversation.

"What do you think happened at the mansion? . . . What are you going to ask Madame Langlois? . . . How much do we confide in these Technologists?"

Caitlin had no answers and didn't offer any. Barbara had put a dent in her confidence and she was trying to hammer that back into shape.

Galderkhaan is real. Jacob is in danger. I have to get back there.

Several times during the sixty-minute drive Caitlin closed her eyes and allowed her fingers to seek the stone. Nearly a dozen times she caught an energetic whiff of it, the sensations of power and spiritual expansion rising with an almost sexual fervor before dropping again.

The man who had the stone was also on the move, most likely heading to the same place they were.

Ben turned off at Exit 15 and drove toward the Long Island Sound. A series of increasingly narrow streets took them to a gated private road. A guard admitted them and they drove to the curved driveway that fronted the Victorian mansion. It was painted the color of whiskey with white shutters and trim. It appeared to be about a century old, though to Caitlin it felt much, much older.

A van from the New York City Department of Sanitation was out front, along with the SUV that had brought Madame Langlois and Enok from the city. Several other vehicles were parked under a long lattice canopy off to the side.

The gentle lapping of the Long Island Sound could be heard across an indeterminate expanse of flat, rocky coast to the south. Caitlin was drawn to the water as she had been drawn to the harbor on her rooftop. It wasn't hypnotic; it was cellular in a way she couldn't explain.

"They're obviously not concerned that the stone will cause this place to come down around them," Ben remarked as they got out of the car.

Caitlin looked toward the mansion. "Whatever the tile was responding to earlier, it's stopped," she said. "From the South Pole, I'd say. I'm not feeling anything from that direction."

They walked toward the front door. Caitlin walked far enough from Ben so that he wouldn't attempt to take her hand. It was nothing personal; she wanted her fingers free to rove, to sense. It was colder here than in the city and, being past sunset, she really felt the chill. She hadn't been dressed for this colder weather and she suddenly felt self-conscious in clothes that were still ripe with the dirt and water of the previous night. She realized suddenly how much cleaner Bayarma's clothes and body had been in Galderkhaan . . . except for her fingers, but they were dirty with clean, rich earth.

Eilifir was standing on the small patio, tucked behind a column. Ben didn't notice him until they were climbing the short, white wooden steps. The man nodded at Ben but smiled at Caitlin.

"This is an honor," the man said, extending his hand to Caitlin. "I'm Eilifir Benediktsson."

Caitlin shook his hand and they all went inside. The foyer and the salon were dark, the shades drawn. The carpets and wallpaper smelled of an aging beach house.

"If you wouldn't mind waiting here," he said, indicating the salon.

Caitlin looked toward a closed door on the opposite side of the room. "I came to see the tile," she said. "It's here."

Eilifir moved between Caitlin and the door. "How do you know that?"

She raised the two fingers of her right hand. They were vibrating rapidly, beyond spontaneous muscular fasciculation.

"I cannot help this," she said, her voice a blend of anger and desperation. "Let me see the tile, please."

"Do step aside, Eilifir," a voice rolled through the salon as the door opened. "I wish to see our guests."

A man dressed in a long white robe entered the room. He stood about five feet tall and had the same gold eyes, ruddy complexion, and short, dark hair as Yokane. Beside him stood a taller, grizzled man holding a plain mahogany box; the tile was inside. It was buzzing in her fingertips.

Ben looked like he did when Caitlin first met him in a master class on the theory and practice of terminology. He stood silent but alert, missing nothing. Caitlin was trying to stay balanced—open to the tile but guarded to the Technologist.

"I am Antoa," the man said.

"*Ramat*, Antoa."

"Greetings to you as well," he said, smiling. "Mr. Skett you know?"

Caitlin glanced at the other man and shook her head. There was a foulness about Skett, and she turned back to the leader. Antoa seemed an amiable man, less guarded than Yokane, less suspicious than Flora. Perhaps because he no longer had the one and possibly the other to concern him.

"We have just been discussing how much you have achieved in just a few weeks," Antoa said. "More than many of us have in a lifetime."

"It's easy when you can borrow the lives of others," Caitlin said. "I would like to try and establish a deeper connection with the stone."

"That won't be possible," Antoa said. "Not because I don't wish it, but because it has been disconnected from the others. The power inside is once again dormant."

"That power," Caitlin said, moving toward him. "What is it? Where does it come from?"

"The Candescents, we believe," the man said.

"What is your evidence?" Ben asked. He added quickly, "I'm Ben Moss, Caitlin's friend and linguistic consultant."

Antoa regarded him politely. "The evidence is that there is no other explanation," he replied. "That is why we are excited to have this artifact to study. It is a tile, we believe, from the *motu-varkas*, the most powerful set of tiles in Galderkhaan."

"It *is* powerful," Caitlin observed. "I have seen it. I was there with the transcended souls of two Priests."

Antoa's expression was as respectful as it was curious. "I wish to hear everything about your experience," he said.

"I'll be happy to oblige, after I go back and save my son. I believe he is trapped there on the eve of the destruction of Galderkhaan."

Just mentioning that catastrophe caused Antoa's smile to waver.

"I help you go," a throaty voice said from the other room.

Caitlin took a few steps around Antoa and Casey Skett. Behind them, Caitlin could see Madame Langlois and Enok in what looked like a library. The woman was seated in a deep armchair and had an unlit cigar in her mouth. Her son was standing several paces in front of her and to the side, between the door and his mother. Behind them, a fire glowed in a large stone fireplace.

"I am happy to see you again," Caitlin said in earnest. She continued to approach. "You knew something was happening."

"I listen to noise, I see the light, they do not lie," she said.

"What is the truth they tell?" Caitlin asked.

"Yes, they, *they*," the madame replied. "You understand. *They* ask for you. First I thought, 'They *take* you,' but no, you are here. Now I understand."

"Tell me," Caitlin said. She held her hand as she passed the tile to keep it from trembling. "Who are 'they?' "

"The dead."

"Cai, do I even have to say 'be careful?' " Ben said, walking several steps behind her.

Caitlin hushed him with her hand. "Do you mean the dead of Galderkhaan?"

Madame Langlois shook her head. "The dead of the snake."

"The snake. You mean the one I saw in Haiti?"

"The snake *I* saw in Haiti before I leave," Madame Langlois responded.

"Let me talk to them, the dead," Caitlin said.

Ben caught up to Caitlin and stopped her at the door. Her eyes were unblinking, intense. "Cai, please. I don't think you're all here right now. Just come back and sit down, get some input from the others—"

Eilifir had walked up behind Ben and gently but firmly held him back. "Don't interfere."

"She doesn't know what she's doing," Ben said to him.

"What explorer does? Let this play out."

Before Ben could figure out what to do next—as, clearly, the only rational man in the room—Madame Langlois waved her son over. She handed him her cigar and indicated for him to light it from the fireplace. The young man did so, puffing it to life and handing it back to her.

"They see you. They hear. Perhaps they speak." Tucking the cigar in her mouth, Madame Langlois blew three quick puffs at the cherrywood floor. The gray clouds vanished quickly.

The shadows cast by the fireplace rippled on the floor behind each person in the room. Standing beside Caitlin, Ben felt a deep chill and was the first to notice that her shadow had changed. It had the general shape of Caitlin O'Hara but there was a diaphanous shade around it—the contours of a robe.

"Look," Eilifir said to Antoa.

"Casey, the portal is not quite closed," the Technologist said. "Open the box and set it down."

Skett did as he was told and then backed away. The tile glowed faintly and the shadow began to writhe toward it with a pronounced snakelike undulation.

"Is this how it began before?" Antoa asked him.

Skett shook his head. "There was no visible element."

"But the curvilinear shape *was* present," Antoa replied. He held his open hands toward the shadow as if to caress it, to savor its presence. "They were present as lines of power, bent around the earth. It is everywhere in Galderkhaan."

"Why this woman and why now?" Eilifir asked.

Ben wanted to say, *Because I involved her in this. She helped stop a war and save our world yet destroyed another. The question is where does she go from here?*

But he just watched as the shadow moved around the box, covered the tile, created a dark scrim over the golden light.

"Madame Langlois," Antoa said. "Are you causing *any* of this?"

"I just point," she said. "They move."

"The African migration," Antoa said. "Our pieces are everywhere—"

That was the last thing Ben heard before Caitlin screamed.

CHAPTER 22

Caitlin awoke in a gently swaying hammock. There was distant, muted noise and someone sleeping at her side. The room was dark and the physical atmosphere was highly charged.

Her head throbbed as if she had a hangover; it wasn't the drugs from the hospital, it was something else. It came with a floral scent, something other than jasmine, that clung to the insides of her nose.

Caitlin was aware of all that in a moment. It took her a few seconds longer to realize she was back in Bayarma's body, in a hammock on-board *Standor* Qala's airship, that people were very active just a few feet away . . . and that the figure beside her was that of little Vilu. She released a single, breath-stopping sob when she realized she had made it back.

Even in the dim light behind drawn, heavy curtains, she could tell that he was asleep or unconscious; his normal, audible breathing suggested the former. She prayed that Jacob was no longer here, that he was at home in their apartment with his grandparents.

Caitlin eased from the hammock, gripping the mesh as she steadied herself on wobbly feet on a floor that was swaying too. Vials rattled on a shelf behind her, all of them knocking to the left; the airship was twisting in a wide circle.

Bayarma's body was perspiring and Caitlin pulled down the hem of her robe before she made her way through the heavy hide curtains suspended from the low ceiling. Walking proved difficult, and not just because of the motion of the airship: she felt pressure, almost as if she were ascending in a high-speed elevator. It was pushing her down, toward the woven flooring, causing the pitch that sealed it to crinkle audibly. She had to move slowly with an awkwardly wide stance to keep from dropping to her knees.

There was more than just the clear sunlight outside the cabin. She squinted as she saw the yellowish glow that suffused the area just below the rail. She noticed that a section of that rail had been broken, that taut bands of hemp had been pulled across the narrow opening.

Crew members were moving swiftly but without panic along the ropes. It reminded her of the crew of a windjammer bracing for a storm, adjusting the sails, preparing for heavy winds.

Standor Qala was forward. The glow was more intense in that direction, girdling the pointed prow of the ship with a nimbus. Caitlin began to approach the officer only to find herself stumbling forward, dropping facedown on the deck, her arms forward, fingers pointing.

Helping hands gathered round her while voices called for assistance. The *Standor* turned and rushed toward them.

"Bayarma, what are you doing?" Qala asked.

"It's Caitlin," she replied in Galderkhaani. "And you must get away from here."

The *Standor* indicated for two crew members to carry her back to the sleeping cabin. She followed the woman in then sent the two men away. Caitlin curled protectively around Vilu, spooning, cradling his head while Qala approached. Supporting herself on one of the ropes from which the hammock was suspended, the *Standor* leaned over the boy and the woman. Her face was drawn, her eyes pained.

"What is it?" Caitlin asked.

"The *galdani* was using a mineral he discovered—he fell to his death." With a motion of her forehead she indicated the broken rail.

"Was it a stone? One of the tower tiles?"

Qala nodded. "He said that you two felt it first. What is this? What's happening? How are you back?"

"I used one of the tiles . . . in my time," Caitlin told her. "*Standor*, you *must* listen to me. You appear to be heading inland."

"I am."

"I beg you to reverse your course, head out to sea."

"That isn't possible," the *Standor* said as she rose. "I must find out what's happening to the columns. I have been looking inside the *simu-varkas*. Something is causing it to burn from within. Apparently others as well."

"It's the Source," Caitlin assured her. She didn't want to say more unless she had to, lest Qala attempt to stop Vol.

"The expansion of the Source is not yet complete and the conduits to the new tunnels remain closed," Qala replied.

"It's the Source," Caitlin repeated.

"How do you know this? Because you are from the future?"

"That's all I can tell you. The Source is going to release a great deal of energy and it's best that your airship—all airships, if you can signal them—go to sea. Boats as well."

Qala shook her head. "Only the Great Council in Aankhaan can authorize a flotilla. They are prohibited by the Theories of Conflict."

"Then take that responsibility yourself," she said. "You will save many lives."

Qala's expression darkened. "You are not telling me all you know."

"I cannot," she said. "There is too much at risk."

The *Standor* turned her back and stood silently facing the wall. Caitlin held tighter to Vilu. Once again, she didn't know how much time she had here. Her primary goal could not be Qala or the airship. She had to wake the boy and find out if Jacob was still present.

She kissed the boy's temple once, then again. He stirred.

"Hey there, Captain Nemo," she said deep into his ear. Even when Jacob couldn't hear her, he felt the vibrations of her voice.

Vilu rolled his shoulders, reached back to touch the woman.

"Boy of mine," Caitlin went on. "It's time to rise and do something wonderful!"

Jacob opened his eyes and then smiled in recognition. "Mother?"

The boy turned and threw his arms around her so hard he nearly choked her. She let him.

Qala had turned and was watching them.

"You are both here, now?" the *Standor* asked.

Caitlin nodded.

"And you will leave . . . by the tiles?"

"Hopefully," she said. "We will return the bodies of Vilu and Bayarma to them."

"Mom, how did you find me?" Jacob asked.

"Dream magic," she said. "Like in *The Wizard of Oz.*"

"I believe you," he replied, releasing her so he could gesture. "I can hear, now. *That's* magic." The motions came naturally to him and were a beautiful thing to see.

She kissed his forehead. "You know we have to go," she said.

"Home," he offered. "Yes, I know. I miss Arfa. And I'm *missing* school. A lot of it."

"I'll tell your teachers I took you on a trip, which is kinda true," she said.

As they spoke, Caitlin felt the pull of the tower beneath them. It was causing the hammock to sway, to sag. She threw her arms around her son and looked up at *Standor* Qala.

"I'm sorry about the *galdani*," she said.

Qala smiled graciously. "The winds are unusually restive. I must see to the course." She started toward the curtain.

"Thank you for all you've done," Caitlin said. "If this doesn't work, if the boy and I are separated—"

Qala stopped and looked back. "Whoever is here, I will look after him," she said.

The *Standor* left the cabin and Caitlin broke the embrace with her son. "Jacob, I want you to do exactly as I tell you. All right?"

"I heard everything you just said," he said, grinning.

"That's fine, just make sure you do it," she replied. "I'm going to hold your left hand and point to the ground like this." She demonstrated how to extend two fingers out and down. "I want you to do the same with your *right* hand. Got it?"

He nodded.

"We're both going to feel kind of tingly, but that's how we're going to wake from this dream."

"Like Dorothy Gale did."

"That's right," Caitlin said, smiling.

"That's better than being attacked by a giant squid like Captain Nemo did," Jacob said.

"I would think they both present problems," Caitlin replied. She took his hand and pointed. "Just hold your hand like this, no matter what you feel. And don't get itchy like you do before you talk in front of class, because you can't say, 'Hold everything!' and scratch."

"I won't," he said. "This isn't my body. Maybe it won't even happen."

"True enough," Caitlin said, letting go and scooching closer on the hammock. This time she took his hand for real, holding tight to his precious life itself.

As she did, she heard yelling outside, on deck.

"Something is wrong!" someone was crying. "Steam is covering Falkhaan!"

"Stay here!" Caitlin told Jacob as she flung herself from the hammock.

"What about going home?"

"I have to see what's happening, baby," she replied. "Promise me you won't move!"

He crossed his heart. But as Caitlin made her way through the cabin she already knew what was wrong: the tiles were losing power, which meant that something had breached the tower. Pumped outward by the overzealous Source, magma must have broken through under the shallow shoreline and boiled the sea.

Stepping onto the deck she saw *Standor* Qala aft, ordering maximum speed from the flipperlike wings as, beyond, the water surged onto the shore and around the tower. It wasn't a tsunami: water was bubbling hotly, violently around a red maelstrom just off the coast, sending waves slamming into every vessel and structure on that side of the harbor. The *simu-varkas* was cracking from bottom to top and literally sinking into the ground below. The topmost section broke as the tower sank, sending workers to their deaths, destroying the ancestral road beyond, kicking up clouds of sand where structural stones struck the beach. The glowing tiles within fell in arclike pieces, like a shattered ring; they were quickly submerged beneath a wave of silt and water, magma and stone, as well as homes and shops to which people were desperately clinging as they swirled out to sea.

The *Standor* turned and hurried forward.

"All speed to Aankhaan!" she shouted to a crew member on an open platform outside the control room.

"All speed!" a *femora-sita* shouted back.

His eyes settled briefly on Caitlin. "We have to warn them about the Source!"

CHAPTER 23

Mikel Jasso got back in the cab of the dead truck. Sunlight scintillated brightly but evanescently on the liquefying surface of the ice sheet. It sparked, then died, flashed somewhere else, then vanished. Thousands and thousands of beads of light appeared as the thin coating of water spread.

"What is going on?" Dr. Cummins asked thickly. "Is it still that portal you opened?"

Mikel watched through the windshield. "Possibly," he admitted. "The ice should have muted it."

Dr. Cummins looked out at the nearest column of light. "Maybe this *is* what it looks like muted. These tiles—is that what's causing this?"

"I assume they are, but—"

"But what?" Dr. Cummins hugged herself as she waited for his answer. Without power, the car was cooling very quickly.

Mikel did not seem to notice. "You're right, I think," he told her.

"God, if only that warmed me! What am I right about?"

"The intensity of the light is the same in all the locations, and the other tiles are still buried," Mikel said. "This is what the muted light looks like. The question is, will it stay muted for long? The surface of the ice is melting."

"So the tiles are burning through?" Dr. Cummins asked.

"Perhaps."

Dr. Cummins made a sour face behind her muffler. " 'Possibly,' 'Perhaps,' " she said. "Is there *anything* we can pin down?"

"If you'll allow me one more qualified answer, Dr. Cummins, I believe this is true: we are being held here in order to witness this."

That caused her to pause. "Held here by whom?"

"What I witnessed in the pit was brilliance to smoke, luminescence to death," Mikel said. "What we're seeing on the surface is the reverse—smoke to light."

"Which is scientifically impossible," she said.

"As far as we know."

"No," Dr. Cummins insisted. "Smoke does not unburn. There has to be another explanation. I'm guessing that wasn't smoke."

Mikel considered the possibility. "You may be right. It could be that we're thinking too small, too local."

"You lost me," Dr. Cummins said as she tried the engine again.

"It will start later, I'm sure of it," he said.

"Glad you're so confident. But we only have about twenty minutes until we start to lose fingers and toes."

Mikel opened the door.

"What are you doing?" Dr. Cummins yelled.

He hopped down, splattering the truck with water. "There's warmth out here," he said. "Actually, it's more than that—the air is soothing, almost comforting."

The glaciologist eased from the truck more gingerly than her companion and turned around. "Holy crap. You're right. Dr. Jasso, what is this?"

"If I had to guess? Rebirth," he said.

"Of what? Of Galderkhaan? Of its people?"

He shook his head. "I don't think so." His eyes slowly followed the column of light into the fair blue sky. "I think it's a lot bigger than that."

Mikel began walking forward.

"Dr. Jasso, I wouldn't!" Dr. Cummins said.

Mikel half turned and smiled. "It's what I do," he replied. "I have to know what's there." As he moved closer he said, "I have a connection with something on the other side. Something I have felt before."

Less than a minute later he was inside the dome of light, invisible to Dr. Cummins, with nothing but static on the radio.

CHAPTER 24

Impulsively, *Standor* Qala put her arm around Caitlin to steady her as the airship surged forward. Her embrace also had the effect of comforting her at a time when she suddenly felt more helpless and afraid than at any time in her life.

"You will need the tiles of the *motu-varkas* to return home, yes?" the officer asked.

"If they still exist," Caitlin said. The wind felt good on her face, though it bore a frightening hint of eternity: the abyss in which they would find themselves when they reached Aankhaan. Either they would likely perish in the blast or be stranded in a dead world.

"What caused this to happen?" the *Standor* asked.

"Deceit, mistrust, arrogance," she said. "I cannot tell you more."

"Because you're afraid I'll interfere," Qala said.

"It's too late for that," she said. "The process has already begun. I felt it before. I feel it now."

"How is that possible? To have felt it before."

She regarded the officer. Qala looked proud, tall, majestic in her uniform, in her command. "Where I come from, I am like a physician," she said. "Galderkhaani tried to burn and *cazh* with souls in my time in order to transcend. To stop them, I had to come here . . . in spirit."

"Using the tiles?"

"I believe so," Caitlin said. She smiled. "The *motu-varkas* seems to like me. To want me."

"The tiles are wise indeed," Qala replied.

Caitlin felt a surprising response to that—a longing, a stirring, a closeness she had not felt in years.

Qala tightened her grip around Caitlin's shoulder. "What would we find if we turned out to sea?"

"Eventually you'll reach land, a great deal of it," Caitlin replied. "Most of it warm, hospitable, green, with rivers and lakes filled with freshwater. Soil where you can grow things, instead of in the clouds." She looked up. "I believe this airship could make the trip, *Standor*. In my time, others have."

"You will not be there," she said.

"I pray not," Caitlin replied. She studied Qala. "That—that wasn't directed at you," she added quickly. "You're a wonderful soul."

Qala bent and kissed Caitlin. Caitlin kissed her back, hard. She was surprised but also grateful: until now, she hadn't known whether the act was part of Galderkhaani life. The kiss endured long after it ended; it had not only felt natural, it felt right.

Though it isn't my body, Caitlin reminded herself. *Maybe this body is different.* Except that her brain liked it too. Maybe even more.

As the airship plowed swiftly toward Aankhaan, the air became more turbulent, the skies less inviting. There was a taste of ash in the wind. While Qala went to the forward command post, Caitlin retired to the sleeping cabin to be with Jacob, who was still firmly present in Vilu's body.

There was nothing Caitlin could do, nothing she and Jacob needed to talk about. They did what they often did, just enjoyed each other's company. She felt a surprising calm, aware that with maybe only a short time left to them she had to enjoy it. Seated in the hammock, they made up a silly game that involved naming the vials they had seen in the physician's rack. They ranged from Violetamins to Silver-sand, after which they created backstories for each substance. Ruby Pebs used to be Queen Ruby Pebbles, ruler of the Quarry Folk who was ousted by the abrasive Green Salters. Pink Wood grew in the Pink Sea that took its color from the setting sun. Caitlin savored every moment, every laugh, as though it would be the last they would ever share.

Engaged with commanding the ship, *Standor* Qala did not appear until the skies blackened with bloody omen. A dusty, rusty smell accompanied her entry into the cabin. Already, Caitlin could feel the pull of the tiles in the main tower as well as those in the smaller columns that were built in a line to the sea.

"We are within sight of Aankhaan," the *Standor* said. "The *motu-varkas* is churning smoke from its mouth and from the columns that serve as vents."

"I know," Caitlin said. She did not have to see it. The image was still fresh in her mind from her spiritual visit. "What are your intentions?"

"Clearly, we cannot moor to any of the columns," the *Standor* said.

"Nor should you try," Caitlin said somberly.

Standor Qala approached with her hands open, imploring. "Cayta-laahn," she said with obvious effort and respect, "the citizens below are anxious. They gather in groups and many are leaving the city by cart or foot. A few are trying to get to boats, though the seas are rough. Many wave to us. The colored banners for the Night of Miracles are blowing unattended in the courtyards and from parapets. I see Priests and Technologists conferring—"

"They're too late," Caitlin said. "Too late."

"I thought—if you could tell me what I *can* do to help," Qala said. "We can lower ladders, ropes, but I fear a panic, that people will fall, or that the weight of so many will pull us down."

Caitlin left the hammock and stood in front of Qala. She looked up into the woman's golden eyes. They glowed hauntingly in the preternatural darkness. "*Standor*, I say again, I *implore* you—take your crew and head to sea," Caitlin told her, gesturing powerfully in emphasis. "Do this before—"

An explosion from below rocked the airship hard.

Caitlin knew immediately what it was. She had heard it before. "Go to sea *now!*" she screamed as she pushed past Qala, left the cabin, and braced herself against an unbroken section of railing. She was forced to grip it tightly as the ship shuddered from a second and third shockwave. The sound was loud and ugly, like a clutch of thunderclaps layered one over the other.

Below, Caitlin saw the caldera of a volcano on the outskirts of the capital. It looked more like a sinkhole that had opened up in the foothills of a mountain range. There were low white structures around it—no doubt the control center for the Source, the place where Vol had gone and was still present. These stone buildings were burning and crumbling, falling along the sides of the small volcano like pilgrims before an enraged god.

Red fury rose from that circular mouth, knocking down the first of the long line of tall, glowing columns that led from the volcano to the sea. Some distance away, on the opposite side, the *motu-varkas* had been spared.

Caitlin was looking down at the masses of people, at the terrified groups beginning to *cazh*, at the ritual that brought her here what seemed like ages ago. Houses were burning and collapsing, flaming banners fluttered through the sky and died like exotic birds. Then, slowly, knowingly, Caitlin's eyes were drawn toward the dark heavens, for she knew—and feared—what she would find there.

Qala came up behind her, shouting back for the boy to remain in the doorway.

"No, come here!" Caitlin called over to him, wriggling her fingers toward her son. He dashed forward, awkward on the rocking deck, and clutched her hand to his chest. Caitlin pulled him close as her eyes sought the *Standor*. "He must stay with me."

"But it's not safe!" Qala said as, suddenly, her own sparkling eyes followed Caitlin's and were drawn to a glow in the heavens almost directly in front of them. The *Standor* simply stared for a long moment before uttering, "It is not . . . possible!"

Caitlin had to suppress a scream as she tried to process what she was witnessing. There, before them, her back to the airship, hovered the spirit Caitlin O'Hara. She was extending her arms, throwing power toward the ground, disrupting the deadly ceremony. The body of Bayarma reacted strongly to the spirit's appearance, lurching forward as though they were harnessed. Qala had to grab Caitlin tightly around the waist to prevent her from going over the side. The boy dug the heels of his sandals into the deck to keep her close.

"Turn the ship away!" the *Standor* cried to the *usa-femora*. "Head to sea!"

As the young woman acknowledged the officer's command, Caitlin felt herself leaving the grip of the *Standor*, leaving the ship, leaving her body . . .

Magma, boiling water, and ascending souls rose furiously from below, mingling in a holocaust of physical death and spiritual anguish. Caitlin relived the pain. She saw it through familiar eyes, the eyes through which she had seen it at the United Nations . . . when, with the help of Ben Moss, she saved Maanik from an unwanted *cazh*, prevented her from transcending with the dying of Galderkhaan.

She saw her spirit fall away and fade into the churning smoke of a dying civilization. But then the tableau changed. The destruction grew vaporous and unclear. The souls vanished. The fires went from red to orange to gold. There was nothing around Caitlin but light.

I am gone . . . yet I am here, she thought as the glow coalesced around her. And she was certain she was not alone but she was too rapt to try and penetrate the glow. She let it talk to her.

The light was now a small, brightly gleaming band, a circle that resembled the olivine tiles but had neither substance nor size—it could be a wedding band or a galaxy. Lights glittered within; but they were not anonymous pinpoints, they were pulsing threads. They were visible but immaterial, undulating and entwining, and growing. Soon she saw other serpentine lights within the outer layer . . . and more within those.

In her mind, Caitlin wanted to panic. But it was only a thought; she didn't seem able to act on it. She tried to look around for Jacob but she had no body to move and there was nothing to see, save the light and the seemingly infinite gleaming parts that comprised it.

Then the light went out. Simultaneously, in its place was a universe. Space, familiar in its parts but unfamiliar in its crisp definition—or composition. There were red stars within twisting galaxies, nebulae paler than she had ever seen yet no vast distances between them. They were like a drawing Jacob might have made, all the pieces densely arranged, arranged like graceful, overlapping lengths of string that had neither beginning nor end.

String, she thought. *Superstring*.

Caitlin did not know much about superstring theory, only that some physicists believed that strings were both the smallest and largest structures in existence, and that the small might well be one and the same with the large in some curved concept of time-space.

As she looked out, Caitlin wasn't convinced this mightn't be some form of temporary lunacy, or perhaps a delirium transpiring as she died in Galderkhaan. Not her life passing before her eyes but all life, everywhere, that ever was.

There were sounds created by the moving strings. Notes. They rose and fell, had depth and inflection, changed in time with the movement of the strings. It was almost like the Galderkhaani superlatives, arms moving to support speech. Caitlin did not understand, possibly because there was nothing *to* understand, only to experience.

Slowly—*or swiftly*, she couldn't be sure of time—the strings tightened into a ball that compressed into a spot of light so brilliant that it almost seemed to balance the crushing darkness around it. That light that never quite surrendered its autonomy before erupting again in a flash of hot light.

A new universe is born, she thought as the strings enlarged and expanded outward and there were once again infinite lights within. And then the lights merged and glowed and burst and caused more small lights as well as dark clouds of early nebulae. The lights—the proto-stars—writhed around and among the gaseous expanses, burning and dying, exploding and being reborn . . .

Forming worlds. They moved around the stars so swiftly that they seemed to be circles, snakes chasing their own tails. Stars glowed and grew and turned red and exploded, consuming their worlds.

Over and over the process repeated itself, Caitlin's point of view changing from the large to the small as her spirit journeyed through the organized chaos, to a point and time in space, to a world that was newly formed, a planet where the strands of light rose from one end like a microbe with many tails.

The world phased from hot and flaming to cooler and inviting. Caitlin plunged toward it, toward the region ripe with the cosmic strings, to a point where they penetrated the surface. She was suddenly below the crust, where the golden light took on a green patina as it threaded through minerals and rested from its billion-year journey.

The "microbe" she had seen from space was replicated around the core, copied over and over, heated by magma, driven up to the light, the crust, to the new continent, to—

A new home, Caitlin realized.

The microbes did not have thought but they had a collective sentience, and that mind was revealed to her. An unfathomable number of ancient essences . . . *souls* . . . had bonded to survive the destruction of their universe, a previous universe. They had formed a collective to survive a big crunch, a snap back from the ultimate extension of matter as gravity reversed their own ancient Big Bang.

Caitlin thought improbably about Jacob playing with a Slinky. One end of the souls had leaped through time to escape the destruction of the cosmos and dragged the other end with it.

Yet was the thought improbable? she wondered. In the spectacle she had just witnessed, even galaxies didn't carry much weight. The countless lives within them were insignificant, if scale were the only judge. *But it couldn't be, could it?* Every part of every string was a piece of something enormous. Without each part, the structure was incomplete. Incomplete, it was not the perfect structure required to make the leap through time and space. Incomplete, every part of the superstring would have failed.

Either everything matters or nothing does, Caitlin thought. Including a boy with his toy.

The microbes moved beneath a world of muted light, of sunlight seen through water and ice. Then they moved on land. Then they moved on legs. Then they moved the arms they possessed and communicated and bonded and reproduced and cleared the ice and built dwellings and spoke.

They found tiles in which the olivine light, the souls of beings—perhaps an assortment of beings—from the previous universe still resided.

The Candescents.

I am Candescent, Caitlin understood with humbling, then terrifying clarity.

The Caitlin on the airship had been powered by the *motu-varkas*. Through the powerful tiles she had bonded with herself when that other incarnation appeared to control the energies of ascending and transcending souls. She was possessed by the kind of force that countless cultures spoke about, mythologized about when they spoke of gods and demigods, messiahs and prophets, angels and demons.

With that understanding, Caitlin suddenly realized she had *control* of what she was witnessing. Euphoria filled her soul. In her mind, she raised her arms and pointed her fingers and moved through the world and time. She watched, for a third time, the fall of Galderkhaan. She saw ice cover its remains. She moved her hands and was back in her own life, her own eyes, at NYU, in Phuket, giving birth to her son—

And then she came to a very hard, absolute stop.

CHAPTER 25

The cry had all but died in Caitlin's throat when she became aware of Ben hovering beside her on one side, Eilifir on the other.

"Jacob," she said. "Where is he?"

The others looked puzzled. She turned around, past her shadow, at the tile gleaming softly inside the box. Her eyes went to Antoa and then to Casey Skett. They were standing with looks that ranged from puzzlement to concern. She glanced at Madame Langlois, who sat smoking contentedly. Even Enok appeared relaxed.

"You know," Caitlin said to the woman.

"I know they are satisfied," the Haitian replied. "I know the snake is pleased."

Caitlin turned back to Ben. "Call my home now, please! I want to know if my son is there."

"His—his—"

"His soul, yes. Is Jacob in his body?"

Ben fumbled for his cell phone and made the call. While he did, the Technologist leader approached Caitlin.

"What happened?" Antoa asked.

"I'm still connected to it," Caitlin answered, pointing at the tile.

"Where is the tile connected?" Antoa asked.

Caitlin regarded him. "Everywhere."

"Forgive me, but that is a very general term—"

"Everywhere!" she repeated. "With living access to every time that has ever been." She shook her head. "I am taking it with me."

"Hello, Mr. O'Hara? It's Ben," Caitlin heard her friend say. "Is Jacob awake?"

Caitlin watched Ben carefully as she adjusted to being back in a body after the Candescent limbo, back in her body after being in Galderkhaan. Oddly, she could still feel the kiss of *Standor* Qala on her lips.

"He is," Ben said, smiling. "Organizing the drawings into a comic book."

Caitlin exhaled and stifled a choke of sheer joy. They had both returned. She faced Antoa now. He had moved. He was standing beside Casey Skett, who had retrieved and closed the box. Both men had positioned themselves between Caitlin and the foyer.

"The tile," Caitlin said.

"It remains with us," Antoa informed her. "Then, after you tell us what you witnessed, you and the others may go."

Caitlin walked toward the men. "The tile belongs to another," she said. "I will hold it for him."

"Eilifir?" said Antoa.

The man removed a .38 from the pocket of his leather jacket. He leveled it at Caitlin.

"Jesus!" Ben cried. "Eilifir—what are you *doing*?"

"Stay where you are," Eilifir warned him without taking his eyes off Caitlin.

"I posed a question and I require an answer," Antoa said. "What did you see when you screamed?"

"It was not what I saw but what I was unable to hold on to," she said. "I think I know how Lucifer felt after the fall. I know I feel like Lucifer now. My higher angels—they're not present at the moment." She held out her hand. "The box, Antoa."

He shook his head.

Caitlin extended two fingers of each hand as she approached. The box shook at once, light pushing thinly from beneath the lid and slashing through the room.

"I came back with a message," Caitlin said. "Listen to me. It is not through a tile that Candescence will be achieved. You Technologists fought the Priests instead of joining them. Together, you could have achieved Candescence. Not just words, not just the tiles, but a combination of both. Instead, you carved out your fiefdoms and because of that Galderkhaan died. There will be no more death. The tile, Antoa."

"This stone was crafted by *my* ancestors, not yours," he said. "It remains with me."

In her mind, Caitlin saw those ancestors and had to focus to bring her mind back to the present. "The tile will go to the owner to be returned to its home. That is what they wish."

"They? Who?" Antoa asked.

Caitlin replied, "The Candescents."

"And how do you know their wishes?"

"They revealed their journey to me," Caitlin said. "They are ready to leave this vessel and return to the cosmos."

"Why would they share that with you?" Antoa asked.

Caitlin grinned. "I was there. Now I suggest you surrender the box and let us go because the Candescents are going to be leaving."

Antoa stood his ground and indicated for Skett and Eilifir to do the same. It was the last command he gave. The box opened with a flash that dropped Skett and the Technologist leader to their knees. The box fell, the glow punched through the room, and as Eilifir fell Caitlin threw herself at Ben and pushed him toward the exit.

"Get the Langloises out!" Caitlin cried. "There has to be a back door!"

Even as she spoke, the Technologist and his associates burned and screamed and died, their brains pouring forth, the floor beneath them trembling. Enok was already at his mother's side, not helping her up but scooping her up and running off with Ben and Caitlin.

"That way!" Ben yelled, pointing toward the kitchen. Enok hesitated before rushing in that direction, taking a moment to pull his cradled mother closer to his chest. Caitlin followed them, her arms in front of her as she tried desperately not to be pulled back into the cataclysm.

The four emerged in a pool area dimly lit by patio lights. They ran wide around the quaking waters as the pool itself cracked along the sides and bottom, dumping water into the earth. They did not look behind them as they ran toward a stone wall that stood between the grounds and the Long Island Sound. Like Lot and his family, they continued forward as the unfettered power of the Candescents burst skyward, illuminating the trees and stony beach as it tore the house from its foundation. A rolling cloud of dust overtook them and they continued to run along the beach until the air was clearer and the ground solid.

Only then did Caitlin and the others look back.

The estate was a pile of debris less than a story high. Nothing recognizable remained: the wood was a mass of splinters among stone that had been crushed to pebbles. The light was gone and so too was the energy that had been pulling at Caitlin.

Breathing heavily, Enok set his mother on a large boulder. Ben assisted him. The Haitian youth thanked him.

Madame Langlois still had her lit cigar.

"They gone," she said around a puff of smoke. She waved a hand at the wreckage and winked at Caitlin. "Yet not."

CHAPTER 26

As one, the towers gave up their light.

The glowing columns and the brilliant domes from which they had arisen did not simply snap off; they drifted like mist, leaving only a memory that was difficult to recall, exactly.

The warmth left too. Standing near the pit, Mikel immediately felt the cold. But he didn't hurry to return to the truck. The surface of the ice was still watery and slick and the vision of the light had changed the way he saw the world around him.

Because there wasn't just light. There were images, views that were cosmic in scale, unthinkably small, and then—somehow—both. There was age and wisdom and power but also the warmth he had felt on the outside—expanded exponentially. He had felt enfolded, nurtured through a journey that crossed eternity and back.

"Dr. Jasso!" Dr. Cummins yelled to him. She had been standing next to the Toyota and was now skate-walking toward him. "Are you all right?"

"Define 'all right,' " he said, as if surprised by more than his own voice but by his very capacity to speak.

"As all right as the truck?" she said. "It just came back on. We can *go*."

"That's probably a good idea," he said.

She regarded him closely as she walked him back to the truck. The archaeologist was clearly distracted, not paying attention to where he walked, or how.

"Dr. Jasso, what did you see in there?"

He looked at her and smiled. "Death. Birth. Death again. An apotheosis."

"Of Galderkhaan?"

He shook his head.

"Who rose from the dead?" Dr. Cummins asked. "You? Did you— *do you* think you died in there?"

Mikel glanced back at the pit. Clouds of ice were already blowing across the frozen surface as they had for millennia.

"No," he said. "I did not die. But I *was* reborn."

Dr. Cummins stopped by the passenger's side of the truck and helped him up. The radio and phone were alive with voices and the beeps of text messages.

"You're not making a lot of sense, Dr. Jasso, but then so little of this has," she said. "Maybe Bundy and his people can help us figure out what happened."

Mikel laughed. "I don't think so," he said. "But I know someone who can."

"Who?"

"I was the beneficiary of someone else who came into the light," he replied. "Someone who was connected to the tile I found from the bottom of the sea."

The glaciologist went around the truck and got behind the wheel. The heat was on and it felt wonderful.

"Who can explain this?" Dr. Cummins asked as she texted Bundy, letting him know they were fine and headed back.

"My grandmother," he said.

"Dr. Jasso, for a man who was so loquacious for the last few hours you are annoyingly elusive."

"Sorry," he said distractedly. "I'm processing. It's . . . it's in a line she used to quote from Second John."

"Which was?" she asked.

Mikel replied with quiet awe, "This can be explained by 'the lady chosen by God . . .' "

CHAPTER 27

The phone call was not unexpected.

It came three days after Caitlin had returned from Connecticut. Her parents had gone home, the Langloises had boarded a plane to Haiti, Ben and Anita had gone back to work, Jacob had gone back to school, and Caitlin had accepted a leave of absence that was "recommended" to her by her supervisor at Roosevelt Hospital. Police and the FBI from Norwalk had come by to interview her the day after she returned, but she told them she could not shed any light on what caused the explosion—or implosion, as they were calling it, since the mansion seemed to have been pulled in, just like the Group mansion on Fifth Avenue.

"I assure you, I am not the common denominator," she half lied. "Ben Moss and I went up there to collect our house guests from Haiti."

"And at Washington Square Park?" Field Agent Arthur Richardson had asked. "You were seen coming from that mansion too."

"I was in the neighborhood, checking on a patient there," Caitlin said. "Adrienne Dowman. Has the bureau found her or Flora Davies yet?"

"We have not, nor the people who lived in the house in Norwalk," Agent Richardson replied crossly.

Caitlin couldn't tell them anything more. They wouldn't have believed her. Going forward, she realized she had to be careful what she said, and to whom. This was no longer something she could share with Barbara. Certainly Ben, possibly Anita. Jacob, of course. He was his old self again; content to be back in his body with his hearing aids, but signing with a facility that surpassed what he had been able to do before. He remembered everything that had happened in Galderkhaan, and though the language had been forgotten the superlative use of his hands had not.

And there was one other person she could confide in, draw on, learn from. The man she had walked a few blocks to meet outside the American Museum of Natural History.

"There's nothing here of that ancient world to interest you," she said when he approached her at the large front steps beside the statue of Teddy Roosevelt.

"How did you know it was me?" he asked.

Caitlin smiled as they shook hands under the warming sun. "You walk like you're still treading on ice." She looked at his arm. "Plus you have a busted wing in a sling that I could swear was made of *thyodularasi* skin."

"It's a *hortatur* mask I found in Galderkhaan," he said. "Remarkable relic. It allowed me to breathe underground . . . and it's helping me heal. I want to be there if it does anything else."

Caitlin smiled. "There is no one alive who would understand that better than me."

"I know that," he laughed. "Do you want to go inside?"

Caitlin shook her head. "If you don't mind, I want to stand right here. I want to watch the cars and road, the people, the arteries of a living city. I haven't really been able to do that for a while." She looked at him. "That is, if you don't mind the cold."

"This, cold?" he laughed. "No, I don't mind."

Caitlin grinned when she remembered where he had just been. "I'm sorry about Flora Davies," she told him. "I didn't exactly get along with her—"

"No one did."

"But I would have liked the opportunity to get to know her better," Caitlin went on.

"Maybe you will," Mikel said. "She left countless notes, recordings. If you're interested."

"One day, I'm sure," Caitlin replied. "I need time."

The archaeologist understood that as well.

"Are you going to stay in the city?" Caitlin asked.

"I am," he said. "Some of the international figures behind the Group are coming. I want to continue the work we were doing. But obviously with a very different endgame. Not something for Priests or Technologists."

"For everyone," she said.

"That's what 'they' wanted," Mikel said.

Caitlin knew whom he meant. The same beings that Madame Langlois had meant each time she used the word.

"When you phoned, you said you saw me with the Candescents," Caitlin said. "I couldn't see anything but light."

"I didn't actually see you," he told her. "What I saw was a force that I knew was someone who had earned the right to be there. You are the only one who had come as far as I did. I entered the dome of light and I was drawn to you, suspended ahead, shimmering and very much a balance to me."

"How a balance?"

"I think either of us, alone, might have been consumed by the light. Together, we were strong enough to remain anchored."

"Together," she said. "The Candescents survived by joining. The Galderkhaani transcended by joining. So that's the takeaway. Hold hands, teach the world to sing."

"The biggest, oldest ideas are often that simple," Mikel said.

"But us," she said thoughtfully, "there at the same time. Are you suggesting we were *meant* to be there together?"

"I believe that from the very start, everything was designed to bring us there."

"From the start of what?" Caitlin asked. "Was all this set in motion two weeks ago by stones waking up under the ice? That seems a little arbitrary, don't you think?"

"I do," Mikel replied. He glanced at the mask around his arm. "Which is why I believe the sequence of events is older, far older than that."

Caitlin shook her head. "I'm not sure I'm ready to believe that. I have an okay ego, but not big enough to imagine that all of history was orchestrated so that we could have a chat with the Candescents."

" 'Who *am* I, that I should go unto Pharaoh, and that I should bring forth the children of Israel out of Egypt?' " Mikel said. "Exodus 3:11. My grandmother was a devotee."

"I am not a prophet."

"Yet," Mikel said. "You already know the message and you have your patients and your platforms. Give it time. That's what I intend to do." He looked at the sky. "They are out there now, no longer in stones. We may all be changed. We already are."

Caitlin thought of Jacob, who bristled with newfound confidence. She could not dismiss the idea, but she remained cautious. She tapped her shoe on the steps. "The Candescents are down there as well." She pointed with two fingers to the south, toward the harbor. "And out there too."

Mikel nodded. "True. I have to learn to think in many directions. Different dimensions."

"What I mean is, the change may be slow in coming," Caitlin replied. "Assuming we were 'chosen,' they picked a psychiatrist, someone who works with young minds. They selected an archaeologist who understands archetypes in civilization, is familiar with the many ideas of monotheism, pantheism, atheism." The sun warmed her and she tugged open her scarf. "What I'm saying is—baby steps. We shouldn't range too far, try too much."

"No, you're right," he said. He touched the *hortatur* mask. "I could probably spend an entire lifetime just studying this." He laughed. "I probably will."

Caitlin smiled. "And the vision will fade," she said with a touch of longing. "It will seem dreamlike as time passes. Life will not push out the mission but it will intrude on its urgency."

"Maybe that's why the Candescents brought us there in a pair," Mikel suggested. "So we can keep reminding each other."

Caitlin could not, did not, dispute that.

They fell silent as they enjoyed the residual connection they had felt. Finally, Caitlin looked from the park to the museum. "I can't decide whether I should just walk through the park or stroll through the anthropology wing of the museum."

"You should probably take your own advice," Mikel said. "Baby steps. You go in that building, you're going to work."

"If I go to the park, I'm going to think of the last walk I took, through the streets of Falkhaan," Caitlin said. She grinned. "We're stuck, aren't we?"

Mikel nodded. "There is no turning back."

Caitlin's grin became a smile and she hugged her companion, careful not to crush his wrist. She could have sworn she felt something as she leaned against the sling—a comforting familiarity, a sense of being home . . . a kiss.

They parted without another word; Mikel to the curb to catch a cab headed downtown, Caitlin remaining where she was. She continued to watch the traffic and the people, the bikes and the pretzel cart, the nearly barren trees and the sky with clouds—

Clouds that once provided sustenance for a civilization.

No, she told herself with a gentle mental push and a final willingness to surrender. *There was no escaping Galderkhaan.*

EPILOGUE

The green lands loomed below, thick and full of new and colorful birds that flitted above and through the canopy. Whitecaps stormed the beaches with a healthy fury, washing a shore that glistened with countless beads of light set among the seemingly endless expanse of sand. The sound of the surf was energizing.

Not far above, an airship limped toward the coastline. It was battered and worn. Like its crew of twelve and its two guests, it was strained to near collapse, held together by strength of arm and will of spirit.

On deck, an exhausted *Standor* Qala—at her command post for several sleep periods, without having rested—watched the epic vista roll toward them as they soared below the thin clouds.

"I did not imagine such riches existed," *Femora* Loi said from her side.

"She said it did," Qala said.

"Who?"

"Someone quite remarkable," the *Standor* said. She did not want to try and explain that the woman in the cabin was not the woman who had directed them here.

"I wish they could have seen this at home," Loi said, his voice heavy.

"Perhaps they do see," Qala replied.

The *Femora* shook his head. "I do not believe in the ascended," the officer said. "I can say that, now that there are no Priests to prosecute me."

"They were a resilient group, and the Technologists," the *Standor* said. "Others may have escaped as we did."

"I pray you are correct—only for their lives, not their divisive beliefs."

"See to a landing," the *Standor* said. Her eyes drifted to the weakened balloon. "We will have to set down very soon."

"Clearing or treetops?" *Femora* Loi asked.

"Treetops," Qala said. "There might be predators and we have no weapons. We can re-rig the plank to descend from there."

"The balloon?"

Standor Qala considered the question carefully. "Deflate," she said. "It hasn't much more life and I would not see it torn."

"It will be done," Loi replied.

As the *Standor* stood there, her beloved airship drifting lower and nearer to the trees, she heard a fresh creaking on the deck behind and below her. She turned to see Bayarma and Vilu, their eyes on the spectacle ahead. Qala motioned them to join her, and they climbed the narrow stairs. Qala could see that the woman's eyes were damp; she had a birth mother and birth daughter in Galderkhaan, and she had been mourning them in private. But her eyes quickly grew clear, her expression hopeful as she saw the new lands.

"Where are we?" Vilu asked eagerly as he gripped the railing and pulled himself up slightly.

"North," *Standor* Qala replied.

"Lasha said there was nothing to the north but water," the boy declared. "He told us he knew that because he was friends with Tawazh."

"Lasha and the sky god will have to sort that out between them," Qala replied. "For we have gone north, quite some distance, and there you see our new home."

"What's it called?" Vilu asked.

"It doesn't have a name, as far as I know," the *Standor* told him.

"Then let's call it Falkhaan-Qala," he said. "That way people will always know who found it." The boy beamed. "The greatest *Standor* in Galderkhaan, in all of history!"

"I'll think about that," the *Standor* said, her gold eyes moving back to Bayarma. "Will you be all right?"

She looked at Qala with soft eyes. "The poet Vol—you know of him?"

"I do, though only from postings in the courtyards of . . ." Her voice trailed off, unable to say the name of any cities so recently lost. "I have seen some of his words, yes."

"I read his scrolls to my daughter," Bayarma said. "He wrote, 'Nothing is ever truly lost, so long as it is remembered.' I will never forget those who were unable to join us." She stopped gesturing briefly to lay her hands on her chest. "They will always live here. And—"

She hesitated. With a look, *Standor* Qala encouraged her to go on.

"I believe in the Candescents," the woman told her. "I believe they have a plan for us. I do not think we are here by accident."

"We are here by the grace of the wind currents and by the heart of our crew," Qala said. "If those be the work of the Candescents, then we are not here by accident."

"Hull mooring imminent!" *Femora* Loi shouted across the deck to all hands.

The *Standor* put a loving arm around Bayarma's shoulders, picked up the boy with the other, and stepped back from the railing as the great airship sighed its last and thumped onto the sturdy tops of the great trees below. An emotional cheer rose from all quarters of the ship as the crew, save those who were deflating the balloon, turned toward the command post from their stations, toward their leader, waiting for instructions.

"Let us begin our new lives," the *Standor* said as ropes secured the ship and envelope, and the survivors of Galderkhaan moved aft to meet their new home.

ABOUT THE AUTHOR

GILLIAN ANDERSON is an award-winning film, television, and theater actor and producer, writer, and activist. She currently lives in London with her daughter and two sons.

JEFF ROVIN is the author of more than 100 books, fiction and non-fiction, under his own name, under various pseudonyms, or as a ghostwriter, including numerous *New York Times* bestsellers. He has written more than a dozen Op-Center novels for the late Tom Clancy. Rovin has also written for television and has had numerous celebrity interviews published in magazines under his byline. He is a member of the Author's Guild, the Science Fiction and Fantasy Writers of America, and the Horror Writers Association.